NET
WORTH

AMELIA
WILDE

The Propostion

Chapter One

Charlotte

I'm not going to be defeated by a zipper.

My vision blurs. I blow out a breath and steady my hand. The needle loops through the fabric, drawing tight. A sense of calm settles over me. This is working.

The sewing machine would be faster, but I need to do this by hand. Maybe it seems silly to pin my hopes on the fit of my suit. In a world falling apart, this is the only thing I control. This is how I'm holding my family together, stitch by stitch.

Done. I take a step back and lift up the skirt.

"This is going to work," I say, though it's not clear who I'm trying to convince.

"The skirt or the meeting?" Elise's voice comes through the speaker on my iPhone. I perched her on the windowsill so she could keep me company while I got ready.

"Both." The fact that it's raining on the day of the most important meeting of my life isn't going to change a thing. Tiny, spitting raindrops tap on my bedroom window while I pull my silk blouse over my head, careful to keep my makeup intact. Then I pull the skirt over my hips.

"That's the spirit," she says. "Who are you meeting with, again?"

She's fishing for a name. We both come from a world of power and money. If there's a major player in real estate, we know about it. Never mind the fact that my family lost all our wealth, and Elise left hers behind. "The letter didn't say. It's from a corporation called Phoenix Enterprises."

"Are you sure they're not wasting your time?"

"No," I say, honestly, though I don't want to think about that possibility. "But I had the family lawyer look into them. They have invested in some major properties in New York City. And internationally. They've got the money. The only question is whether they'll give it to me."

"Are you wearing black?"

I laugh at her. "Of course. I picked out

2

something last night. Laid it out on the bed. Then at midnight I woke up with this idea for a new suit—a jacket and skirt. I've been awake since then making it. It turned out even better than I imagined."

She sighs, the sound full of longing. "It's criminal that you don't do this full-time. I want to wear only Charlotte Van Kempt pieces for the rest of my life."

"Get in line," I say, teasing her. She knows I'll make her clothes any day of the week. Unlike my Etsy shop, which has a waiting list a mile long. I'm grateful for that little shop. It's been supporting my family for over a year now. The problem is time. I only get to sew at night. Each piece costs a lot, but it also takes days to make.

"I would," she says, "if you'd hire a seamstress."

I make a noncommittal sound. We've been over this. I have dreams about having my own fashion line. Or at least expanding my online shop. But that requires time.

All my time is spent trying to save the family business.

Elise doesn't understand. Or maybe she understands too well. Elise Bettencourt cut ties with her rigid family and built her business. She started selling cupcakes on DoorDash. Now she does cakes, and they've been featured in major bridal magazines.

"All I have to do is finish the Cornerstone development," I say, repeating what she already knows. It's been my mantra for the past twelve months. "Once I do that, the business will be solvent again. We'll be able to hire a proper CEO. And I'll be able to focus on my clothes."

"Shouldn't your dad be the one going to this meeting? It's his business that's about to fail and put you out on the street, not yours."

"It's a family business." I turn this way and that in front of the mirror. Fashion is a cutthroat business, but even I have to admit it looks good. No one would guess it hadn't walked down the runway at Prague. It could be hanging on a rack at Saks. Whoever I'm meeting with at Phoenix Enterprises probably won't care, but I'll know.

"Oh my god," she groans. "I love you so much."

"Really? Because when you say that, it sounds like—"

"Like I'm making fun of you? I am, but only a little bit. Who looks at bankruptcy as a great opportunity other than you? I love that you're helping your family, even if I wish you would focus on your own dreams."

"We're not bankrupt," I say, scolding. "There's still time."

"How much time? An hour?"

I laugh at her, but it's mainly to cover up the clenching fear at the pit of my gut. Elise's right. We don't have much more than an hour. Days. A few weeks at most. We have to come up with the cash or the Cornerstone development will be a pile of rubble. "I'll figure it out."

"Are you trying to convince me or yourself?"

"You." It comes out slightly forceful. "All I need is enough time to go to this meeting. And I'm going to be—" A glance down at my phone screen. "Shit."

"See? This is why the alarms aren't enough. You have to answer my calls, otherwise you'll be late. Okay, go. Call me after and tell me everything."

"Bye." I end the call while Elise is telling me she loves me. I'm forgetting something. The outfit isn't complete. I scan it one more time in the mirror.

It's jewelry.

My hand goes to my throat, even though I know the necklace is missing. All of my jewelry has been sold over the past year. Every single piece, even the necklace my mom gave me on my eighteenth birthday. It was my great-grandmother's—a teardrop diamond set in platinum. Now it belongs to a pawn shop in exchange for paying off six months of our electric bill. We started out with what my parents called "estate sales" to bring in serious buyers. Now there's no estate to sell.

I feel naked without it. Like I'm going out into the world without armor.

Which means I have an opportunity to find something even better.

First I have to put on my plain Target heels. Once upon a time, I would have worn Louboutins. I had a closet full of designer shoes. I scrunch my nose a little at the sight of the heels in the mirror. The people at Phoenix Enterprises aren't going to pay attention to my shoes. They'll be so excited about the Cornerstone development that they'll sign a deal.

The hall outside my bedroom echoes the sound of my heels. It's not just my shoes and clothes that had to be sold at those sales. It was *everything*. Antique tables that held vases of fresh flowers. The carpet that used to cover the big staircase leading down to the center of the house. Any piece of art that hung on our walls.

My heels clack all the way down the bare spiral staircase.

"Where are you going, sweetheart?" My father's voice travels down from his office on the first floor. He heard me coming. It's impossible not to, now that the carpet is gone.

"Into the office. I'll be back later, Daddy."

"Call if you need help," he says, but I know he doesn't really mean it. In a few hours he'll be halfway through a bottle of vodka. And he hasn't been to the office in months.

I haven't told him about the meeting. It would only raise his hopes. Or worse, he would reject the entire idea. He refuses to really accept how dire things are at Van Kempt Industries. The business is drowning in debt. Our personal finances are no better.

A pile of mail on the kitchen counter grows higher every day. Bills, of course. Bills we can't pay, so I leave them unopened. We don't have any money left.

Not until we finish the Cornerstone development.

My mother's out in her observatory off the kitchen, surrounded by roses. Pruning and pruning with a furrowed brow, like there's nothing to worry about but the roses. My mother pauses in her pruning and looks up at the glassed-in roof of the observatory. The rain's getting louder.

She was raised to be a society wife, to host parties and sit on the board of charities. Now that we're broke, she doesn't know what to do with herself.

That's why this meeting is so important.

We need an infusion of cash to finish the Cornerstone development. We need an investor, because we ran out of money halfway through.

Without walls and ceilings and finishes, the development is just steel and concrete. It was my father's last deal. He poured our money into the land, into the demolition of the old buildings, into the foundation. He believed in the Cornerstone development. Then construction went over budget. Our foreign investor backed out. Everything came to a standstill. And my father never recovered. His drinking habit took over his life.

There's a covered walkway to the garage, but rain hits me sideways. I push through the door along with a gust of wind. There's a black town car inside. It's all alone in a space big enough for eight vehicles. This is the last one standing. The last one that wasn't worth enough to sell. I open the driver's side door and toss my purse inside.

The town car rattles when I start it up, but the engine settles quickly enough. I go slow down the drive to make sure it won't shake itself to death on the way to the city.

Our house was a mansion once. Technically, it still is.

Two big pillars flank the front doors, surrounded by windows and brick. When I was growing up, a crew with a white truck came and men washed the windows once a week. That doesn't happen anymore, and it's not the only thing that's fallen by the wayside. The whole house is crumbling. Shingles have come off the roof, leaving holes like missing teeth. Cobblestones have cracked in the drive—another reason to creep around the drive at four miles an hour. If we don't repair the drive, the potholes will be vicious by next year.

It was easy enough to brush things off at the beginning. What difference did it make if the fountain in front broke and had to be wrapped in industrial-strength plastic? We'd get the roof fixed when Van Kempt Industries was thriving again. Have someone repave the drive as soon as the credit cards were paid off. Replace the faltering bricks in the front of the facade as soon as the Cornerstone development was done.

Something more urgent always came along. My dad took us off the company health insurance to save money on the premiums. I didn't find out until my mom got sick last winter. The ER visit cost twelve hundred dollars. I didn't know the credit cards were maxed out until Christmas, when the envelopes with FINAL NOTICE printed in red started coming.

I didn't realize I'd be the only one with the will to figure it out.

Which is tougher than I thought.

I've had to negotiate with credit card companies and debt collectors. It's almost impossible to talk to the same person twice, and all of them use a different set of rules. I've prioritized the phone bill because that's the only way I can get anywhere—by being the last one to blink in the game of hold-music chicken. I've tried my best to make friends with everybody I talk to on the off chance they'll give me a break. It's worked a few times.

It's not enough.

The balances owed are too high to manage with minimum payments. And that's not including the new bills coming in. The business is a house of cards ready to come down.

Stop thinking like that.

I'm going to the meeting that will change everything. The Cornerstone development will get the cash it needs to be completed. Once we sell that, the company will be solvent again.

And our family can rebuild.

A gentle push on the gas takes me past the broken fountain. The plastic wrapping has come undone and slipped down, and in the rain, it almost looks like it did when it worked. I'll fix the fountain, along with everything else. Whatever it takes.

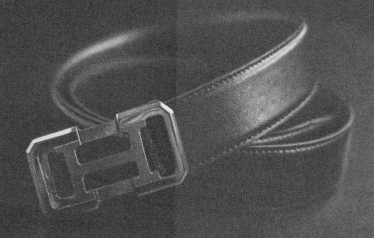

Chapter Two

Mason

I don't get excited for meetings. Some CEOs get hard for them. They get off on the attention and the ass-kissing. I like a good display of power. I like a signed deal. But the meetings themselves don't do it for me.

Except this one.

The anticipation of this meeting is so fucking delicious I can't pay attention to my phone conversation.

"—intercepted from an estate sale in Northern California. Once it arrives on the mountain, I'll confirm the provenance." Cyrus Van Kempt is going to be here any minute, and everything I've planned will be in motion. "I gave a man at Sotheby's a heart attack for you, Mason, and you're not paying attention."

"You love terrorizing people. Consider it a gift."

"I'm wounded."

"Bullshit." I'm almost certain it's impossible for him to have hurt feelings about anything. I met Hades after he outbid me at an estate auction. I'd traced a few pieces of my mother's jewelry to that particular sale. After she and my father died and everything fell apart, we lost everything, including her jewelry.

I'm in a position to get it back. More than a few of those pieces have ended up with Hades, on the mountain where he lives and where his diamond mine is located. I gave him shit about it early on—the fact that he lives on a mountain, even though he's filthy rich.

And then he sent the pictures.

It's not some survivalist cave with steel-framed bunk beds. It's like my penthouse, if the penthouse were the size of a small city and literally carved out of black rock and gold.

He laughs. His laugh gave me shivers the first time I heard it. I'm used to it now, mostly. "You're distracted."

"I have a meeting."

"Is it more important than the fact that I've located another impossible-to-find piece? More important than a ten-carat emerald nestled in diamonds?"

"Yes."

"Well then, tell her I said hello."

He hangs up without waiting for an answer, and I'm left with my folio full of documents and several minutes to savor the black words on crisp white pages.

The intercom on my desk beeps. "Mr. Hill, your four o'clock is here."

I stand up from my seat, the ache in my knee barely registering. "Show him in."

It took fourteen years to build my fortune to this level, for this deal, for this day.

Fourteen years.

Now it's here.

I cannot fucking wait for this.

Except it's not an older man who walks into my office. It's a woman.

It only takes a second for me to understand who came instead. His daughter.

I have a few vague memories of Charlotte Van Kempt. Pigtails. Blue eyes. She should be the image of her mother now. Pretentious and fake, the way society women are supposed to be. Bred to be. Instructed to be.

My throat goes dry.

She's come from the rain, that much is clear, and droplets cling to the perfect twist of her hair like diamonds. The reality of her batters me like rain batters the windows of my office. Flushed cheeks. A delicate jawline. The pretty shape of her lips as she murmurs a quick thank-you to my secretary.

Her sapphire eyes meet mine. They take me in, standing behind my desk, and widen for a fraction of a second. It's less than a breath, far less than a heartbeat, but I feel my own response like I would feel a bullet through flesh. The force of the impact. The shock of recognition. The muscles around my right knee become part of this cascade of muscle and bone, tightening around the ligaments, mired in memory.

What the fuck did she see? I'm struck by the urge to tilt her face to mine so I can stare into her eyes. As if that clear-cut crystal would reveal the thoughts in her head.

She only saw what I wanted her to see.

It's an impossible thing, to feel this hot rush of desire for Charlotte Van Kempt.

I thought Cyrus Van Kempt would show up to

his own destruction, but I guess not. He sent his daughter to face my wrath.

She'll be my revenge. She'll be the person I'll carry it out on. Her family's sacrifice.

There's no disappointment, really.

It will be even sweeter this way.

If she knows this, it doesn't show on her face. Her features are delicate and strong at the same time. She doesn't look smug as she approaches my desk, her skirt suit moving with her body as if it was made for her. The outfit gives her the illusion of being older, but she's not. Charlotte Van Kempt is twenty. She's twenty, and she looks serious. Determined.

And if her expression is slightly veiled, then it's because she's trying to cover her nerves.

She stops at the edge of my desk and extends her hand. "Charlotte Van Kempt. It's a pleasure to meet you."

For fuck's sake.

That voice. It sounds like a rustle of silk sheets. It feels like a fist around my cock.

I take her hand in mine, and touching her is like hearing her speak. Electrifying in a way it definitely should not be. "Mason Hill. A pleasure to have you here, Ms. Van Kempt."

She has no idea how much of a pleasure it is. And an unexpected one. This was supposed to be a meeting with the cunning asshole who ruined my family. Instead I'm left with his young, determined daughter. But I don't get the impression that she's foolish. Naive, perhaps. Far too innocent to be in this room with me.

Far too innocent. Look at that hope in her eyes. The slight tremble in her voice gives away her own anticipation. And the scent of her—fresh and clean with a hint of the raindrops caught in her hair.

A beat passes after I drop her hand, and she uses it to watch me, not breaking eye contact. She's bolder than I expected, and more afraid. The expanse of my desk isn't enough to keep me from her. It's an illusory shield. I could reach across and touch the hollow of her throat, which rises with every breath she takes. Charlotte Van Kempt isn't aware of it, or she'd be trying harder to hide it.

If I touched her there now, would her pulse be quick as beating wings? Would she be ready to fly?

I want to know.

I want to know everything about her.

"I understand you've come to discuss my offer."

Her next breath is deeper. "Yes. I'm very excited to talk to you about it." She's excited about something, that much is clear. The pink of her cheeks sets off the blue in her eyes. "Shall we have a seat?"

"I'll stay standing."

"Okay." Her eyes slide to the chairs on either side of her but come back to mine. "I've gone over the terms, and I think a partnership between Van Kempt Industries and Phoenix Enterprises would benefit both of us. We've got a piece of prime Manhattan real estate already in development, and both parties stand to make a good return."

Christ, she's adorable like this, talking about benefits and returns like she knows a goddamn thing. She doesn't. I can see that in her eyes. See it behind the confidence she's projecting. Her nervousness burns, lighting up all that blue.

"So," she continues, "I thought we could come to an agreement today and move forward."

Yes, I want to say. I want to say it so badly. *Yes, Charlotte Van Kempt, with your blue eyes and rosy cheeks and little black skirt suit, yes. We will come to this agreement and your smile will be enormous. The gray skies will be nothing compared to the blue of your eyes.*

No—fuck no. That's not something I'll ever say to anyone, much less Charlotte, much less the daughter of my enemy.

It's the anticipation. That's what this is. The compulsion to jump the gun, to end the game right now. It's been a long time, but I'm not going to fuck it up here and now. Not after everything I've done. Not after everything I've had to do.

"No."

It brings her up short. This is not how she imagined this would go.

This is not how I imagined this would go.

Charlotte Van Kempt is a surprise. I'm taken with the nip of her waist and the promise of her thighs underneath the prim black skirt. Taken with her parted lips. Taken with her bravery.

Her hand tightens on the strap of her purse. "You're saying no to an agreement?"

"I've had time to consider, Ms. Van Kempt," I tell her, flipping a page in the documents in front of me. "And I doubt it's as mutually beneficial as you say. Why would your family business be worth that much? Isn't it falling down around your ears?"

Her lips part, and her hand comes up to the hollow of her throat. There. I've done it. Shaken her confidence. Her fingertips brush against the skin there, as if she's looking for something. No doubt she is. That delicate flesh screams for diamonds. She needs them. Charlotte used to have them, I have no doubt. Something to ground her. Keep her here on earth.

She swallows. "But you—you made the offer."

Indeed I did.

"Yes, and I'll consider it. For a majority stake."

Her eyes fly open, no subtlety to it this time.

This isn't what she expected. *I'm* not what she expected. Well, turnabout is fair play. I wanted to embarrass her father at a meeting, and I got a society girl instead. More than a society girl. "It's Van Kempt Industries. Our family's name is right there. We can't give it away."

I let the smirk move slowly over my face. God, she's exquisite. Let her see how much delight I take in this. "Would you rather file for Chapter 11?"

Charlotte's chin lifts. "That would be impossible, because my family's company isn't bankrupt."

"Isn't it?" A deeper red on her cheeks. I keep telling myself they can't get redder, and then they do. There are other parts of her I'd very much like to experiment with in this way. See how red they can get. See how fast the tears come. "Isn't that why you're here on your knees, begging for a deal?"

"I'm not on my knees. And I'm not begging."

"Not yet."

She gasps, reaching for her throat, and this time she realizes what she's doing. It's too late. Her secret is already mine.

"Never." The tremble in her voice now isn't from nerves. It's from anger, and it's lovely on her face. Flashing in her eyes. Charlotte Van Kempt is doing her best to keep it close. It's riveting. One deep breath, then another, and a brief flutter of her eyelashes. "Van Kempt Industries has a lot to offer. Any business would be lucky to invest in us. If you aren't interested, I'll find someone who is."

"You have one thing to offer, and it's the location of the property. That's where your value begins and ends." I let my gaze linger over her curves. Her beautiful breasts. The flare of her thighs. I long to get between them. Patience, patience. "Well, I suppose you have some other value."

Her cheeks flush, but she doesn't take the bait. "The construction on the Cornerstone development is already in progress. The design is—"

I laugh at her. Interrupt her. Cut her off. "The design is atrocious. I won't attach my name to the project until I'm in charge of it. Who approved the plans for those apartments, anyway? I'm guessing it was your father, and from the looks of them, he was in the middle of a bender when he agreed. They're going to need an engineer to sort through them."

"The apartments will be beautiful," she insists, and her eyes cut to the floor for a blink. So it was her. Innocent Charlotte Van Kempt had a hand in this. "They're going to be—they'll be highly sought after. There's a lot of money in this for you."

"A lot of money in saving a business on the brink of collapse? No, Ms. Van Kempt, there is not. What you're asking for is charity." I tap my knuckles against the papers on the desk, and she can't help it—she looks. Her eyes move down, and without all that blue clouding my vision I can drink the rest of her in. The dip in her throat where I could feel her pulse. The elegant slope of her shoulders. She's dressed for the meeting to hide herself from me, but she failed. I might not have noticed how well my hand would fit around her neck if she'd already had diamonds. "You and your family don't need an investment. You need a rescue."

"That's not what this is. I'll admit that we have a problem. Of course we do. Otherwise I wouldn't be here. But I—*we*—don't need to be rescued."

"A company like mine doesn't partner with a disaster like yours."

"Then why did you send the offer?"

"It got you here, Ms. Van Kempt. Surely you know that the first offer is never final. It's only the opening move."

She didn't know, and I get the pleasure of watching her understanding come in real time. So sweet. So naive. The offer I put together was a lure, and she was desperate enough to bite. "You did all that just to get a meeting with me?"

"Are you surprised?"

"I thought you were an honest businessman."

"Right," I say, my voice dry. This coming from

Cyrus's own daughter. A more dishonest business-man doesn't exist. She's been working with him. She must know the dirty details, even if she looks pure as snow. An idea forms in my head. I can get revenge on the father in more ways than one. I can fuck his daughter. And God, will I enjoy it.

I have a short, intensely erotic daydream involving the slow unraveling of one society brat. The shock. The tears. *Fuck yes.*

"If you didn't intend to keep the offer, then you're wasting my time."

"Let me be clear." Her eyes come to mine and pain trips through my knee. Damn the adrenaline. Damn the scent of her in the air between us. Damn the memory of that slim skirt, hidden from me by my own desk. "It took no time to make the offer. It will take even less to withdraw it. I can invest my money in a thousand buildings in New York City. I could have you escorted out of the building in the blink of an eye, but I don't think you want me to do that."

"How would you know?" she challenges, and a gust of wind picks up a spray of raindrops. It hurls them against the window. Sharp like hail. Sharp enough to cut this soft, innocent thing standing in my office.

"Because you're still here. You haven't taken one

step toward the door. You're probably wet from how badly the money turns you on. Your company's on the brink of bankruptcy. Not to mention the sad state of your family's finances. You want this deal, Ms. Van Kempt, but that's not the worst part."

She can't help herself. "What, then? What could be worse than that?"

"How desperately you need it."

Chapter Three

Charlotte

I hate Mason Hill.

I hate the perfect fall of his dark hair, and I hate the cruel curve of his lips, and I hate the brilliant green of his eyes. They shouldn't look so deep, so vivid, in the gray, natural light of his office. He takes up all the air available to breathe. Even his clothes feel like a scold. The dark, flawless suit was made for him. I can tell by the precise stitching and the way the sleeves fall just so on his wrists. His jacket moves with him, with no ill-fitted tug at the shoulders, and all of it might as well be an advertisement for what has to be a perfect body underneath.

God, he's such an asshole. *Such* an asshole. I

know why he wanted to stay standing now. So he could tower over me. Make me look up at him. It's tiring, standing in heels. Standing up to him.

What I hate most of all is how right he is. The glint in his eyes when he said *how desperately you need it* made a cold knot form in my gut. It also made my face burn.

And the word *need* in his mouth while the rich green of his eyes settled on my skin—

I don't feel like I'm standing in an office building on 6th Street. I feel like I'm standing in the lion's den. I feel like someone pushed me in and slammed the gate behind me, and now I'm in here with an apex predator.

But Mason Hill isn't dangerous. He's just a prick with the most beautiful face I've ever seen and a killer suit. His hands move at the button, and I look. I can't help it. The jacket parts to reveal the perfect tuck of his shirt over what must be carved-out abs.

It reveals the leather stripe of his belt. And the buckle—it's a Tom Ford, a thousand dollars at least. It's like a magnet. Draws the eye. It's an understated style. It looks like it was made to be around his hips. Like it only found purpose in the loops of his slacks. Oh, god, his hands would look so good, unbuckling that belt, so strong and right.

I can't look away until I do, and then there's nowhere to look but back into his face.

His smile gets sharper. It makes me feel strangely powerless, even though I'm the one standing closer to the door. I could walk out and never speak to him again. I should. He's being awful. Insulting. He knew I would look when he undid that button on his jacket. He's pushing me. Almost as if he's trying to make me give up and leave.

Not today. Not this meeting. I came here to fix things for my family. And I'm going to fix things for my family.

No matter how much it rankles that he's right, we do need him. Far more than he needs us. He doesn't need us at all. We're nothing to him. And he's the only hope I have right now. Mason Hill's offer is the only one that's come in. There's no one else.

"If you want a majority stake in the company, I'll have to take this back to the CEO."

"Yes, yes. Your daddy will need to sign. I'm sure he can be convinced. Someone needs to pay for his next bottle of vodka."

Mason's eyes glitter. The color there takes my breath away, but so does the comparison. My father's the CEO of a company on the brink of failure, an alcoholic with no power, and Mason could not be more powerful. It radiates from the hard muscles beneath his clothes. I hate him, and I would kill to see him without the slacks and the shirt—I want to know what all that strength looks like when it's not hidden by cloth. It's a terrible thing to want.

It shouldn't throw me as much as it does to hear him talk about benders and bottles as if he's been in our house. My father's drinking problem is supposed to be a secret. It's not supposed to be something that people like Mason Hill, in their gleaming high-rises, use in business negotiations.

I summon all my disdain, but it's impossible to look down my nose at him. He's too tall. He has the advantage. He's tall enough to tower over anyone. With his height and his icy control he'd be the king of any room he walked into. But I draw myself up anyway. "What my father does with his money is none of your business."

"Of course it is. It's his company you're pleading with me to save. It's his habit that has Van Kempt Industries halfway to its grave. If he's spent the last ten years drunk, it's my business."

My mouth drops open and I snap it shut. Too late. Mason saw, and what flashed across his eyes was pure satisfaction. Fresh hate scorches the back of my neck. "What happened in the past isn't relevant." Oh—that was the wrong thing to say. Mason's jaw tightens, and the part of me that senses danger screams to back up a step. But I don't. Those small expressions on his face never last. "What matters is that I'm here to deal with you now."

"You, instead of your father. You, instead of the CEO himself. Tell me again how it's not relevant that he can't be bothered to show up to a meeting and save his own life."

"He didn't know about the meeting," I shoot back.

And freeze.

Delight flares across Mason's eyes, his face. The carved planes of his face make him look like a Greek god. Like something to worship. "He didn't know," he muses. "You kept it from him. Little Charlotte Van Kempt planned this all by herself. Things must be much worse than I thought."

"No. They're not. I wanted to handle it by myself. Then once we've worked out the terms, I'll bring it to him."

Mason Hill is breathtaking when he grins, even when that grin is pure evil. It's there for a blink, settling quickly into an expression so piercing that it shoots down my spine and makes my thighs engage underneath my skirt.

Shit.

Please, let him not have noticed.

Another flare in his eyes—of light? Of heat? I can't tell, and I can't look away.

"If you're handling this yourself, then you'll want to take special care not to tell him about the final clause in the new offer." It's lighting me on fire to look into his eyes like this, but he'll see if I look down at his body. He'll use it against me.

"What is it?"

"You'll spend a night with me at my apartment."

If I weren't already standing, I'd be out of my seat. All I can do now is take several steps back. At least now I'm out of his reach. My face burned before. Now I feel like a house fire. Images flicker through my mind at high speed. Mason Hill. An apartment as gorgeous as this high-rise. His hands on me. His body. "This is a joke."

At *joke*, the delight in his eyes hardens to ice. Or maybe it was always frozen through and I didn't notice. I've angered the god, and I hate, down to my bones, how beautiful anger looks on his face. Artists would fall all over themselves to paint him. "Is anyone laughing?"

"You're disgusting."

He raises an eyebrow. "How badly do you want your family's company saved, Ms. Van Kempt?"

"Not badly enough to do that."

"To do what, exactly?" He's mocking me now, and I know because his tone hasn't changed. Mason Hill sounds like we're having an actual business meeting, and that makes it worse. He's in control of himself, and I'm not. I believe, with all my heart, that the world is a good place, but Mason Hill is not a good man. "Tell me precisely what it is you won't do to save your parents."

"I won't come to your apartment."

"You're afraid of seeing a real luxury apartment, then."

"I'm not afraid."

"Are you sure? Your face is red and your pupils are all blown out." Mason's eyes drop to the front of my throat. Damn it. Now that I'm aware of my breath, I can feel how shallow it is. "You're either terrified or extremely aroused."

"I'm neither of those things." He's definitely going to believe me now that my voice shakes and I said it too loud.

"Is it the fantasy of saving your family that

turns you on so much, or imagining all the filthy things I could do to you?"

"I came here to make a deal with you, not to be—not to be played with like this." I've never been so humiliated in my life. Not when we had to start selling our furniture. Not when I had to make excuses at the office to cover for my father's absences. Not when I had to make hours of phone calls to debt collectors. This is the worst. This is rock bottom.

"We've had a misunderstanding if you think I'm joking, or playing." Mason's voice fills the room. He owns every square inch of this place, and probably every inch of the building we're standing in. "Go out into my offices and ask anyone. See if I'm in the habit of fucking around."

Even his cursing is precise. Like he's taken the words and made them into his own sharp arrows. Which means that when he made me this deal, he did it with precision. Not fucking around. To hurt me. I force myself to be sharp, too. "I'm not fucking around, either."

"No?" His eyes rake over my body, head to toe, and I regret stepping back so far into his office. It means he can see all of me. I don't have the protection of his desk. "Then it's interesting to me that you're pretending to be above this. You're most certainly not, Ms. Van Kempt. You have a gorgeous body and you've managed to dig up some last-season couture, but no one could miss the cheap cardboard shoes you're wearing."

Oh. *Oh*. Pride hits first, just before new embarrassment. He thought my clothes were couture. I made these. *I* made these, and nobody else. But he's right about the shoes. I bought them on clearance at Target with a coupon, and they're too cheap for this office. For this kind of deal. Shame flutters down over all my other feelings like a blanket thrown over a piece of furniture. Cover it up and move it out. Sell it for money.

That's what he's asking me to do. What he's demanding that I do, actually. There's nothing about Mason Hill that makes me think he'd ask.

He's telling me to trade my body for the money we need.

I wish I could hide, somewhere here in his shining, perfect office. The world outside is nothing but rain and slate-colored clouds, and I have the lurching sense that he could make the windows disappear and let in that rain. It wouldn't touch him. All that water, all that wind. But it would destroy me. Rip my handmade clothes to shreds. Tear apart the cardboard shoes.

"Do you have a real offer or not?"

Mason narrows his eyes. "I've been clear about the terms."

"Then you're just an asshole who likes wasting people's valuable time." I'm glad we're both standing now. It makes it easier to turn my back on him and leave. On the first step, the heel of my cheap shoe wobbles in the plush carpet. Fine. I accept it. I accept that I'm desperate, but I'm going to fix this. I don't care what Mason Hill says. I wrench open the door with one hand. "I have a business to run. A development to build. If you don't want to invest, someone else will. And you're done wasting my time."

I almost make it out without looking back.

Almost.

But even now, even in my hurt and embarrassment, I don't want to slam the door in front of Mason Hill's secretary. I put my hand out to catch it, turning my head, and—

Mason smiles at me from behind his desk, standing up tall and unflustered and perfect. "I'm done with you," he says. "Until you beg." Then the weight of the door meets my hand and pushes me away from him.

Chapter Four

Charlotte

This could not be worse. *He* could not be worse. The rain. Mason Hill. The falling-apart car. The falling-apart life. What am I supposed to do?

It takes forty extra minutes to get home. The rain comes down in bucketfuls, too fast for my shitty wipers to keep up with, and I crawl along the highway and into the suburbs. Storm clouds have sunk down to street level. It's probably all the rain that keeps coming through the vents and hitting my cheeks. Definitely not tears. Not over Mason Hill.

Our driveway is overflowing when I finally rattle onto it. Water collects where it's not supposed to, drowning the grass on either side. Ditches are starting to form in irregular places in the yard. The lawn service stopped coming last August. The landscapers before that. I never knew that lawns could deteriorate like this.

Nothing I can do about it today.

Hot tears threaten at the corners of my eyes, but I'm done crying for today. I'm done. Done forever. I'm never going to think about Mason Hill again. Never going to think about the suit that fit his body so well it made my mouth water. Never going to think about those green eyes. I caught a bit of every shade in those eyes. Striations of dark forest and new leaves. The kind of color pattern that calls for a simple garment because it's so complicated.

The adrenaline goes out of me as soon as I pull the car into the garage. Rain beats at the roof. My hands are sore from gripping the wheel. My hair's wet from the walk to the parking garage. Worst of all, I imagined that night in his luxury apartment. How forbidden it would be. How wrong. The things he might do before the sun rose.

I've never done anything like that before. Nobody has ever made me feel breathless or needy enough to do it. And with Mason Hill…

I didn't hate the idea. For a second, I didn't hate it.

What is wrong with me?

The car door slams behind me—*too hard, Charlotte*—and my cardboard shoes squeak against the concrete on the way into the kitchen. It's bright in here. Cheery. Recessed lights under the cupboards shine down on pristine countertops. They're naked countertops. Bare. Every kitchen appliance that could be sold has been, all except the coffee maker.

My heart sinks at the pile of bills, waiting right where I left it. No one else has gone through them. Why would they? Neither of my parents are in a position to do anything about them. My mother's observatory is empty. She'll be upstairs, taking a nap. The sound of rain gives her migraines, she says.

"Are you home, sweetheart?" My father's drunk. Four words is all it takes to know it. He thinks he's hiding it by making his speech more precise and not less, but it's a dead giveaway. He might as well be slurring and stumbling from one room to the next. My father doesn't slur, and he doesn't stumble. Maybe it would be better if he did. Maybe then someone else would have noticed.

Someone *did* notice. Mason seemed to know plenty about it today.

"Yes," I answer. "I'm back."

"Come talk to me."

I don't want to talk to him. I don't want to talk to anyone.

Too late now. I've already had the worst conversation of the day. I kick my shoes off and gather them into my hands. "Hi, Daddy."

He's sitting behind his desk in his office.

According to the house plans, this room was meant to be a library with floor-to-ceiling shelves. He left the shelves but made it a private office instead. I used to think this was the best room in the house. I'd find excuses to be here on the weekends. I'd work on sketches of dresses I wanted to make, and he'd work on real estate deals. Never mind that half the time those deals ended in raised voices and threats to ruin the other person.

My dad looks up from the laptop perched on the desk in front of him. "How was the office?"

"Good," I lie. "Things are going to be back on track soon."

His eyes are too bleary to care one way or the other. He lifts a heavy glass from the desk and uses it to gesture at my outfit. "You make that one, too?"

"Last night. I thought it might be nice to wear for meetings."

A sip out of the glass. He can pretend he's not drinking the whole bottle when he does it a little at a time. I've never seen him with more than a finger or two of alcohol in front of him.

It's exactly why he doesn't go to the office. Doesn't go to any of these meetings. He might not look blackout drunk, but he is. He signs things without remembering them later. He didn't notice that the foreign investor had backed out of Cornerstone for two months.

It's better that he doesn't remember.

"You don't have to make your own clothes, Charlotte. It's small time. Your talents are better used at Van Kempt."

I take the seat across from him.

Up close, it's even worse. His hand has a subtle tremor around the glass. Unlike Mason Hill, he couldn't insist on standing for a meeting. He'd have to sit down to cover up the times when he forgets he's standing at all.

"I'm using all my talents all the time," I tell him. "I wanted to ask you a question, actually."

His dark eyes gleam. Another sip from the glass. Here, in his office, he's not a failure who's let his family down. He's a businessman who's taking time to plan. "Which manager do you want to fire? Give me his name, and I'll place the call myself."

I put on a smile I don't feel. "It's not about firing

anybody, Daddy. Have you ever heard of a man named Mason Hill?"

His lip curls back, eyes narrowing, and for a split second it looks like he might snarl out loud. By my next blink, it's gone, and my father's sipping at his drink again like nothing happened. My heart thuds. What the hell was that? "I've heard the name before. Mason Hill." He tests it out, his eyes sliding to the left. "Someone in real estate?"

"I think so."

"Why do you ask?"

I could say that someone brought up Mason's name at the office, but judging by that change in his expression, that would get someone fired. "His name was in one of the magazines we get at the office. One of the architecture ones."

"He wouldn't know a damn thing about architecture."

So he *does* know about Mason.

The glow from the lamp on my father's desk doesn't seem bright enough to combat his mood, or the gloom in the office. I get up and go around to the other side of his desk. Lean down to kiss his cheek. There's so much alcohol in the air that it stings my throat. "I'm sure he wouldn't. I'm going to go up and get changed. Want me to bring you anything?"

"Look in on your mother."

He's glowering into his glass when I leave.

It's a relief to be out of that room, but it's short-lived. Now that the deal with Phoenix Enterprises is going nowhere, it's time to figure out where we stand. The pile of bills from the kitchen counter is heavier in the crook of my elbow than I thought it would be. Some of them slip out when I get to the top of the stairs, fluttering to the floor like thick feathers.

Every one of them has FINAL NOTICE printed on the front.

I shouldn't waste the water on a second shower, but I have to scrub the humiliation and disappointment off me. I'm lucky our water heater hasn't broken. I'm lucky there was a sale on my favorite scent of Suave shampoo. I'm lucky, lucky, lucky to be able to do this for my parents.

Ironically, the last expensive item of clothing I have left is a lounge set in cashmere. No one would buy it because it doesn't look like it's worth anything.

Maybe Mason Hill didn't want the deal because I don't look like I'm worth anything.

No. Stop. I won't think like that.

My mom is a still crest in the sheets, her hair spread out on the pillow behind her. The two of us have the same blonde hair. She kept hers shoulder length for years with monthly trims from her personal stylist, a man named Chris who came to the house with a team of three other people. One person's entire job was to be on hand if my mom wanted a drink. Now it's down past her shoulder blades. If it gets any longer, she goes to the Great Clips at the strip mall and refuses to take off her sunglasses so that no one will recognize her.

I've tried to tell her that this is impossible— no one we know would ever go to that strip mall. That conversation ended in tears. I haven't brought it up again.

My phone is vibrating when I get back to my bedroom.

"Hi," Elise says as soon as I answer. "I was going to wait to call you, but I couldn't. How did it go? Did you knock their socks off? Of course you did."

"Well." Tears ball up in my throat, but I'm not going to cry. I'm not going to break down over this, or sob, or panic. "Nothing got signed today."

"Is that a good thing?" Elise's cautious but optimistic. "Like, maybe you're still negotiating the terms and it'll be a done deal by next Friday?"

"Not with Phoenix Enterprises."

"Who did you meet with?"

"A man named Mason Hill."

She gasps. "Are you serious? He's not just *at*

Phoenix. He *owns* Phoenix. I can't believe they didn't tell you you were meeting with him."

"Yes, I'm serious." I flop down on my bed and watch the rainclouds roll overhead through my window. "He was an asshole. Not interested in the deal after all." It's on the tip of my tongue to tell her what else he said. A night at his apartment. His vile suggestion.

But then—

He didn't actually say anything. I was the one who made it seem dirty.

"What a dick." Elise's pissed. I can hear her pacing back and forth in her apartment. "A total dick. How could anyone look at you and not want to work with you? What the hell?"

"When I got there, he said the original deal wasn't good enough. He wanted a majority stake in the company. And… he wanted a time commitment from me."

"Wait. Wait." Her pacing stops. "Like, he offered you a job?"

"It wasn't really a job."

Not a job at all. His apartment for a night— that's not a job. That's an arrangement. That's—

I won't let myself think of it.

The words hover in the air. I think about telling Elise, about her getting offended on my behalf. She'd

42

probably march over to Mason Hill's office herself and tell him off. Does it count as sexual harassment if I don't actually work for him? "It doesn't matter," I say. "He was an asshole. A major asshole. The deal's never going to work."

"Shit," she says on a sigh.

"Yeah." I pull the envelopes onto the bed with me and rip open the first one.

"Uh-oh," says Elise. "Going through the mail?"

"Not mail. Just bills. Just a huge stack of bills." She stays on the line while I open envelope after envelope. More money owed in each one. The water bill is overdue. The electricity will be past due next week. The bank wants an updated repayment plan for Cornerstone. Everyone wants money. I don't have any. Above my head, a shingle detaches from the roof in the rain and rattles down the side of the house. Everything is falling apart. "I can't pay these."

"I'm sorry," says Elise.

"But…" The papers cover my lap and half of the bed. I'll have to dig my way out before I can do anything. "If Phoenix was willing to offer me anything, then someone else might."

"Who?"

"Someone. There has to be someone out there. A company that wants to be part of the Cornerstone development. And this is a chance—this is a chance to find them. I'll take the proposal I did for Phoenix and send it to my father's old contacts. Somebody will bite."

Someone other than Mason Hill.

"Of course they will," says Elise. "Maybe you'll even get Hill to reconsider."

"I don't care if he does. I'm never going back. I'll do this myself."

Chapter Five

Charlotte

I 'm not going to be defeated by one man in a perfect suit with a cruel mouth and gorgeous eyes. I'm just not. So the new proposal gets every bit of my attention, and none of it goes to thinking about Mason Hill.

I've positioned Van Kempt Industries the way I would a piece of my clothing I wanted to sell on eBay. All the good things front and center. It concentrates on how it'll feel to make a profit off Cornerstone, which is practically guaranteed once it's finished.

All I have to do is sell it.

I smile confidently at nothing in the waiting room, trying to get the rest of my body on board.

The racing pulse is excitement, not nervousness. The ache in my abs is strength, not tension. I don't know how to categorize the vague sense that I might throw up. Intense anticipation, maybe.

The secretary appears at my side. She's dressed in slacks and a sleeveless sweater. More casual than I am, but then, it's a Saturday. The only opening in the schedule when we made the appointment early in the week. "Mr. Morelli will see you now."

Mr. Morelli's secretary wears a kind smile while she leads me to a pair of double doors set into the wall. The smile has to be a good omen. I'll take anything at this point. Any sign this will go well. She pauses with her hand on the handle. "Ready?"

"Yes. Yes, I am."

She pushes the door open. "Ms. Van Kempt for you, Mr. Morelli."

He's already in motion when I step into his office, striding through a space that's natural light on dark neutrals. His eyes come up from the folder in his hands. They're a steely blue. He snaps the folder shut with one hand and offers me the other. "Ms. Van Kempt. Thank you for coming. How was the traffic?"

"Thank you for taking the meeting. You

probably have better things to do on a Saturday, so I appreciate it." I sound great. So sure of myself. "The traffic—it was fine."

The corner of his mouth quirks up. "It was atrocious, but I admire your optimism. Please, sit."

He motions me into a chair that turns out to be surprisingly comfortable and takes the one at his desk. I never saw Mason sit down. I probably never will. I'll probably never think of him again.

"About the proposal. About the Cornerstone development." I fold my hands over my purse and look him in the eye. He looks back, and sweat pricks underneath the ballet bun I've worn for the meeting. It feels like he can see right through me, right to my cardboard shoes. Like Mason. Shit. Not again. "I thought we could discuss—"

"I can't make you an offer."

No. That's not what he just said. It's not. I put on a bright smile, as bright as I can make it. "I haven't made my pitch yet."

"One of my least favorite things is having my time wasted on bullshit, so I won't waste yours by pretending this is going to go anywhere. I hate to be so blunt, Ms. Van Kempt."

Disappointment comes in waves, lapping against my shins, my knees, my thighs. It creeps into my stomach. "Do you? Hate being blunt, I mean. I thought you were known for that."

Real amusement flickers into his eyes. "You flatter me."

"Fine. You're known for being demanding. You're known for being—" I almost *say cold*, which would be true. From everything I've read about Jax Hunter, he's a difficult person to convince. "Calculating."

"And you think I've made the wrong calculation."

"I think you haven't given me a chance."

He really doesn't seem cold and calculating, though his face is made for heightened emotion. A beautiful canvas for it. He's a beautiful man, with his dark hair and bright eyes. It's hard to look at him when I feel this panicked. This let down.

Better to look at the frame on the shelf behind his desk. It's a wedding photo. Him, with a dark-haired woman in a fall of white, looking absolutely gorgeous in a shaft of sunlight through a church window. They look taken with each other, as if nobody else at the wedding exist. Mr. Hunter is laughing in the photo, leaning in to kiss her, and I'm so painfully jealous that I can hardly breathe.

"Your wife is beautiful," I say into the silence.

"Cate is the most beautiful person I've ever

met," he says, and I realize he allowed that silence. Let me stare at the pictures behind his desk.

It takes all my willpower to meet his eyes again. Every Internet rumor about this man paints him as a ruthless, unfeeling person with a snappish temper, but there's no frigid resolve in the air around him. No cold that cuts like a knife.

I felt more of that coming from Mason Hill.

Damn it.

Jax puts his fingertips to my proposal. "You have a worthwhile piece of property here, but my company won't be investing."

I swallow curdled confusion. "You're the last one."

"Last one of what?" Jax's hand flattens on the documents, all his focus centered on me. I wish he were more distracted.

"You're the last meeting. I've had eight meetings this week, and—" I'll resort to tears if I have to. I will cry to get this done. But if I cry, it's going to be on my own terms and not because I break down in a rich man's office. "Everyone keeps turning me down. It's a good property. It will make a ton of money when it sells. This isn't that complicated."

Not the sales pitch I wanted to make, but this is beyond frustrating. Beyond infuriating. My face is hot with it for the eighth time this week. More shingles fell off the roof of our house last night. Another contractor pulled out of Cornerstone early yesterday morning. My entire life is coming apart at the seams, and all of New York is conspiring to make it happen.

"I disagree." Jax Hunter's tone is shockingly level, shockingly gentle. "The situation appears to be quite complicated, Ms. Van Kempt. I'm not sure you're aware of just how involved it is."

"There is nothing involved about this beyond a development project. I know luxury condos need more hands-on management than retail space, but—"

"It doesn't have to do with the kind of development."

"Then what does it have to do with? If someone would just tell me, for the love of God, then maybe I could write a proposal that won't get laughed out of every office building in Manhattan."

"Your proposal is solid," he says, and I hate this, I hate this so much. I hate that he's having to walk me through this problem when I should have been able to see from the beginning that it wasn't going to work. Except I can't let myself think that. I have to hope it'll work, I have to make it work, because I don't have any other choice. "One of the better ones I've seen."

"Don't. You don't have to—" Coddle me. Try and make me feel better. Then again, I don't get the general impression that Jax Hunter spends a lot of time soothing people's feelings. "Tell me why everyone I've met with this week sends me out the door with a sad smile and some bullshit promise to follow up if anything changes."

"Ms. Van Kempt—"

"Jax?"

I'm staring at him, waiting for him to reveal the big secret behind everyone's wholesale rejection of my offer, so I see the way his face changes at the sound of that voice. The blue in his eyes brightens, and there's a brief flicker of surprise, like he's thrilled to hear his name. Like he's been waiting all his life to hear his name said just that way.

"I'm so sorry," she says, and I finally turn to see her. It's the woman from the photos. His wife. Cate. She's got the door propped open on one elbow, a gorgeous, sheepish grin on her face. The green of her summer dress brings out her eyes. One shift of her weight, and I see what else it's meant to do—show off her baby bump. "I didn't realize—"

"Excuse me," Jax says, and then he's up, my proposal abandoned, this entire embarrassing meeting abandoned.

I stand up after him. There's no reason to stay and talk this out. It doesn't matter why everyone is turning me down, only that they are. I'll try something different.

He pushes at the door with one hand, doing something so that it's held open. It will be even more awkward to go out the other side of the door, so I don't. I pretend to search for my phone while he angles her away from me, his hand dropping down to rest for a moment on the swell of her belly. It's so intimate and sweet that my throat tightens. The way she looks at him makes the rest of the world seem like a painted backdrop.

I get my phone into my hand and swipe at the screen, glancing up one more time to see if there's an opening to flee.

I don't see one. I see Cate in her dress the color of sweet mint and Jax in his dark suit, and past them, his secretary's office and a wide hallway. At the end of that hallway is a glassed-in meeting room.

And in that meeting room is Mason Hill.

He leans against the table, arms folded over his chest.

He's looking right at me.

A wolfish grin spreads across his handsome face, and my gut plummets through all the floors of the building below me. Frigid cold flashes through my veins. The burn comes next, along with the steep drop of understanding.

This is not a random coincidence. He's here because he wanted me to see him here. After eight meetings, he wanted to watch the final rejection himself. Well, he didn't get to see it in person. He didn't. Because the doors to Jax Hunter's office are heavy and opaque.

It doesn't matter. He can see me now. He can see me in my handmade skirt suit and my cardboard heels. He can see me armorless. Defenseless. Defeated.

Screw that. I'll never let him see me defeated.

I lift my chin and meet his eyes, even though I'd rather sink down to the floor and curl up in a dramatic ball until everyone went home for the day and I could go home in peace.

His grin gets wider. More sharply satisfied. My heart pounds. I tried to forget about Mason Hill, but he didn't forget about me. He's been pulling the strings on all these rejections. Getting to each company first. Whispering in their ear about how they shouldn't trust me. How they shouldn't sign a deal with me. He probably talked about my cheap shoes and my father's drinking problem and all the things I've failed to keep together.

I wouldn't be surprised if this building collapsed under my feet, just like everything else.

He would love that.

Mason Hill would love to destroy me.

Chapter Six

Mason

Jax is almost finished cursing me out when I toss my keys at my building's valet and punch the button for the elevator.

"Next time you ask me for a bullshit favor like this, I'm making you sit in on the meeting."

"There won't be a next time."

"There sure as hell won't. Just ask her on a date, Mason. Don't have your friends do it."

I snort a laugh into the phone. "This has nothing to do with romance."

"Of course it does. Women love fucked-up games like that from bastards like you." I don't know whether his tone is best described as sarcastic or venomous or both. "I want an explanation. A real one. I just turned down a real deal for you. And almost made her cry."

Did Charlotte Van Kempt almost cry? It would be good if she did. My revenge plot has been twisted inside out by her arrival in it, and it makes me feel feral. She has added a certain dimension to all this. Charlotte isn't revenge in the abstract—she's a blushing, pissed-off woman who has run around the city trying to find other deals. She won't win, but I've had to leverage my connections.

Jax did me a favor when I showed up at his office five minutes prior to the meeting. I had to trade on our friendship to get it done. I was acquaintances with him years ago because we both ran on our respective prep school track teams. Anyway, we move in the same circles now that I've built the family business back up.

"I'll tell you at the next card game. Or at the benefit." Some bullshit happening at the botanical gardens. I almost never show up to those things.

"Liar." He hangs up before I can say anything else, which is fine, because the elevator is letting me out into my penthouse. I shrug off my suit jacket in the foyer and hang it on one of the hooks there, then go to the other end of the open-plan great room, where there is a large dining table. Sit down in the nearest chair. Stretch.

My knee burns today, in addition to its usual ache. Like the tendons might snap.

It'll let up with a few minutes of peace, looking out through the oversized windows at the skyline.

Forget that—one minute of peace. I can hear the elevator going down already. Gabriel will be coming up with it. He's always slightly early, like he's afraid he'll miss something crucial if he's even one minute late. It's a life philosophy I find simultaneously irritating and accurate. Lives can be ruined in the space of minutes. Seconds. In the time it takes for a building to catch fire and for that fire to burn out the floor. The ceiling. Everything.

The elevator arrives some forty-five seconds later. "Mason?"

Gabriel practically sings my name. I don't know if he remembers that our mother used to sound like that. Like our names were a melody. She's been dead a long time. There's no telling which intangibles have been lost to the years.

I could ask him if he remembers. But I won't.

"In here."

I get up before Gabriel enters, one of my kitchen staff coming from the opposite direction. Pots clang together in the kitchen, muted by the doors. I'm hoping having extra staff will keep tension to a minimum and keep everyone on their best behavior for this first brunch. Namely Jameson, who is never on his best behavior. Hasn't been for years.

Neither of my brothers are going to ruin this. Not today.

Gabriel approaches the dining table still on his phone. He has the same dark hair and green eyes as me, but we look nothing alike. I'm dark where he's light. I'm serious where he's playful. I'm a hardass where he's the consummate charmer. He taps out the rest of his message.

"Rude as fuck, Gabriel. Get off your phone before you enter a room."

He gives me a delighted grin. It's a smile that's closed million dollar deals. "You could do the right thing and cancel this brunch. Reschedule it for… never."

"Why would I do that? You love to visit home."

"Sure. It's your sunny personality I came for." Another grin. He's a favorite at every party he walks into, God knows why. A favorite at every event he puts on.

I make an expansive gesture at the table, set with my finest china. "I set the table just for you."

"You don't set the table yourself. You have staff

for that. It's Saturday. Why are you dressed for the office?"

"None of your business."

"You're not going to tell me?"

"No."

"Oh. Then I guess I don't give a fuck about being rude." Everything he says is light and measured. Playful and cutting. People want to be around Gabriel.

I worry about the easy way he moves through the world.

It's too normal for the lives we've led.

On the surface, everything is fine. He's busy. He's social. Always in meetings. Always at parties. He was the first to move out of the penthouse and carry on with his life like our parents' deaths were a minor hiccup. Always on his way somewhere. Always leaning close to talk to someone at a party. But for all he lets people know about him, I still have no idea what he's thinking most of the time. What he's really doing. No idea, and I can't make myself ask him. He'd brush me off. I wouldn't get an answer.

"You'll give more of a fuck while you're in my house, asshole."

Gabriel laughs, then saunters around the table and drops into one of the chairs. One of the staff comes in with a covered tray. He gives her a megawatt grin as she puts the tray in the middle of the table. "Thank you," he says with a wink, making her blush. "Where's Remy?"

"She had a project for her Greek Classics seminar."

"That's bullshit." Jameson delivers this pronouncement five minutes late, like always. A T-shirt and jeans look like they might have been on him since last night. He sidesteps the server on the way through the great room, narrowly avoiding a collision. He gets all his thrills from brushing shoulders with death. I have no idea how to explain to him that he doesn't have to go chasing it. It will find him whenever it wants. He throws himself into the seat next to me. "Why does Remy get to skip the family brunch but I don't?"

"Because she's doing something important."

The server reappears with a pitcher of water and steps around us, filling our glasses. I've arranged to pay her several times the normal salary to ignore it if tensions reach a rolling boil. That, along with an ironclad nondisclosure agreement, will allow us some privacy to try and be a family and not the splintered thing we've been lately.

"I was doing something important, too." Gabriel makes a show of putting his phone facedown on the table, light in his eyes, his posture relaxed. "And I still had to come."

"Fucking a random person every night is not important."

"It is if you do it right." Gabriel grins devilishly. "But for the record, I don't always fuck. Some people just like to talk."

"God knows you can't shut your mouth."

Jameson groans. "Should I let you two have some privacy?" The way he's slumped in his chair is an invitation for me to slap him across the back of his head, so I do. He punches back. It's a practiced movement, habit more than anything, and he straightens up to the table. "You can just say you want me here, big brother."

"Not for the pleasure of your company," Gabriel points out. "This is about keeping us where he wants us. Close to his heart, so we can't get into trouble."

"Yes, Gabriel, omelets are what keep the two of you from destroying the family. If only they'd convince you to join Phoenix Enterprises."

"This way is better," Gabriel says, the response coming easy because we've had this talk a million times before.

I have no idea why he's being so obstinate. Gabriel is a natural dealmaker. He's convincing and charming and people want to please him. It's why his small real estate brokerage is successful. But his lack of interest in business management is holding him back.

If he'd just join Phoenix, we'd both be better off. We would make his business an international player, and his skill would make us the best in acquiring new properties.

"If it's the money you're worried about—"

"I thought one of the rules of this little family brunch is that no one gets to talk about work." Jameson takes the cover off the tray in the middle of the table. Three stacks of pancakes. He stares at them for several moments. Blinks once. "What's this?"

"Pancakes, Jameson. Are you high?" I'm joking, but not entirely.

He cuts a glance at me. "*The* pancakes?"

"If you mean is it Dad's recipe, the answer is yes."

"Wow." He looks like he might be genuinely pissed, in which case…

"What the fuck is your problem?"

"There's no problem." He picks up the serving fork, sticks it through three pancakes, and tips them onto his plate. He doesn't meet my eyes.

Gabriel watches this with a smirk, then glances at me. "You really don't know?"

"Who the hell has a problem with pancakes?"

Jameson says nothing. He butters the top pancake with the kind of concentration I wish he'd give the business. His hair is long, almost brushing his shoulders. Unprofessional. I'd never allow that in someone who works for me—except for him. He gets away with it because he's, unfortunately, brilliant. My brother can tell the cost and the ROI of a piece of property at a single glance. He's made a fortune on the kind of community revival projects that usually bleed money.

He can make miracles out of train wrecks when he applies himself.

And then he'll disappear for several days. He'll ignore properties I've assigned to him. He's one delayed reaction away from a deadly car accident, but he doesn't seem to care.

It's maddening. "Jameson."

"Gabriel texted me on his way in," he says, pushing the syrup carafe into my hands, though I don't have anything on my plate. "He said you're taking secret meetings."

"Oh, for Christ's sake. I wasn't even in the goddamn thing. I just waited in another room."

"You're spying on other people's meetings?" Gabriel reaches for the bowl of fruit and tips assorted berries and melon onto his plate. "That's not very professional of you. How can I merge my company with yours when you're involved in corporate espionage?"

I unroll my napkin, letting the silverware tumble to the tablecloth. My knee throbs. The fork is convenient enough to stab in Gabriel's direction. "I don't need to resort to that bullshit, so shut the fuck up. And you." A stab at Jameson misses his arm by a fraction of an inch and gets his attention. "Tell me what's wrong with the pancakes."

He scoffs. "Nothing's wrong. They're great."

"Then why are you being such a dick about it?"

Jameson's jaw tightens. "One of the rules of brunch is having polite conversation, fuckface."

"One of the rules of brunch is not being an obnoxious jackass, you piece of—"

"This is good watermelon." Gabriel's everything's-fine, nothing-is-wrong tone isn't enough to smother the rising argument. "Ripe. Juicy. Like a certain blonde I spent last night with."

I don't bother to look at him. Jameson locks eyes with me and shoves an enormous bite of pancake into his mouth. "Absolutely nothing wrong with the food," he says around it. "But you're in a terrible mood. If your knee is bothering you, you can just tell us. Excuse yourself and take a rest."

It's not my knee that's bothering me.

I didn't expect to feel anything but satisfaction

when I saw Charlotte Van Kempt again. But when those office doors opened and she watched Jax and his wife have a conversation—

Things became more complicated.

As complicated as the longing in her face. As complicated as the jealousy that shot down my spine. Jealousy that she was looking at him and not me, even though he's married and there's no way he has any interest in any woman other than his wife.

I saw them, just like Charlotte did.

And then she saw me.

It was a priceless moment. The moment she'd know who had come after her. The moment she'd know I was the one pulling strings all the way across the city, and that I wouldn't stop until I got what I wanted.

Well. I want to destroy Charlotte Van Kempt.

I want to break her in every way there is under the sun.

I want to put her back together afterward and break her again.

That's the part I'll never admit out loud. If she's a smart woman, she'll run the other way. She must be fairly intelligent, since she's been single hand-edly keeping her father's company just above water for at least a year now. No business degree. No help from her father.

Not a single note of complaint in her sapphire blue eyes.

She could have gone straight to Jax and told him what an unholy prick I was being, but she didn't. Charlotte shook his hand, allowed herself to be introduced to his wife, and left with her head held high. Then Jax disappeared with his wife, and I left for brunch. Fine. I owe him an explanation. He'll have it later.

"My knee is fine. You're the one with the vendetta against brunch. What do you want from me?"

He takes another bite of pancake. "Are you going to have any?"

"I don't know. If I have to watch you eat them, maybe I'll never order these fucking things for brunch again. I thought you liked Dad's pancakes. You make them with Remy."

"But she isn't here," Jameson says back. "Is she?"

"Is that what you're pissed about? That Remy didn't show up?"

"You're the one making a big deal about having brunch with the family."

Keeping this family together has been my sole focus since our parents died. We were left orphans. Practically penniless. I fought to get custody of my siblings. We lived in a shitty apartment while I worked shitty jobs. Remy was pulled out of private school and sent to a place with metal detectors and shooting drills.

Yes, the brunch is important. Because family is important.

Gabriel attempts to change the subject. "Jameson, do you—"

"Tell me." I cut into whatever polite, skin-deep question Gabriel has for Jameson because I can't stand it. Not after I saw her in that office. Not after she looked back at me without flinching. If I have my way with Charlotte Van Kempt, I hope there's more of a struggle than the nonexistent fight she put up this morning. "Now. I don't want to spend this entire hour arguing with you about—"

Jameson drops his fork onto his plate with a loud clang of silver hitting china. "A pleasure as always. I'm so glad we had this little brunch. The table is yours."

"Sit down, fucker."

"No."

I'm out of my seat before he can get around the table, my glass going over in the process, a plate hitting the floor. I catch Jameson with one fist in his shirt, my knee aching, and use all my body weight to put him up against one of the windows. "I can't fix it if you won't tell me what the hell is wrong."

Jameson glowers at me.

Then he throws a punch.

I deflect it in time to stop him from hitting my temple and return both hands to the task in front of me. Another punch. This one is harder to stop. I throw one on instinct and get Jameson across the cheek.

"I can't believe you outsourced the pancakes." The hint of a crooked grin, but I don't buy it. "Dad's special pancakes that he made for us. His own recipe. And you just hand it off to a chef, like what? Like it's a goddamn task on your to-do list?"

"I thought you liked them," I say, but there's a sick feeling in my stomach. Somewhere in between building Phoenix Enterprises and seeking revenge, I've lost my hold on the family. The brunch was supposed to fix that. Instead it's made it worse.

"What's next? You have your secretary buy us Christmas presents? You pay actors to sit around at Thanksgiving pretending to be Mom and Dad? Jesus Christ, Mason." Jameson punches me toward the back of my jaw, and now I'm going to kill him. Now's the day I stop being Jameson's older brother and safety net, I stop worrying about him, I stop noticing the hurt in his eyes. "Remy's not even here. If we can't all be here, just cancel it."

"That's the entire point. We're here because we

can't all be together. We can never be together again. This is all there is."

This is all we have. And I know, I fucking *know*, that it would be better if our parents were alive. But they're not, because of me. This bullshit fight is just another piece of evidence that I wasn't enough to stand in for them. Another vivid reminder of just how much we've all lost.

Jameson swings his body hard enough to loosen my grip. I know by his stance he's planning to tackle me. That's how he is—all or nothing. He doesn't know the meaning of moderation.

I draw my fist back to hit him, to end this, but I catch Gabriel out of the corner of my eye.

He's up out of his seat, close enough to reach out and stop me if he wanted to try. His expression is open. Easy as it always is. He puts a hand out.

"Maybe we should make them together," Gabriel offers.

Fuck. What am I doing?

The fight dissipates. I let Jameson go.

The three of us sit down in our spots. I put pancakes onto my plate. Butter. Syrup. "How do you want to do this, if it's illegal to let my chef cook them?"

"Make waffles," Jameson says, voice struggling between flat and his normal jackassery. "Don't hand out the recipe like it's another one of your projects at work."

Christ. Of course he would be pissed about this. When our dad would make pancakes on the chef's day off—and whenever else we wanted them. He was a billionaire and a businessman, but he always took time for his family. He was always there for us… until he wasn't.

"This isn't about the pancakes," I say, my voice hard.

"At least your chef got them right," Gabriel picks up his fork, because clearly the worst is over. Even though a couple dishes were casualties in the fight. A server appears from the kitchen with towels in her arms and a calm expression on her face. I'm glad, now, for the outrageous salary.

"It's about the family," I say. It's always about family.

Jameson narrows his eyes at me. "Go fuck yourself."

"I'll make sure Remy works on her school projects on other days. Next time she'll come to brunch. And we'll figure out something else to eat. We're a fucked-up family, but we're going to meet once a week. That's the way it is."

A heavy silence. Then: "Good."

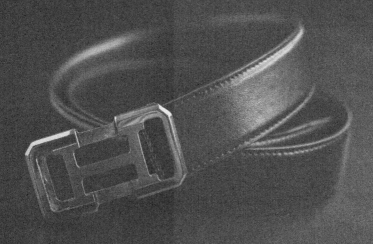

Chapter Seven

Charlotte

I have no idea what I've said to Jax Hunter or his wife. None. I could have said anything. All I remember is his brow knitting and the careful way his jacket lay against his shirt. It doesn't matter anyway. I'll never go back there again, or see them again. I'll go to people in different cities. I'll find an investor who's never heard of Mason Hill, even if I have to drive this town car all the way to California. I don't care, I don't care, I don't care.

I arrive home hours later due to the New York City traffic.

The day ends with me pulling the covers over my head and retreating into despair.

The rest of the weekend I simmer in a state of humiliation and rage.

It boils over when I wake up on Monday morning. I dress with exaggerated care, almost as if I'm as drunk as my father. Not with alcohol. With a sense of righteous indignation. How dare he? The town car doesn't like starting today. I ignore the protesting sputter and gun it toward the city.

This asshole's not going to strut around his office thinking he's won.

He hasn't won. *I'll* win, and he can deal with it.

Adrenaline flows like sparkling wine all the way out of our suburb. All the way into the city. Up three levels of the parking garage until I find a spot. Every heartbeat pumps more angry heat into my veins. More acid humiliation. I'm all out of kindness today. I'm not out of hope.

People bustle through the lobby of the Phoenix Enterprises building, going in and out in the cool of the air-conditioning. Heads turn when I shove my way in through the rotating door, cheap cardboard heels loud on the floor. No, I'm not the most graceful person in the room. Not the most well-dressed. At the counter inside the door, I slam my ID down on the marble top. "I need a visitor pass. Please."

The security guard presses his lips together like

he might laugh, or might scold me. I don't care what he does. "Who are you meeting?"

"Mason Hill."

A low whistle. "I feel bad for him, then."

He pushes a temporary pass across the counter to me. I'm not pinning it to my jacket. I'll throw it in Mason Hill's face. I'll make him understand that he doesn't need passes like this because he's a terrible person who does terrible things and all of that will come back to him one day. A man at the elevator steps out of my way and doesn't follow me in. Good.

It lets me out onto the beautiful thirtieth floor. One wall is taken up with glassed-in offices. I stomp past two desks by the windows on the other side. Mason's secretary sits at a rounded desk outside the big door to his office. The oversized door is meant to be intimidating, and maybe my stomach does clench at the sight of it. I'll never let him know that.

His secretary's eyes get wide, then wider, and she hangs up her phone call.

"I'm going in," I tell her.

"Ms. Van Kempt, you're not on Mr. Hill's schedule—"

"I'm going in."

She doesn't have time to stop me because I'm

already wrenching open the door to his office and bursting inside.

This might be the only time in my life that I catch Mason Hill by surprise. He stands up behind his desk in a rush, shoving the chair back with the force of his body. The angry motion is nothing compared to the complicated storm in his eyes.

My body reacts to it before my brain can figure out what I'm seeing. A bolt of fear. Dark leaves thrashing under lightning flashes in the sky. Impending doom. Immediate danger. Goose bumps spread like wildfire across my shoulders, pulling the hair on the back of my neck up. The hazy sky outside his huge, pristine office windows has turned from blue to iron gray. The muscles in my legs tense like I might take a step back. Like I might do the very smart thing and get the hell out of this room.

I didn't come here to run away.

So I go toward him instead.

He won't let me do it. Mason Hill is such an asshole that he won't even give me the desk for comfort. He strides around in front of it, and through all my fear and anger and disappointment I see something. Something about the way his clothes move as he walks.

I plant my heels on the rug. God, he's terrible.

74

He hasn't so much as touched me but he's still bending this moment to his will. Blocking my path. I know there's nowhere for me to go once I reach the desk, except for the windows on the other side. But I wasn't ready to stop yet, and now he's here. Keeping me off-balance. Keeping me right where he wants me.

"What the hell is your problem?" I've never been this pissed in my entire life. "You didn't want to sign a deal with me, so you're going to stalk me all over the city and sabotage everything?" I slice my visitor pass at him. "You are the worst."

He covers his mouth with his hand, his eyes dark and glittering. "You stopped for a visitor pass."

I throw it at him. It flutters to the carpet before it can touch his Burberry suit jacket. "You're a prick, and everyone in the city knows it. Are you going to answer my question or not?"

"Did you ask one? You're just so cute with your visitor pass and your righteous anger, it's hard to pay attention."

"What did I ever do to you?" I take another step toward him. A gust of wind curls against the tall pane of his window. This high up, the wind is stronger. "I came here with a way for you to make money, and you didn't want me."

A gorgeous, cutting grin curves the corner of

his mouth. "I want you very much, Ms. Van Kempt. In many different ways. I thought you weren't on the table."

"I'm not."

"*You didn't want me,*" he mocks. "Are you hurt that I didn't strongarm you into the contract? Did you dream about me touching you last night? Sometimes our words give us away when we're not fully in control of ourselves."

"You're the one who's out of control."

"Am I?"

"Yes. You have followed me around the city and interfered in my meetings. You told people to turn me down. You probably have surveillance cameras on the Cornerstone development. Or you have phone taps on Van Kempt Industries' phone lines."

"No, but that's a good idea."

"I saw you in Jax Hunter's office. I know you told him not to make an offer."

He laughs, and another burst of heat and ice spirals down through my core. It's a beautiful laugh. He has a beautiful voice. The most beautiful voice I've ever heard, and he only uses it to hurt me. "My god, you are precious. You're quite sheltered, Ms. Van Kempt, so I'll let you in on a little secret—no one tells Jax Hunter what to do. I simply gave him all the relevant information."

"What information? If it's about my dad—his drinking has nothing to do with this."

Mason's eyes widen. "You think I spent valuable time making calls and traveling around the city to tell my business associates information they already know?"

"No." Blood bumps through my veins, thick and hot. "Yes."

"It's a well-known fact that Daddy's a drunk who can't finish a project to save his life. Or yours." A smirk that cuts to the bone. "I thought they should know about the meeting I had."

He's too happy to tell me about this. Too thrilled. My burning, righteous anger falters under a cold wind. There's something happening I don't know about. "What meeting?"

"I met with the commissioner at the Department of Buildings."

"About what?"

"About your project." The green of his eyes darkens. A trick of the light. No—not a trick. It's getting darker outside. A summer thunderstorm, rolling over the city. "Cornerstone isn't just a half-finished eyesore. It's a liability. Everyone who walks by is in danger."

"It's a construction zone. There are signs to warn people—"

"Are there?"

"Yes."

"Are there enough? Are you sure?"

He's the one to step forward now, and—what is it? What is it?—something about the way he moves is different. I would be curious if I wasn't so angry, if I wasn't so scared. More terrified by the minute. "No," I admit. "I'm not sure. But I bet you are, because you're a stalker with nothing else to do but ruin my life."

"Ruin your life?" Mason puts a hand to his chest, a mockery of compassion. "I'm saving your life, Ms. Van Kempt. Can you imagine the lawsuits if a person were killed by your father's recklessness? It's not a construction zone if there's no crew."

"One contractor quit. Not everyone."

"No, it's all of them. No licensed contractor will work on a project that doesn't have a permit."

"We have a permit."

He waits, and my stomach turns to knots, tighter and tighter until I can't breathe.

"You got the department to revoke it."

"Oh, yes. Safety is so important to the reputation of our city. Can't have residents and tourists in harm's way. I was only doing my civic duty."

"We can't build without that permit. Even if I—even if—"

"Even if you went to an outside firm, someone who had no knowledge of the city, they wouldn't take the job." A mean, beautiful grin. "The commissioner trusts me. I have been fucking meticulous when it comes to safety standards in all my projects. In all my investments. They won't grant Cornerstone another permit unless and until I'm attached to the project."

The air in the room is so thin, but the force of it presses in tight around my body. This was a trap. I should have known it was a trap the minute I met Mason Hill. But I didn't know. I was foolish, and I was hopeful, and I thought this would be simple. Not necessarily easy, but simple. Signatures on paper. Notarized documents. Bank transfers.

There's a knot in my throat. "And you won't be attached until I agree to your terms."

"It's a pleasure to watch you arrive at this conclusion, Ms. Van Kempt. But you'll have to do more than agree."

"What more?"

Another dark grin. *Not until you beg.*

That's what he said to me as I stormed out of his office, hot with shame and justified anger. I was sure I would never beg him—not for anything. But here I am, needing something.

I don't know whether I'm numb or on fire. I think it might be both. I reach for my necklace without thinking and my fingertips brush over soft skin. Mason's eyes track the movement. The suit, the office—it's all to create an illusion that he's not a dangerous man. That he's not a predator hunting prey. But that's what he is.

And I'm cornered.

The pressure intensifies. My parents are waiting at home right now in a house that's falling to pieces around us. An empty, rattling house that won't be able to keep itself standing. Cornerstone will crumble soon enough if the construction doesn't continue. Every day that passes without construction crews makes it less likely that the project will ever be finished, and more likely that we'll lose our house.

Salt stings the corners of my eyes. My chin is doing that thing it does when I'm about to cry.

Nothing has ever been this bad.

He's so close now that the scent of his skin is in the air between us, already touching me. And worse than the obvious glee he's taking in doing this to me, far, far worse, is that he smells so good that I've shifted my weight forward. Like my body wants to be closer to him.

"It won't be the same offer as before." I manage to say this without shedding a tear. It won't be long, I don't think. "It'll be worse now. Won't it?"

"A matter of perspective." Mason is like a magnetic field. I feel pulled toward him, almost desperate to touch him, to see if he's real. If a person can actually be this cruel and this attractive at the same time. "It'll be significantly more entertaining for me."

"Tell me what it is."

He puts one big, strong hand under my chin and tilts my face up in a firm grip. I shiver in it, though his hand isn't cold. His touch is warm. Possessive. As if this is already a done deal and not something I could walk away from.

Right. Because I can't. I have no other choice. No choice but to agree. No choice but to look into his eyes. They take my breath away. Not just green—a sunburst of yellow around his pupils.

"Not just one night, Ms. Van Kempt. Every Friday until the project is complete."

I swallow, and his eyes drop down to where his hand is a quarter inch from my beating pulse. "And you'll make sure Cornerstone gets built? There will be a schedule? We'll sell the property after it's done?"

"Your cut will be enough to dig Daddy out of debt and then some."

A nod that he barely allows. "What are you going to do to me?"

The smile is a sunset that burns down into a glittering night. All of those grins, all of those smirks—they were hiding what was underneath. His expression now makes my pulse race. It makes my face burn.

I'm terrified. Humiliated.

And…

I can't say it. Can't think it. Can't let him be right one more time.

"Are you sure you want to know, Ms. Van Kempt?"

"Yes," I whisper.

He leans in close and lets his breath brush the shell of my ear. Lets his grip on my chin tighten by slow degrees until I gasp. "Whatever I fucking want."

Mason seals this promise with a deep, vicious kiss. So hard that I cry out into his mouth. So violent that I kiss him back.

He pulls back far enough to study me. His eyes burn my skin. "You're not finished yet," he says.

I know what he wants.

He told me himself at our very first meeting. He'd planted the vision in my head. Me, on my knees. It might be better that way. His bruising grip on my face means I can't hide. There's no distance.

He wants me to beg.

My mouth goes dry. "Please."

Mason scoffs. "You don't want this."

It feels like blades on my insides. "Please. Offer us a deal. Offer—offer *me* a deal."

"I'm still not convinced, Ms. Van Kempt."

"I don't know how to do this. I don't know." I'm not a person who gets panicked, but he makes me feel that way. He makes uncertainty rise until it crests. "No one has ever made me—"

"Figure it out," he snaps. "You'll do many things for me that you haven't done before. Start now, before I lose interest. You're very pretty, but too proud."

Tears prick my eyes. "Please sign a deal with me. *Please, please, please.*"

He shakes my face, a quick, possessive jerk that makes my skin combust. "If you're going to beg, you'll need to include a reason. What do you want, Ms. Van Kempt, and *why*?"

A single tear escapes and runs down my cheek. "Please sign a deal with me," I beg, my voice choked with fear—with more than fear. "Please. Because you're the only one in the city who can— you're the only one who can save us. We need you. *I need you.*"

He drops his hand and steps away, and I almost do it. I almost drop to the floor and keep begging. My entire body trembles. My knees—they want to give out.

Mason walks back to his desk, his expression verging on bored, and picks up a leather folio. He holds it out to me without a word. "Don't come back without the correct signature." My dad. My dad is the one who will have to sign off on it. He's the CEO, if only in name. "He won't make it easy, I'm sure. But that's okay. Lord knows you need the practice."

"Practice with what?"

"Begging."

I have no choice but to approach his desk and take it from him. When my hands make contact with the leather, he holds on. I don't want to look him in the eye. I do it anyway.

What I find in his green eyes isn't boredom.

It's an unreadable, unnameable expression. It's like a forest fire. It's too much for words. It's a promise of all the things he'll do to me this Friday—and for many Fridays after that. In that blaze I see both sex and ruin. I see sensual violence. I work so hard to craft these clothes, but he's going to peel them away from my skin. He's going to see everything, touch everything. Own everything.

Mason releases the folio, and releases my balance with it. I catch myself just in time.

What will be left for me?

Not dignity. Not pride. Not even a majority share in my family's company. *Nothing.* That's the answer written in his green eyes. They're hard as emeralds.

He'll take and take, until there's nothing left of me.

NET WORTH

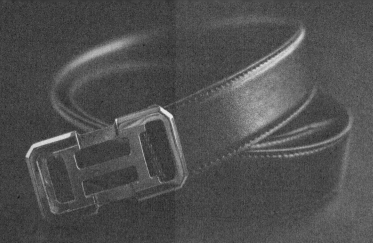

CHAPTER
ONE

Charlotte

Rain sweeps against the windshield so hard I can't see the road. My wipers are so old and shitty they hardly make a dent. If one of them flew off right now, it would be a perfect fit for this afternoon. Summer humidity presses into the car, choking off the air. The AC struggles against it and I can't get the settings right. It's fogging the windshield from the inside. I only have a vague impression of thrashing green trees on either side of the road.

It reminds me of Mason Hill's eyes.

Damn him, and his eyes.

I've been going to meetings since my dad started drinking too much to handle it. I've been holding his company together with both hands for a year and a half now. But the meeting I just left with Mason Hill was the worst.

He's sabotaged all my other chances of saving my father's failing business and our crumbling home and our family's financial future. He followed me through the city, making sure I'd have to come crawling back to him. Not literally. I will never actually crawl for him. Never get on my knees for him.

My face heats. I can think *never* in the safety of the town car all I want, but I will do those things, if that's what Mason wants. If that's what he decides to do with me.

Because Mason Hill is the only one who can get us out of this spiral into bankruptcy and homelessness. He's the man standing in the way.

It was one thing to agree to the deal with him. One thing to look into his dangerously green eyes and know he would only accept one thing in exchange for his help.

Me.

It's going to be another thing entirely to get my father's signature. For all the work I've done, he's still the one in charge of the Cornerstone development, the last project we have at Van Kempt Industries.

A leather folio sits on the passenger seat, raindrops beading on the cover. My clothes are soaked through from the walk to my car. A wild burst of hope—maybe the rain will have destroyed the papers, too, and I won't have to do this. But I know it hasn't. Everything Mason Hill owns is bulletproof. The Phoenix Enterprises building in the city gleams with glass and light. The contract will be intact. It's me who might not end up that way.

I shiver under my wet clothes. My hair was destroyed by the rain, and even though it's summer, the cold is sinking into my bones.

Or maybe it's Mason Hill.

What are you going to do to me?

He'd looked at me with those green-gold eyes, his grip tight on my chin.

Whatever I fucking want.

The kiss was more final than any signature. A hard, bruising kiss, like I was already his property. My lip aches. I brush my fingertips over the place where his mouth touched mine. It felt like he'd whipped up the storm clouds himself just to prove he could, but that's impossible. It's impossible for a man to have that kind of power.

It's all the other kinds he has.

Our gatehouse guard waves me past, and it's hard not to think he knows. That everyone behind these gates knows what I've done already. Promised myself in exchange for losing everything.

That's the one part I won't tell my dad. Mason laughed at me when I asked him how I was supposed to get him to sign when all Mason's terms and conditions for me are written out in black ink. His eyes sparkled at how naive I was. *Did you think I'd add them to the main contract? No, Ms. Van Kempt, you'll sign a separate addendum. I'll file it here in my desk drawer. That way, your daddy can't get in my way.*

But my dad can still get in the way of the main deal, and that would be a disaster. For him. For my mom.

For me.

I know what's waiting for me when I get back to the house. A pile of bills we have no hope of paying, a mother buckling under the stress of losing everything, and a father who's exactly as much of an alcoholic as Mason Hill said he was. Down to our last pieces of furniture and my mother's roses.

The turn onto our driveway feels rougher than normal, and a wild laugh bubbles out of me. Why did they pave the driveway with cobblestones? We have winters in New York. I never thought about cobblestone driveways and how they need to be redone every few years in states like this until ours started falling apart.

Did I start falling apart the moment Mason kissed me, or did it happen earlier? Did it happen when I walked into his office? When I decided to take that meeting at Phoenix Enterprises?

It's a struggle for the garage door to open, but it makes it. That's the spirit. That's the attitude I need right now. You might be on the verge of failure. That doesn't mean you can shut down. Not yet. Maybe not ever. Picking up the folio from its place on my passenger seat feels risky, like it might burn me. But the papers haven't done anything. It's Mason himself who's setting my skin on fire.

My cheap, Target shoes fold under the weight of me, and my face burns again. Mason was right. He was right about my shoes. And he was right that I need him. I yank them off one by one as soon as I'm in the back door and let them tumble to the floor.

And then...

Go back for them.

They're my only pair of heels. I need to keep them nice.

I can already picture, in vivid detail, his expression when he notices my half-off shoes in his apartment. The hot delight in his eyes at how little I have. At how little I am.

No. Not little. I'm worth something. I'm worth enough that he wanted me. Unless he just gets off

AMELIA WILDE

on getting as much power over people as possible, in which case—

I can't think like that.

The approach to my father's office gives me just enough time to get control of my breathing. Sticky air from outside has followed me in, settled into the hallway. Our central air hasn't been turned on yet this summer. How are we supposed to afford it?

All we can afford is enough to keep my dad comfortable with a portable unit in his office.

The office door stands open, but I knock on it anyway as I round the corner into the only cool air in the house. My clothes stick to my skin. "Hey, Daddy."

He looks up at me from his desk. A wide ledger covers the surface in front of him. I don't ask what he's doing with it, or who it belongs to. I know better than to ask. Anything written down like that is old—old enough to be private. "Hi, honey. How was the office?"

"I didn't go to the office today." I take the seat across from him. I've never been more desperate to change out of my clothes, but I'm also desperate for this conversation to be over. "I had a meeting in the city with a potential investor."

My father's eyes track the folio as I place it equally between us. He raises narrowed eyes to me

94

with a set jaw. "Investors, Charlotte? For a business venture of yours?"

"No. For Van Kempt Industries."

He lets out a bark of a laugh. "The company isn't looking for investors."

"We need an investor, Daddy. It's the only option we have left. I've had meeting after meeting with the team, and we all came to the same conclusion." Steely rain lashes the window behind him. My dad bristles in the yellow light of his desk light, but I have no choice. I have to keep going. He might not remember that he's had to fire almost everyone at Van Kempt Industries. He might be denying it to himself. But the team—there's practically no one left. It's me and a handful of people who have been trying to keep the Cornerstone development from imploding. "The only way to go forward with construction is to form a partnership with an outside investor."

He reaches out a white-sleeved wrist to pick up the tumbler on his desk. Only a single drink waits for him in the glass, and he downs it in one. I know that's not all he's had. I know he's been drinking all day. Wearing his nice office clothes can't disguise the tremors he's beginning to have. The liquid in the glass doesn't lie. My dad brings it back down to the desk with too much care. It scares me, how careful he is. How hard he's trying to disguise the amount he's had.

It's worse when he's not trying.

"I never have partnerships."

"But…you did. You've had lots of them."

"I don't have them anymore." He's put the glass down but he hasn't released it from his grip. "They're dangerous. They're shitty. They always end with someone getting hurt."

Partnerships *are* dangerous. More than I ever realized. Mason hasn't just demanded my time. He's also demanded my body, all but guaranteeing that I'll get hurt.

My stomach turns over. Am I really considering this? Selling myself to him to save my family?

Oh, god. I *am* considering it. I've already taken it for granted, but it's only now that I'm home that reality is setting in. Mason will touch me. He'll do more than that. He'll use me in every possible way, ways I haven't even considered yet.

Is it worth giving up my dignity to save my family?

An expression flickers over my father's face in a blink. Shorter than the flash of lightning outside. But I see it—I know I see it. His lips draw back from his teeth. They're out. Bared. Not a smile, but it makes me think of satisfaction. And then he's scowling again. The leather folio on the desk feels almost alive. He glances down at it like it might bite.

"Daddy." Folding both hands over my purse presses wet fabric into my lap. "I've found an investor for us. This contract guarantees the construction of the Cornerstone development. It guarantees a minimum sale price for the property after it's finished. The money will be enough to pay off the company debts and all of our family debts and start fresh. All it needs is your signature."

"Charlotte."

His tone is mildly scolding, and the urge wells up to admit that I'm in over my head. It was always this way growing up. I felt so guilty every time I stepped out of line. The smallest mistakes felt like enormous failures. "I think you should take a look at the contract."

My dad snatches the folio up into his hands and I bite back another wave of that old habit. It would feel good not to lie to him, but that feeling wouldn't last. I would have to shoulder the guilt of watching my parents' house get put up for auction after the mortgage payments stopped. Watch the town car get repossessed by whichever creditor got to it first. Our humiliation in front of New York society would be complete. Right now, at least, we can hide from it behind the doors of the mansion. My mother can pretend to her friends that she's not up for parties. My dad can pretend he's exploring new business ventures. Right now, everything has a chance to work out.

He thumbs through the pages. Too rough on them, but Mason Hill used thick, heavy paper for this. If he wanted the contract to feel like the only real thing in a cardboard house, he did it. The sound of the rain almost drowns out the subtle swishes of the paper. I need to check the bucket in the upstairs guest suite. It's sitting under a leak that gets bigger with every storm. I hope it hasn't overflowed.

A sigh, and then a slow, deliberate turning of the pages. All the way back to the beginning. Another bolt of fear—did Mason lie to me? Did he put the terms of our deal on the first page, where my dad would definitely see them? The hair on the back of my neck pulls up. Oh, god. If he did that, if all this was a cruel game, then it will be worse than rock bottom.

I take a slow breath. He didn't do that. Mason Hill might be an asshole. He might be the meanest person I've ever met. But somewhere, even if it's buried deep, there's good in him. There's good in everyone.

There has to be some good in everyone.

"Phoenix Enterprises." The name sounds

unfamiliar in my father's mouth. Not the way he's said *Van Kempt Industries* all my life. There's no pride in the way he says *Phoenix Enterprises*. Only resignation with a hint of suspicion. "This is Hill's company."

My shoulders sag. Thank God. I'd been going through scenarios, trying to figure out how to describe it while giving him the minimum amount of information, but he already knows. No hiding it now. "Yes."

A muscle in his cheek twitches. There's no telling how much he's had to drink, and I don't know if it'll make his pride duller or sharper.

"Find another investor." He moves to close the folio. I lurch forward in my seat, my purse falling wetly to the rug, and block his hand. My heart thuds. If it weren't for the storm, he'd be able to hear it.

I tried to find another investor. I couldn't. Mason is doing everything in his power to stop me from finding a deal with anyone else, and he has significantly more power than I do.

"There are no other investors." I'll break down if I have to. My dad never liked tears. He never liked what he called *theatrics*. But that's because they work. The problem I was having would be solved in a matter of hours. "I've looked. There's no one else. You don't have to deal with Phoenix, Daddy. I'll do all of that. All I need is one signature."

His lip curls and my stomach sinks. He's not going to sign it.

"Cyrus?"

My mother's voice filters down from the second floor. He stands at the sound of his name in the tired voice, shaking my wrist off as he does it. I stand, too, but not to go to her—to grab for the folio and a pen from the holder on his desk. The electricity flickers as I step into my father's path. Irritation darkens his face. "Excuse me."

"Sign it."

I feel as desperate and small as I did in Mason's office, but I won't let it show. That's not how you get things done. Without breaking eye contact, I flip open the contract to the correct page, marked with a red tab.

My dad snatches the pen out of my hand. His cheeks are as red as the tab on the page, and I don't move. I hardly breathe. I just stand still, blank-faced, as expressionless as possible while he takes off the cap. He's been in business a long time, and he doesn't sign things without reading them. But right now, today, he's drunk. My mom's waiting. His eyes move over the page. Cursory. Unseeing.

The tip of the pen hovers over the line.

It trembles.

My dad seems to notice it at the same time I do. He curses under his breath, scrawling his name in big loops on the line. Then he tosses the pen down onto the paper. It leaves several droplets of ink. They remind me of blood. He brushes past me on his way out of the room. "I'll expect a copy on my desk by the end of the week," he says as he disappears into the hall.

Outside, lightning flashes over the trees at the edge of the yard. They bend and twist in the wind, looking for all the world like they're screaming.

CHAPTER
TWO

Mason

I wonder if she's going to show.

Wondering anything about a woman is an unfamiliar habit. There have been a few over the years who served as useful distractions, but no one has ever made such an impression that it kept me awake at night or snatched away my attention during business meetings. Keeping the family intact has taken the bulk of my focus for the past fourteen years, followed closely by building Phoenix Industries. Those two projects dovetailed. I needed money to keep us together, and to keep my siblings in school and then in college. I needed the business to prove to anyone who might come knocking that we were fine.

So that's what I did. That's what I've done.

Until Charlotte Van Kempt.

I thought of Cyrus's wife and daughter in the abstract before. As pressure points to be manipulated.

Charlotte could not be more real.

And now all I can think about is her body in that skirt suit. Her red-faced rage at me for ruining her plans. Her curiosity. She's twenty and sheltered, new to the world of men like me, and it is fucking intoxicating.

But I'm not here to be intoxicated. I'm here to observe the property I'm about to own. Charlotte will show. Naive as she is, she understood that she had reached a dead end. No other choices but to bend to my will. If she hates the idea, all the better.

The Cornerstone development has one positive attribute: the location. From this rise at the edge of the property I can look down into the open rib cage of what Cyrus Van Kempt tried and failed to build. Steel beams rise from a concrete slab at the bottom of the basement.

Of course, everyone with half a brain knows that location is crucial in real estate. I'm of the opinion that it's a key part of any project, but not the only essential consideration. With enough investment any area's desirability can be increased. Business districts and neighborhoods can be manipulated to a person's will as long as he has enough money and drive.

Cyrus had neither. He ran out of money before the initial construction stages could be completed, and the man has only ever had enough drive to fuck people over.

I have personal experience with that.

I'm not the only one.

His daughter didn't look so pink-cheeked and white-faced at our meetings because she has time to fix any of this. The situation at Van Kempt Industries is far less rosy than she painted it in her proposal. When she said *a versatile team is already in place*, she meant that the staff originally hired to work the project are down to a skeleton crew. Most of them are doing the jobs of three people or struggling to make work for themselves in the absence of any actual development to do. It's not just the man's family he's let down. It's families across the city, some of whom were no doubt counting on him to keep them employed.

They've made a poor assessment.

A black town car turns the corner at the edge of the site. It's clearly struggling, the frame juddering in a way that suggests a problem with the engine, or the transmission. Things I don't generally bother to care about, except for the fact that this town car is carrying Charlotte Van Kempt. She grips the wheel with small hands. Hanging on for dear life. The innocent heat of her mouth comes back to me in a hard push at the base of my spine.

I don't want her hands on the wheel of that car. I want them elsewhere. Clasped and begging, for instance. Or wrapped around my cock.

It's a slight problem, that wanting. Wanting is not strictly part of the deal. At least not want for Charlotte specifically, though it is her body that's been on my mind. Her eyes. Her taste. The feel of her delicate bone structure underneath my palm.

It's her body that will bear the brunt of my revenge.

I see the moment she sees me, standing next to my Escalade. Charlotte can't or won't meet my eyes and her teeth dig into her bottom lip. She concentrates very, very hard on parking behind my car, leaving a good twenty feet of space behind the back bumper. The curve of her neck when she leans over to take something from the front seat makes my already-hard cock harder.

Fuck.

One slim ankle out of the car, then the other, then the rest of her. Charlotte wears a black sheath dress made from the same fabric as that little skirt suit, a narrow belt around her waist and those same cardboard shoes. No sunglasses, so I have a clear view of the adorable determination in her huge blue eyes. She grips the leather folio like it's holding her upright. The muscles around my right knee tighten, layering a more acute pain over the ever-present ache.

I'm going to wreck her.

She approaches with her head held high, though her pert chin drops as she gets closer. Charlotte Van Kempt can't help herself. I know what I look like, towering over her next to a monument to her father's abject failure as a business owner and a man. I know how she'd fight me if I forced her to her knees. I know how she'd secretly be relieved.

Charlotte slows a few feet off. Out of my reach. Her eyes dart over me, head to toe, in a flutter of her eyelashes. Suspicion needles at the back of my neck. That she's seeing more than I want her to see.

Not possible.

She clears her throat. "Mr. Hill, I've brought—"

I take one step toward her to put her within my reach, shove my hand between her dress and that little belt, and yank her closer. Charlotte gasps. She almost goes over, tumbling off her heels and into me. It's a disappointment when she doesn't, and a sheer pleasure to watch her straighten up with her face blazing red.

"Now you don't have to shout."

Her hand comes up to her throat, to the naked hollow there, her fingertips hiding her nervous swallow from view. Charlotte brushes a single lock of hair away from her face. "I've brought—"

"Look at me."

She drags her eyes up from the folio to meet mine.

"You're free to be nervous, Ms. Van Kempt. You're free to be angry. You're free to be humiliated. But you're not going to look at the ground when you speak to me. If I want your eyes lowered, I'll tell you."

"Okay." It's just above a whisper. Embarrassed, but steady.

I let my smile come slowly. Let it turn into the expression that brings meeting rooms to dead silence.

The hollow of Charlotte's throat dips. She needs a diamond there. So fucking badly. Is that what used to be there? Is that what she keeps reaching for?

"Okay, Mr. Hill." A breath of a pause. When I don't interrupt, her shoulders relax. "I've brought the signed contract."

She offers the folio to me and I take it. Look her up and down one more time, then flip it open to double-check the signature. Her chin comes out so she can look over the folio with me. Make sure it's still there. I want to put my hand around her neck and feel her pulse. I want to stop it for a few brief seconds so she knows I can. I want to make her understand the sins she's going to pay for.

But I won't do it yet. Patience.

I snap the folio shut and she blinks, startled. Curiosity ignites all down my spine. It's not particularly loud, or particularly violent. It's leather on leather. Something happened with it while it was out of my sight—while she was out of my sight—or else it's me she's reacting to. This is how I want her. Wide-eyed. Innocent. Breakable.

There's another folio, identical except for the papers inside, balanced on the trunk of my car. Charlotte's eyes follow my hands as I switch them out. Open the second one in front of her. "Now it's time for your signature."

A deep breath. "I never sign anything without reading it first."

"Did your daddy teach you that?"

"Yes." Defiance sparks in her eyes. "No matter what you think of him, it's good advice."

"You don't think there are ever occasions when it's better not to know?"

"I think it's always better to know." Uncertainty in that big blue gaze. Another swallow.

"Read, then."

Charlotte doesn't reach for the folio, and I don't offer it to her. I hold it in front of me so she has to step a little closer to read the print on the page. One big, deep breath, like she's getting ready to jump into the ocean, and she begins with the first paragraph.

Her face gets redder. This is a game that's going to be difficult to give up when I'm finished with her. I want to know, down to the shade, exactly how hard I can make her blush.

On the third paragraph she presses her lips together in a thin line.

On the fourth, her hand comes up to her throat. I'm intensely jealous of those fingertips on that fine flesh, but it's fascinating to watch. This is the paragraph that undid her. That made her forget I was watching. She's given herself away.

One more paragraph.

I've kept the document concise. It will be simpler, contract-wise, to trade her body for her father's debt than it is for me to take charge of Cornerstone. Cyrus Van Kempt's signature essentially gives me the power, as a partner in the venture, to modify existing building contracts to ensure the completion of the project. Doing those things requires hundreds of other decisions and signatures. An electronic forest of legal documents signed and stamped by my lawyers.

Charlotte's signature gives me—

"This is everything." Barely above a whisper. She remembers what I told her about not staring at the ground and looks back into my eyes. "This says—" Charlotte glances around, like she's worried someone might have crept up to peer over her shoulder. "This says you can do anything."

"I won't accept less."

Another glance down at the page. This is the moment Charlotte Van Kempt could come to her senses. She could realize that her asshole father isn't worth putting herself in my hands for.

She could understand that there are larger forces in play than the building. Than the deal.

That I have a deeper motive than simple cruelty.

"I don't—" Charlotte's hand splays out at her throat like it's possible to protect herself, and my knee tenses again. It aches. It hurts. On the verge of locking up completely. If she walks away from me now, I won't chase her. I won't have to. I will make my presence known everywhere she goes even if I never step foot in those buildings. I'll haunt every meeting. I'll be the death of any business deal she tries to make before it has a chance to breathe. I'll do all this despite the fact that I'm here at the end of fourteen years of excruciating patience, waiting to get back at her father, and she's still fresh and sunny and—

"Finish the sentence, Ms. Van Kempt."

"I don't have a pen," she whispers.

There should be no sense of relief at this, but I feel it anyway. I take the pen from my pocket and hand it to her, the folio balanced in my other palm.

The weight of her pen on the paper is so light. The meaning of her signature is so heavy. Charlotte gives me the pen with a shaking hand. She straightens her back. "What now?"

"What do you think? That I'll put you on your knees here in the street?"

Oh, that shade of red. I want it captured in a painting. It's burned into my memory instead. "You could do that," she admits, and I hear it in her voice—reality setting in.

"My team will be visiting the property in an hour to make assessments." I close the folio and toss it on top of the car. It lands neatly on top of the one she brought with her, freeing my hands to reach for my phone. "You'll be at my apartment on Friday at sunset." I send the address in a text message. "The address is waiting on your phone."

"Okay." She glances at the concrete and steel beams. "And right now—"

"Right now you'll turn around, get back into your car, and drive away."

"Shouldn't we talk about Cornerstone?"

Charlotte stands so close that it's nothing to take her by her ridiculous little belt and haul her closer to me. She panics, trying to pull away, trying not to fall into me, but I have her by her clothes. I hold her there until she stops struggling. It doesn't take long.

"A piece of advice, Ms. Van Kempt."

"What? *What?*" Breathless. I fucking love it.

"If I give you the choice to walk away from me, take it. This is the last time I'll give you a second chance."

I release her, though I don't want to, and Charlotte turns on her heel and runs.

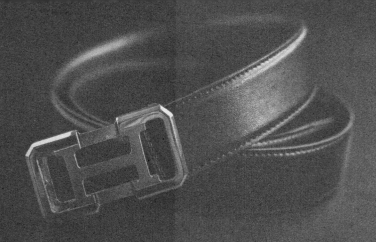

CHAPTER THREE

Charlotte

The town car trundles through the gates of the parking garage underneath the building where Mason Hill lives, and the first thing I'm confronted with is a sign that says VISITORS MUST STOP AT SECURITY STATION.

It should make me feel more comfortable. We have a gatehouse in our neighborhood, and I've been waved through every time I came home since I was sixteen. My heart continues racing. I ease past the sign and pull up next to the guard station. A man in a dark uniform steps out and motions for me to roll down the window. I do it.

"Do you have a pass, miss?"

"I—yes. Yes. It's right here." I meant to have it out and in my lap before I got here. It arrived to my house by courier with a note that read *Sunset*. I get it into the guard's hand without dropping it. A small miracle.

He checks the pass, then peers into my face. It feels like everyone in the world knows what's going to happen to me in Mason's apartment tonight. I'm the only one who doesn't know. All I know is that it will be all right, in the end. It might be…embarrassing. It *will* be embarrassing. It'll be out of my comfort zone. But I'll be saving my family. I'll be saving myself.

It will be worth it. I know it will.

The guard directs me to a spot in a near-empty row and I take the elevator up to the lobby of the building. It lets me off in the front corner of a wide, modern space with a gleaming tiled floor. A swath of carpeting runs along the center. On the right-hand side of the space, a wide archway leads to a bar. The Middlegame, according to the black marble sign above the archway. An outline of a chess piece decorates the sign next to the elegant letters. A floor sign near the archway points to a hallway. *Dining*, it reads.

Voices drift into the lobby on the air. I can only

see one man sitting at the bar, but it feels like a crowd is watching.

Two doormen wait behind a small counter on the other side. Their conversation blends with the soft noise from the restaurant. None of it is louder than my own racing heartbeat.

One of them lifts his head and waves me over. It wouldn't be the worst thing in the world if he ended this now. If he said he had a message from Mr. Hill that I'd proved myself to him, and we didn't have to play this game.

"Good evening, Ms. Van Kempt."

My face heats. They're waiting for me, then. Everyone knows what's happening. They all know what I am, and what I've done. I put on a smile anyway. "Hi. I'm meeting Mason Hill."

"You'll need the private elevator. The main one won't take you to the penthouse."

Of course.

"Do I need—" Oh my god. This is not the first nice building I've been inside. I grew up in a mansion. And I feel like I've never visited the city before. I feel small. Unsteady. "Do I need a pass for it?"

"You'll need a code, provided to you by Mr. Hill."

At that moment my phone vibrates in my purse. I reach for it like a lifeline. Mason's name is on the screen, along with a code. 0-6-0-7. Relief thunders through me at the name. At the numbers. Relief, and a flash of anger. He's in control of every moment. He decides if he wants to save me or let me dangle in front of the doorman.

"I have the code," I announce brightly while I read each of their name tags. "Thanks so much for your help, Derek. Steve."

They go back to talking as I go over to the elevator. A keypad by the side lights up when I'm close enough to touch. The doors don't open until the code is in. I've never been more relieved to have those same doors slide shut behind me.

On the inside panel there are four buttons, three unlabeled, one that has a slim metal plate that says PENTHOUSE. I pick that one. I try not to think of the fact that Mason Hill not only owns the penthouse, he owns the top four floors. He probably owns the entire building. Pays the men at the counter. Everything I can see and touch belongs to him.

Including me.

My pulse is racing too fast to feel individual heartbeats by the time the elevator doors open.

Directly into the foyer of Mason's penthouse.

That explains the code, and the two doormen. There's no outer hall. The elevator itself is the only transition between the rest of the building and his private space.

And him.

He stands in the center of the foyer on shining marble my mother would approve of. Feet planted, but there's possibility in his stance. He could do anything.

Run. The instinct hits at the same time the cool air does, all over my skin. I give in to it, but the only place to go is toward him. Into his house.

It smells good in here. Fresh. New. Like someone might have painted recently. Like someone took great care with every part of this place. Including the man in front of me now. He's tall and strong, nothing like those thrashing trees in the storm, but that same energy fills the space around us. Is it him or me? Or both of us together? It's one thing to look at slicing branches from the safety of your bedroom. It's another to stand below one while the lightning cracks.

Mason looks me up and down. "How was traffic?"

Three words. It should be a simple question, the way it was when Jax Hunter asked it. In Mason Hill's mouth it's a challenge. Every syllable is another reminder that I'm here in bargain-bin cloth and cardboard shoes. No jewelry. No armor.

"It was terrible," I tell him. Mason looks just as

gorgeous and cutting as he did at his office and at Cornerstone, but he's changed out of his suit. Slacks and a button-down, all of it crisp and perfect, even the sleeves rolled up to his elbows to show off strong forearms. Those are the arms he'll use to…do things to me. "Mid-morning would be a better time to meet in—in terms of the traffic."

He laughs, and the sound gives me shivers. It's mean and beautiful and makes me feel like I've lost a layer of clothing or a beloved necklace. Something I came in here expecting to keep. Maybe it's my dignity. But no—I still have that, for the moment. "You'd rather me cancel meetings for you?"

"I'm sure you're in charge of your schedule. You could make it work."

"This works for me." A gesture in my direction. He takes in my clothes. My shoes. My burning cheeks. "You, struggling through traffic and fumbling your way past the doormen. I like it when you're nervous."

"I'm not nervous."

Mason takes a deliberate step closer. Then another. Fine. Okay. I'm nervous. I'm terrified. The back of my neck goes hot, then cold, then hot again. How long is it going to be before he makes me get on my knees? There's a dark suggestion in everything he says, and I don't know him. I don't know him at all. I'm not sure whether he's the kind of man who will want to drag out my humiliation as long as possible or get right to it.

"What about now? Is your heart beating faster?"

It is. "No."

"Really? Your pupils are enormous."

"Really," I insist, and it sounds like a breathless lie, because it is. "I'm not afraid."

He's close now. Close enough to smell him. And I'm mortified to find that he smells so, so good. Clean. Masculine. Something vaguely spicy I can't name. I haven't taken another step but adrenaline runs rampant through my veins. My heart crashes like I'm being chased through those storm-laden trees. This scent would be in the air seconds before he caught me. I remember what he said about looking him in the eye and I do it. His eyes make me think of those trees. All that violent motion. It's a clear night. No sign of rain, or lightning. His focus has the same intensity as that storm.

Worse than the storm.

He wouldn't take off his jacket and cover me with it, if we were out in a storm. He would let me get soaked to the skin.

"Not afraid," he echoes, like he's testing the shape of them. Tasting my fear on the air. "I'll fix that."

How?

One step takes the last of the space between us. I don't ask the question. I'm fighting for every breath. God, they're so loud. It's so obvious that I'm afraid.

"Look at that," Mason murmurs, almost to himself. "You think you're terrified."

"Fine. I am. I admit it." A new wave of shame heats my cheeks. "I'm terrified. But I'm still going to do this."

"Of course you are. You don't have any other choice."

"Doesn't that—doesn't that bother you?"

He cocks his head to the side and his perfection is like a hem done by a master tailor—once you see the best, everything else looks ragged and less-than. It makes me jealous. It makes me hate him even more. It makes me wish—

I won't get into what I wish.

"Does what bother me, Ms. Van Kempt?"

"That I obviously don't want to be here?"

A noncommittal noise. "You very much want to be here. You're desperate to be here. You're so desperate for it that you're panting."

"I'm—" I force a few slow, deep breaths. "I'm not panting. I'm nervous. I already admitted it. What more do you want?"

He laughs again. It cuts into me. Double-edged. It hurts, to be laughed at like this. It hurts that he's enjoying my fear so much. And I want to know what he sounds like when he's not being mean. The curiosity comes in an embarrassed ache. I shouldn't want to know more about him. It's because he's standing so close. It's because he's so handsome. There are other reasons. If I keep breathing, I'll have time to think of all of them.

"I think we're past what I want, Ms. Van Kempt. At this point it's more about what I'll take."

Mason has already taken all the space in his foyer, and now there's nothing left but me.

I can't do it. I can't look him in the eye for this. For whatever's about to happen. So I end up looking at his chest. At the beautifully sewn buttons of his shirt. The movement of his arm as he reaches for me.

His fingertips burn across my forehead, brushing a lock of hair away from my face. Gentle but perfunctory. Getting it out of his way. I hold my breath. There are other things in his way, like my dress. Like my panties and bra. I'm still standing in his foyer.

He follows the line of my jaw with a fingertip, then digs the pad of his finger under my chin and forces my face up. "You're free to lie to me about being afraid, Ms. Van Kempt. I like the way you sound when you try to convince me. You're not free to hide."

The terrible thing is, he's beautiful. It's not just the soft, expensive lighting in his foyer. He is just absolutely gorgeous. Mason Hill could have stepped out of a fashion magazine, with all his lean muscle and elegant bone structure. "It's hard to hide from a person who's touching you."

"Bullshit," he says. "You're trying to do it right now."

His fingertip moves down over my throat. Over the hollow. Down to the neckline of my dress. My brain skips ahead along the path he's following. Down and down and down. The space between my legs is unbearably hot, but I can't move. Moving my thighs at all would tell him that I've thought of it. That here, in this moment, I'm imagining his hand there. He has big hands, and I'd have to spread my legs to let him—

A palm on my hip startles a gasp out of me. He makes a sound that's almost like approval, and part of me bursts into flame. This is bad. This is worse by the second. I can't want his approval. I can't want any part of this. I don't want it.

"Yes," he says, like he can hear my thoughts. "You hate it when I touch you. Aren't you lucky?"

"Why—" It takes so much energy to stay

standing. It would be better to fall. At least then I'd be on solid ground. "Why would I be lucky?"

He bends, and something about the movement—I notice something about it but it's subsumed in the scent of him. In the heat of his breath against the shell of my ear. "You're lucky, Ms. Van Kempt, that the contract doesn't require you to want this."

"That's absurd." His lips brush the soft skin behind my earlobe and my whole body tenses. It feels good. It's not supposed to. Somehow he's angling me against him, angling himself against me. Every time I think he's touching me everywhere, it changes. "You couldn't control my feelings even if you wanted to."

"I don't need to control your feelings. You loathe this." A kiss to my jawline. "And I don't fucking care."

I open my mouth to argue, to fight, to say something, but I never get the chance.

Because he kisses me for real.

All the rest—I don't know what that was. The kiss bowls it all over. He's all power and strength and possession, a hand locking around my jaw, another one warm and solid on the small of my back. A cage. I'm caged in by him and he's not using anything but his body. But it's worse than that, because everything with Mason Hill is worse than it seems. It's worse.

Because I want to be kissing him. He kisses me like he's known me forever. Like he's demanded entrance to my mouth with his tongue a thousand times before. Like he expected me to react by letting him in.

Which I do.

I do.

It's terrible.

It's wonderful.

I hate it.

I want it.

I've never known anything to be so good and so cruel at the same time. He's playing with me, proving his power over me, and I just have to stand here and take it. His tongue. His teeth. The cold, clean taste of him. I don't know I've put my hands to his chest until he moves and I feel him there, all hard muscle and control.

His grip on my chin tightens. Mason takes one last, desultory lick of my mouth and then he breaks the kiss off. "No," I hear myself say.

I have the impression of glittering green, and then he kisses me again, laughing behind it, the sound so dark it makes my vision shadowy. Unclear. He's moving us and I can't make sense of the direction. He'll take me inside. To a bed. A couch. A carpet. He'll take my dress. He'll take everything.

I feel the wall, inches away from my back, but

his hand keeps me from touching it. His teeth graze my lower lip. Tease at sinking into the flesh. A warning of what he could do. Of what he's probably going to do. Fear and confusion and desire braid themselves together down my spine. A movement. A sound.

And then he pushes me backward into his elevator.

I catch myself on the railing, barely upright. "That's all?"

He's pushing at a button on the outside, but when he steps in front of the open doors, there's no sign he was ever kissing me except a glint in his eyes and a lightning-storm energy about to crest.

The expression that comes over his face is the same one he wore when I saw him in Jax Hunter's meeting room. Cruelly satisfied. "That's all you get tonight," he says, and then the doors close.

CHAPTER
FOUR

Mason

Here's the real problem with letting Charlotte Van Kempt stand in my foyer. Here's what it is. I can't stop thinking about her there. Every time the elevator doors open, I think of her. Every time they close, I think of how hard she gripped that railing. How huge her eyes looked. How red her cheeks were.

All for a kiss.

A *tame* kiss in comparison to what I wanted to do to her.

Her trembling in the foyer was very different from the woman in my imagination. I pictured a society ice queen. I got the opposite. Charlotte Van Kempt is like the sun fighting through thick clouds. The scent of her reminded me of fresh air. Of possibility.

Many, many filthy possibilities.

God, this revenge will be even better. I'm glad Cyrus didn't attend the first meeting. That would have been satisfying, but this is much sweeter.

Those possibilities are currently interrupting my work. Again and again and again. There are some silver linings to the situation. Namely, I'm in my private office at home, and I don't have to stand up all day. I can stretch out my knee under the desk while I exchange emails with the new team leads for the Cornerstone project. I had interim people in those positions before. Some have been promoted. Some have been returned to their regular work. Everyone who has even a tangential part to play in this development has been made aware that I'll be an enormous pain in the ass until this is finished.

Some projects require a more hands-on approach.

Obviously, this is one of them.

An email comes in from Hades while I'm in the middle of an extended back-and-forth about the numerous contractors we'll be hiring over the next few days. He emails exactly like he texts, which is an accurate representation of the way he is on the phone. A rare consistency to find in a person.

SUBJECT: Necklace

I've located a piece that matches the description. The lot is out of Italy and will be on the mountain in three weeks.

–H

He doesn't bother saying that he'll send photos as soon as the lot arrives. He always does. It's an obnoxious process, finding this jewelry. It dredges up old memories I'd rather forget. And then there's the secrecy. Rebuilding my family's fortune means we're back on the radar of the world at large and anyone who happens to own pieces from the estate.

As for the people who took it from us in the first place…

They're still out there, too, the fucking cowards. That's an information game, same as the jewelry but buried deeper.

SUBJECT: RE: Necklace

Three weeks? I thought we were friends, motherfucker

Mason Hill

CEO, Phoenix Enterprises

A knock at the door. It opens before I've said anything, and Gabriel comes in. He sits down in one of the chairs on the other side of the desk without looking up from his phone. I don't doubt he's been up—and out—all night, but he looks fresh as a daisy. It's one of the most obnoxious things about him. Nothing touches him. Nothing so much as wrinkles his shirt.

"In some circles, it's considered rude to barge in on someone who hasn't invited you."

He gives me what I call his party grin, which for some reason I can't fathom makes people want to talk to him at social gatherings. "It's brunch day. And you can't get enough of me."

"Were they disappointed when you left early to come harass me?"

"Yes," he says. "Our conversation was finally getting somewhere. They thought it was cute that we spend so much family time together. Which is ironic, because you never answer your calls but are now demanding a weekly brunch."

"Please. It was one call." Last night, after I'd sent Charlotte away. The reason I didn't answer is because I was in the shower with my cock in my fist. It hurts to get off like that, with my knee protesting every second, but not more than my cock hurt from wanting to fuck her.

From wanting to destroy her.

"Mason," Gabriel says.

Shit. He's been talking. "Yeah?"

"I need you to talk to your friend at the DOB. My new property in Chelsea needs a historical designation, and they're dragging their feet."

"I'd already have talked to them if you were with Phoenix."

After last week's brunch, I sent him an updated merger proposal. It would cost him nothing to merge with Phoenix. It would make him several fortunes over. And if anything happened, Phoenix would absorb the losses. It's a safer bet for everyone.

"I'm not with Phoenix, though. Luckily, my favorite brother owns it."

"You want a signing bonus, is that it?"

He laughs. "My independence is priceless."

"Your independence is going to hang you out to dry one day. You, and all the people who depend on you. Why not offer them some job security?"

Gabriel finishes with his phone and drops it onto my desk. "They have job security. I'm the best in the business at acquisitions."

"You could be the best in the business at Phoenix. Better than you are now."

"No," he sings, a two-note melody that's both irritating and exhausting. "I didn't come here to fight with you, big brother. I just need a little help. A couple of strings pulled. Anyway…"

He keeps talking, and my brain takes a left turn. Charlotte didn't make it this far into the penthouse. I planned on bringing her inside. Of course I planned on it. But then she was so nervous, so high-strung, and I wanted to take every advantage of her where she stood. Naturally, there were competing interests. It would be a waste of her fearful anticipation to take everything in our very first meeting. It would leave very little for her to lie awake about.

So I didn't bring her to the living room, or the office. I didn't bend her body over the desk and cut away her clothes. I didn't tie her to it with my belt just to watch her struggle against the bonds. Patience is a virtue. It's also torture. In the moment, I thought if I got her out of the penthouse, I wouldn't be able to imagine her in any of the rooms. I thought I'd buy myself a little more patience.

It's been an outright failure. All I can think about is how she'd look naked and shivering, her hips against the edge of the desk.

"Rude." Gabriel drums his fingers on my desk. "You're not listening."

"Not really. Go ahead and start over."

"Hey, Gabe." Remy pads in and takes the seat next to him, curling up in it like she'd rather still be in her bed. She has a study group on Friday nights that keeps her out late. I agreed to it because it happens in a building I own near her college campus, on a block that I mostly own, and so security isn't a problem. It *does* mean she shows up at five most Saturdays this semester. "Did you just get here? Did you have fun last night?"

"Yes. I've been trying to talk to our eldest brother."

My sister runs both hands over her bedhead. "It's not going well?"

"I can hear you," I point out. Another email arrives in my inbox.

SUBJECT: RE: RE: Necklace

The seller was a nosy bastard who wanted to know if you had any involvement with the sale. I told him I'd never heard of you. Poseidon is off the coast and will pay him a visit after a suitable interval.

–H

Well. Everyone counts as a nosy bastard to Hades. What's unusual is for him to ask his brother—a pirate who masquerades as a shipping magnate—to gather information. It explains why he hasn't rushed the shipment, or given any indication that it contains something I want. Since the seller brought up my family name, it makes it more likely that the necklace is the correct one.

SUBJECT: RE: RE: RE: Necklace
Thanks. I'll send you a gift basket for your trouble.
Mason Hill
CEO, Phoenix Enterprises

The necklace reminds me of Charlotte Van Kempt's naked throat and how quickly it rose and fell in the foyer. I didn't let myself touch her there. Did not allow myself to press the pad of my thumb into that space to feel her gasp and swallow. I settled for her chin, which is enough to know that a little light choking would make her hot. Telling her she hated every moment made her blush deepen.

It would be satisfying if she did hate my touch, but the poor thing didn't. It's a far better revenge to make her want it.

Make it terrible for her, and make her want that, too.

"All I want from him is one whisper in the ear of his buddy at the Department of Buildings. It's practically nothing."

"I want him to let me go to Greece. Maybe I can get him to agree while he's not paying attention," says Remy.

"You know my terms for studying abroad."

She lets out a theatrical groan. "Mason, I can't be the only one who takes a team of bodyguards to the field. They'd get in the way, and everyone would think—"

"I don't care what everyone thinks, little sister. Your safety is my top priority."

Remy purses her lips. She's going to school for a degree in archeology. "When am I going to age out of your obsessive overprotectiveness?"

"When I die."

"Mason—"

"It's not a battle worth fighting," Gabriel says. "Trust me."

Remy drops her head back against the chair. "At least you got to pick your own team."

Gabriel snorts. "You think Mr. Obsessive let me choose when I was in college?"

Her eyes go comically wide. "He didn't?"

"It didn't matter." Gabriel grins at her. "I befriended them all so they wouldn't tell my secrets."

"I paid them to keep your secrets, asshole. Don't listen to him," I tell Remy. "He hires his own people now and he *still* befriends them because he's addicted to gossip and mind games."

"Are you talking about me?" Jameson ambles in with bloodshot eyes, his hair windblown, a tear

134

in the knee of his jeans and a dark streak down one of his arms. A grin on his face, like this is all a very good joke.

"Oh my god, Jameson." Remy hops up from her chair and fusses over him, tugging at his t-shirt, peering at his arm. "Where have you been? Sit down."

He shoos her away but takes the seat she left, throwing a hand over his eyes like the light in here is too oppressive to bear. "Why are all of you in here?"

"You'll be surprised to discover that we weren't talking about you." Gabriel watches Jameson with an unreadable expression.

"Who's playing mind games, then? You?" Jameson uncovers one eye and peers back at Gabriel. "I heard you were at your favorite club last night."

Gabriel ignores this entirely. "Mason. It's one phone call."

"No, don't go back to that." Remy perches on the arm of Jameson's chair and gives me sad puppy-dog eyes. "It's not even an entire semester. It's, like, six weeks. And there will be plenty of other people around. It's not like I'd be going into the field by myself."

"Correct. If you go, you're going with your entire security team, so you won't have to worry about being lonely. Jameson, tell us where you were and if the cops are going to knock on the door of the apartment."

"It's six weeks," says Remy. We've been talking about this for at least six weeks. It feels like fourteen years.

"There are no cops." This, from Jameson.

"You can't avoid this discussion forever," says Gabriel.

My knee seizes under the table and I grit my teeth against the pain. It aches constantly whenever I'm standing. Sitting down is usually the solution. But now, with all of them on the other side of my desk, in my office, on Saturday fucking morning, pushing and pushing and pushing—

"It wasn't me this time," Jameson says. He's sitting up now, watching. "Do you want an Advil?"

"No."

"Bullshit."

I get up from my seat to prove it doesn't hurt. Jameson's correct. This is bullshit. It hurts to stand up, and it hurts to stay standing. I swipe my phone from the desk and text the chef to tell her we're eating in the den. "Remy. Pick the show."

"I have a meeting," Gabriel says.

"The fuck you do." I level the phone at him. "You're staying for brunch, and today we're eating in the den." Things are not always better at a dining table. If I'm going to make this work—and I am—then it will take some adjusting. After our parents died, we didn't have a dining room. Maybe this will be better.

Jameson gets up next. "I'm going to bed."

"No," Remy says. "Come to brunch. Please? You can go to bed after."

This is an old, old act we're participating in. The only question is whether Jameson and Gabriel are going to play their parts. Lately they haven't been. I see Jameson at the office more than I see him at home. Gabriel denies that he feels any tension. He puts on that smile of his and disappears back to his business.

But Remy has always had the upper hand. She was about to turn seven when our parents were killed.

When they died.

"What, Jameson, you can't go another hour without a nap?" Gabriel arches an eyebrow at our brother. "You're losing your edge."

"I thought you were abandoning our sec-ond-ever brunch for a meeting," Jameson shoots back. Remy's eyes move between the two of them. She bites at her lip, forever hopeful that things won't fall apart. The catastrophe, of course, happened four-teen years ago.

Gabriel rises, making a show of tapping out a message on his phone and sending it. "There. I canceled it. Your move."

Jameson grins, rubbing both hands over his face. "Give me ten minutes." He cuts a glance at me. "If it's more pancakes—"

"It's waffles, prick. And scrambled eggs."

"Thank God." He goes out into the living room and turns toward the bedroom. Remy goes through the larger living room and into the den. Gabriel's already protesting her choice of show, but he'll let her have the final say.

My phone buzzes. More email.

SUBJECT: RE: RE: RE: RE: Necklace
Don't bother with a gift basket, you insufferable bastard. It was no trouble. After all, we're close friends.
–H

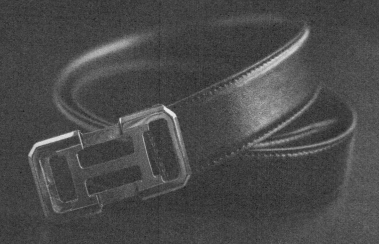

CHAPTER FIVE

Charlotte

Elise's late for our lunch date, which is good, because I haven't figured out exactly what to say. It feels weird to sip cucumber water at the little place by her apartment in the city like nothing happened. It wasn't nothing. I definitely haven't lain awake all week over nothing. But it wasn't what I expected. None of this is how I expected.

"I am so sorry." She leans down for a quick hug, then takes her seat. "A last-minute order. I thought I could get it done in less time."

"It never turns out that way. Literally never. I say that every time I make a dress."

"And you're wrong every time." Elise slips her sunglasses into her purse and peers at me. "Now stop being so cagey and tell me what happened with Mason Hill. It's not fair to be so stingy with the details."

My face heats. "Okay, well…this new deal."

I told her I signed with him, but I didn't tell her anything else. I'm not sure why I thought it would be easier in person. At least this way, when she judges me, I'll know it's happening. I won't have to guess.

"You said it was like a job, and you didn't take it, but now you have taken it, so…what is it? Secretary work? Are you filing papers in his office? Aren't you supposed to be at Van Kempt?"

She's talking about my weekly responsibilities for the company, which I took over months and months ago. Someone from the family had to be in the office. My mother can't do it, and my father won't stop his drinking, so that left me. I work days at Van Kempt for nothing and make clothes at night.

I take a quick look around the restaurant to make sure there are no familiar faces. It would be like Mason to know I was here.

Coast is clear.

"Like I said, it's not really a job. What he offered me is more of a…more of an arrangement."

Elise leans in, curiosity sparkling in her

eyes. "Tell me right now, Charlotte. That sounds incredibly…illicit."

I take a deep breath. "I have to see him every Friday night."

She blinks. "That's it?"

"No, that's not—I have to be available every Friday night at sunset. At his apartment."

This sounded way dirtier in my head. Way more illicit. Like it sounded when Elise said it.

"Are you telling me—"

The waitress comes back to the table and Elise leans back to let her pour more cucumber water. She orders her sandwich and mine, as quickly as possible, with a big smile on her face. Her expression turns serious the moment the waitress steps away, and we both lean back in. My heart beats fast. I would never make it as a spy. People would definitely notice the furtive looks and the lowered voices.

"Are you telling me you already saw him?"

"Last Friday."

"Tell me everything," she demands.

"Okay. He lives in a penthouse. Like…a really nice building. I think he might own the whole thing. You have to have a code to the elevator, and the guys in the lobby—"

Elise waves this off. "We can talk about the guys

in the lobby later. What was he like? What did he do? Was he still an asshole?"

"He was waiting for me when I stepped off the elevator."

She nods. "Okay. Okay. That's normal. That's not serial killer stuff. If you invite someone over—"

"It's not really an invitation kind of situation. I'm required by the contract."

"There's an actual contract?"

"Yeah." Her eyes have never been wider, and I know, I just know, that she's going to ask me what it said. There's no way I can repeat it out loud in this restaurant. "It's every Friday night. So I showed up last Friday, and he was waiting for me."

She folds her arms beneath her, leaning forward another few inches. "Oh my god. What did he do?"

"He…" I replay it in my memory. How long was I there? Fifteen minutes, maybe. "He talked to me. He wasn't…you know. He wasn't nice."

"Did he insult your clothes again?"

"No." He ran his finger along my neckline and made me think he might tear the whole dress from my body and send me out without anything to wear. "He was kind of taunting me. Telling me how much I hated it."

Elise's eyes sparkle. "But obviously you didn't."

142

"Right. Obviously, I didn't—" No. No no no. "Wait. No. I did. It was terrible. He's terrifying."

"Because he's so hot."

"Because he's so mean," I correct, though it's not really a correction. He *is* hot. Thinking of him now, his presence in that space, the smell of him, the height of him, all that muscle. "The only reason he's helping with Cornerstone is because I signed this deal with him. He can do anything he wants."

Both eyebrows go up. "Anything?"

"Anything."

She takes a deep breath. Takes a sip of her cucumber water. "Did he fuck you?"

"No."

"What? Oh my god. Did he kiss you?"

"Yes."

"And was that it?"

"He touched me."

"Did you…" She mouths the words *get off*.

"Oh my god, Elise. No. It wasn't like that. It was just a kiss."

It was *not* just a kiss.

It was the farthest thing from just a kiss on the entire planet. It sank into all my cells. I can't stop thinking about it. Can't stop replaying the taste of him. How powerful he seemed. But when I describe it, when I say it out loud, it seems like nothing.

Did he do that on purpose?

Probably yes.

"What did you wear?"

"The blue dress."

"The boat-neck one?"

"Yeah."

"Okay. I love that dress on you, by the way. But you need a power outfit. You need to wear black."

"Yes. Yes." I can't stop thinking about next Friday, but making plans—that's better. That's the way to deal with a scary situation. An…exciting situation. Plan to be my best. "Do you think I should make a new one?"

"Do you have fabric?"

"I have a coupon."

Elise nods decisively. "Then yes. More of like a—" She traces the shape on her own chest.

"A sweetheart."

"A sweetheart neckline. But then…" We both lean in again. More state secrets. "Then there's the slit."

I can absolutely see it. How it'll look when I put it on. How he'll look when he sees me in it. I take a long drink of cucumber water. It feels impossible to stop nodding.

Elise reaches across the table and puts her hand

on mine. "Do you want to get our food to go so we can go to the fabric store?"

"You're my best friend," I tell her, already on my feet.

A last-minute dress like this begs for optimism. It requires optimism. The less I think about begging, the better.

Anyway.

I only have tonight to work on it. Tomorrow I'll be in the office at Van Kempt and I have to leave soon after five to make it to Mason's penthouse by sunset. It has to be done before I go to work in the morning.

And it has to be perfect. So perfect that he doesn't make a single comment about it. I won't be terrified in this dress. I'll be powerful.

I won't even miss my necklace.

It's damn near perfect by the time I fall into bed three hours before my alarm on Friday. It waits for me on the back of my closet door while I throw myself through a bleary shower. I drink too much caffeinated tea at the Van Kempt Industries offices and tell everyone who's left they can leave at four. This dress needs makeup to match. Not the sweet look I wore with the blue dress, though it was my favorite. The one I feel most comfortable in.

If anyone's going to make me feel uncomfortable, it's going to be me. And I'm going to do it before Mason Hill.

But once the dress is on, once my makeup is done, once I'm in my Target heels…

I'm not uncomfortable.

Oh my god.

I look so good. The best I've ever looked. I try out a sultry expression in the mirror and end up pointing at myself in congratulations, which ruins the effect.

The town car's radio is broken so I turn the volume all the way up on my phone and toss it into the passenger seat for the ride into the city. I intend to take this mood in through the parking garage. All the way through the lobby. All the way up the elevator. All the way into his foyer, and—

"Your keys, Ms. Van Kempt," says the guard at the security station.

"What? Why?"

"We'll be parking your car for you tonight. Mr. Hill has requested that you meet him in front of the building."

A request from Mason isn't really a request. It's an order. My confidence ticks down a notch. The guard gives me enough space to open the door and step out, but then I have to go around to get my purse and my phone from the passenger seat. I have trouble with the door—it sticks, and won't shut all the way sometimes—and a second guard hops behind the wheel and pulls it closed for me.

"Okay," I say to no one in particular. It looks like every Friday with Mason is going to start with my face on fire.

My heels click and clack all the way out of the underground garage.

He's waiting for me in front of the building, that beautiful, infuriating smile on his face. A shining black SUV idles at the curb. Mason looks me up and down as I approach.

My heart is the first to respond to him, even though I don't want to. I want to be cool and collected and untouchable. It's a lost cause. My heart knocks against my ribs with every step I take. My skin goes hot at the sight of him in his flawless dark suit. He's the untouchable one. All perfect dark hair and eyes turned a deep green in the glow from the lobby of his building. Sunset comes late in the summer. After eight. It's burning down the sky behind him. Melting into a darkness that's as forbidding as he is.

And as alluring.

Damn it.

"Are you leaving, or are we going somewhere?"

His mouth tilts up at the words. "I have reservations for a late dinner. You'll be coming with me."

Dinner. With him. I don't let the shiver of nervousness show, I just climb into the SUV. It smells brand new. Nothing like the end-of-life leather smell of our town car. Mason gets in after me, and his driver comes around to shut the door. There's more space back here than I thought. Enough for him to stretch out his legs, which he does. There's something about the way he moves. The fit of his clothes...

I can't put my finger on it.

There would probably be rumors about him on the Internet. Speculation. Gossip. But I haven't put his name into a search engine. It gives me secondhand embarrassment to think about it. I didn't want to know how much money he had after that first meeting when I turned him down.

"Don't you think it's early to be taking me out to dinner?"

His eyes meet mine in the half-dark of the back of the car. "Compared with what? Is there a regular schedule you follow with the men you sell your body to?"

It's so blunt, so harsh, that I start to suck in a gasp.

And stop. That's what he wants. Of course that's what he wants.

"You're the only one I've ever done this with, Mr. Hill." It's hardly my voice. It's the voice of someone who's sure of herself. Whose life isn't falling apart.

He shifts closer to me. Close enough to feel his heat across the narrow space between us. Close enough to put one hand on my thigh, over my dress. A shock runs through me like he's coaxed my knees apart with his hands. I inch them apart before I can stop myself.

A laugh, and then a big hand comes down and turns my face toward him. All the lights are different shades and colors, and they swim through his green eyes as he stares down at me, tracing paths on my skin over and over again.

"You can't stand this."

It's a lie. He knows it. I know it. He just watched me attempt to spread my legs for him. Oh, god. It cannot get worse.

A little voice in the back of my mind whispers that it can. It will.

"No," I agree with him. "It's awful."

He gives my face a little squeeze and I want to fight. I should push his hand away. Slap him away, if necessary. But I've agreed to do this. And a dark, twisted part of me likes the feel of his grip on my face. It's not right. In fact, it's very wrong. My body trembles with the contradiction. I agreed to let him do this in exchange for saving our lives. He wasn't lying when he said I sold my body to him. I did.

"You've never done anything like this, Ms. Van Kempt. Does that mean you've never been fucked?"

The question reminds me of begging him for a deal in his office. It's that same tone. That same power. Trying to hide the answers will only make him meaner. Only make me want him more. And I can't do this.

"No." The smallest pause urges me on. "I've never been f-fucked."

"What about this criminally fuckable mouth?" His thumb brushes over my bottom lip.

I clear my throat. "No."

"Good," he says lightly. "That will make things considerably hotter when I take your throat."

My entire body, head to toe, every inch, knows what's coming next. I might be a virgin but I'm not so naive that I don't know anything. I do. And what I know is that Mason is about to touch me. He's about to make me say the most humiliating things out loud. He could make me do it over his lap, with my dress pushed up around my waist. He could—

The car pulls over to the curb, and he lets go of me.

150

It's a sudden loss but I catch myself on the door handle. Mason steps out of the car and comes around to open the door for me. I put my hand in his with an angry, mortified push.

I don't know why I'm embarrassed at all. He didn't do anything.

He didn't do *anything*.

One measured step, and he's in front of me, blocking the entrance with his height. His hand comes up and glances over my throat. A light squeeze. His grip comes up under my chin and he forces my eyes up to meet his.

His brim with heat and cruel laughter. "You wanted me to ask. Oh, Ms. Van Kempt. You wanted to give me all those answers."

"No," I lie. "What I want is for you to stop calling me that. It's so—it's so—" I hate the distance of it. If he's going to embarrass me like this, if he's going to take everything from me, the least he could do is stop pretending he doesn't know my name. "Everyone calls me Charlotte."

"You sweet little thing," he says, and he makes it sound like an insult. Worse than an insult. "Charlotte. Have you been fucked in any other holes? I already asked you about your pretty mouth."

"I haven't. I told you. I haven't."

"Feel better?" he croons.

"No."

"Perfect." He leans down and brushes a kiss to my lips. I lean into it, trying to take more from him than he's giving, but he doesn't let me. He straightens up and calls for his driver, who comes to his side carrying a black box. Mason flips the top open.

There are jewels inside. Jewelry. He lifts out a necklace first. A diamond necklace. Real. I know it by the way the light from the restaurant glints off the facets.

He reaches around me, standing so close I can smell the heat of his skin underneath that spiced-rain scent, and fastens the clasp behind my neck. The square-cut diamond solitaire falls into place at the hollow of my throat. He pulls back to look at it and makes a low noise in the back of his throat. Then he's reaching for the box again.

It feels like he's dressing me up like a doll.

Earrings next.

His fingers are deft at my earlobes. He's been close enough to know my ears are pierced, and now he's close enough to guide the post through the hole and slip on the backing. Mason holds up the second one in the light so I can see it. They match the necklace.

"What are you doing?" I murmur. Like it might be dangerous to startle him when his hands are on me. Though I'm not sure he can be startled.

"Dressing you appropriately for our company."

I thought I couldn't be more nervous.

"What company?"

He glances over his handiwork and then he's moving, putting himself next to me. It's too deliberate. Too graceful. A man who moves that carefully is hiding something. I don't know what. He tucks my hand into his elbow and reaches across us to skim his fingertips over my jawline. I turn my face to him. "Don't embarrass me in front of the investors. Be very good, Charlotte."

"Fine."

I move to take a step, but he holds me back. Turns me to face him. Anyone looking would think he was being gentle, but he's not. He just disguises it with gentleness for everyone else. I end up with his hand fully around my throat. More pressure this time. I keep getting lost in this. I keep going the wrong direction. "What did you say?" he asks lightly.

"I'll be good," I whisper. "I'll be very—I'll be very good."

"That's better," he answers, and then he's guiding me inside the front doors of the restaurant, my nerves on edge, my cheeks blazing.

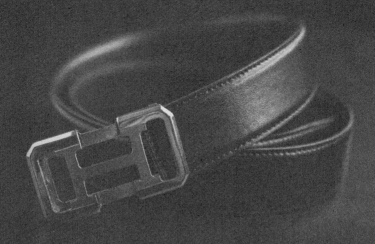

CHAPTER SIX

Mason

It's captivating, watching Charlotte get ahold of herself despite how ashamed she is. By the time we're inside, the red on her cheeks has cooled. Her back is straight. Head held high.

The jewelry is helping. A woman like Charlotte Van Kempt belongs in jewelry like the pieces I've put on her tonight.

And the dress.

What the fuck.

The dress has already done several numbers on me, which is why it was so necessary to put her in her place out there on the sidewalk. That hint of defiance in her big blue eyes makes me want to drive her back to the penthouse and take it all out on her. All these years I've waited for revenge. All these years, and now it's here, but it looks nothing like I thought it would.

She is so fucking sweet.

We're the first to arrive at the table and Charlotte has all of a minute to prepare herself for the investors. Four men from around the city who deal in real estate. None of them are in my circle of friends. The only reason they're here is to discuss whether they want to play a role in the Cornerstone project. Once the first building is completed, there's more opportunity in the surrounding areas. I haven't decided whether I want Phoenix to take on all of the risk.

Hence the dinner.

Charlotte greets each one of the men with a smile that makes their faces light up. I'd be jealous if I allowed myself to feel that kind of jealousy.

"Where have you been hiding her?" one of them says. John. Twenty years older than me and constantly hunting down women Charlotte's age.

"Away from you." He laughs at my joke as we take our seats.

"How did you meet Mason?" Brian. A guy who has too much money and not enough time on his hands. He's good to tap for this kind of project.

She glances at me for help, and I drop my arm around the back of her chair and run my fingertips down the bare flesh of her arm. Charlotte leans into me. It's an act. She's doing what I told her to do. But it feels so real that something happens near my heart. Probably an artery shutting down. I don't know.

"I saw her outside my office and had to know more about her," I say, gazing into her eyes.

Charlotte goes bright red. Redder than I've seen her. "Yeah," she says softly. "That's how it happened. Isn't it crazy, how things turn out like that?"

And then she smiles, and my entire heart leaps for it like it's trying to reach the edge of a window-sill before a long, hard fall.

Someone at the table whistles. Charlotte laughs. I feel the strangest urge not to turn away from her, but I do it. This is a fucking business meeting. This is part of my revenge. I'm half-expecting her to lose it halfway through the meal. To let the truth bubble out of her. That I'm making her do this. That we're not really dating.

I have a vision, clear as anything, of her rising from her seat and pointing at me. *How can you believe him?* Her voice would tremble. Her hand would shake. *How can you believe I'd be with him?*

None of that happens. What happens instead

is that every man at the table wants to be the first to buy her a glass of wine.

Charlotte has three glasses, sip by sip. By then, she's feeling awfully comfortable at the table. Jumping in to answer questions if I leave the smallest space. Talking up the Cornerstone project like it wasn't dead in the water two weeks ago.

They can't stop staring at her neckline.

I can't stop staring at the damn thing. I can't stop listening to her voice. I can't even bring myself to interrupt her thoughts about Cornerstone.

I even compliment her on a few of them.

Charlotte knows what she's talking about.

She's got excellent business sense.

I wouldn't have taken this deal if it wasn't for her.

That last one's true.

Everyone at the table listens to her and to me with rapt attention. I offer my own commentary. Lay the groundwork for the future deal.

Charlotte inches closer and closer to me until, by the end of the meal, her chair is an inch from mine and my knee is a ball of muscle tension and pain. What the fuck? This is essentially a business meeting. It's not any reason to get worked up.

"That was fun," she whispers to me as everyone stands. There are handshakes all around the table.

Pointed promises to see the both of us again soon. When we step away to leave, she puts her hand on my arm without hesitating.

Warm summer air greets us on the sidewalk. It feels so good after the too-cold chill of the air-conditioning that my knee reacts mid-step. I cover it by stopping to look for the car. My driver is a few cars down, getting himself out of traffic and to the curb.

"You're nicer than I thought," says Charlotte as I help her into the car.

It's like hitting the ground from a great height.

Adrenaline spikes. I'd recoil from the SUV if it weren't for my knee putting up a fight. I've made a mistake. I've made an error. This tipsy, giggly thing can't start to believe I have any fondness for her beyond her usefulness to me. Charlotte Van Kempt is here so that I can use her the way I want. The way I need.

What was I thinking, looking at her like that in the restaurant? Praising her ideas? Giving her all the space she needed to talk to the investors?

I get in after her. "Charlotte's house," I tell my driver, a guy named Scott. Everyone who drives for me memorized her address after the contract was signed. I never want any hesitation on their part.

The corners of her lips turn down. "What do you mean?" She slides a little on the seat. Charlotte's a lightweight. They were full glasses of wine, but still. She's tipsier than I realized. I reach over her and she turns her head to follow my hand. "What are you doing?"

"Keeping you alive for the trip home." I click her seat belt into place as the driver pulls out into traffic.

"My house? You're taking me to my house?"

"Were you expecting to get behind the wheel and drive yourself home drunk? I think not."

A giggle escapes her. It's so light. So sweet. I can't let her be like this. I can't let her have that power over me. No one will ever have that kind of power over me. Turning my spine to pure warmth with the sound of one laugh? Fuck that.

This isn't about kindness. It's not about convenience. It's not even about sex.

This is about revenge. All this is about is revenge, and I've been foolish. I've never been more frustrated with my brothers. With Gabriel, for making it so damn difficult to do the right thing and merge our companies. With Jameson, for losing himself to the city more often than not. It makes me a hypocrite. I haven't been focused enough on the things that matter.

Like hurting Charlotte's family the way they hurt mine.

She settles her body against mine and I let her

159

stay there. The wine has gone to her head. Charlotte looks out the window the whole drive, pointing things out and giggling. This funny sign in a store window. A slice of beautiful sky, visible despite all the buildings. A woman in an incredible dress. "I'd love the pattern for that." She reaches longingly for the window, but the woman is already gone. "It would look so good on me."

I want her in the dark for this. That's what I tell myself. I let her lean against me and laugh and be delightfully tipsy because I want her off guard for what happens next.

More of her weight falls against mine as the driver makes the turn onto the driveway. It's a long-ass, pretentious-as-hell driveway and we rattle over it like it's a dirt road on someone's farm. They haven't been keeping up with the property, then. No surprises there. The condition I found Cornerstone in was no better.

The driver pulls to a stop in the circle drive and Charlotte reaches for the door handle. I put my hand over hers. "Wait."

Another soft giggle. "See? You are nice."

I get out. Go around. Help her out onto the drive. Her heel catches in a missing cobblestone. It hurts to walk on the uneven surface. The rest of the house shows wear, too. Burned-out porch lights. Peeling paint. A rotting mansion.

"You don't have to walk me any further," she says at the door, more laughter in her voice. Bright as day in the dark of night. It's not particularly late.

"Oh, I do. You have something that belongs to me."

"What—"

I take the solitaire diamond in my fist and snap the necklace. No time for fucking with the clasp. Charlotte freezes, the only movement coming from her breath. I take the earrings too. Shove it all in my pocket.

"Those are only for when you're with me."

"Thank you," she says, and my whole knee balls up into pain. "For letting me wear it tonight."

"Aren't you adorable? I wouldn't thank me for anything just yet."

I raise my hand and knock hard on the door, then go for the handle. It's not locked. Charlotte grabs for my arm on the trip across the threshold.

"Mason," she says, keeping her voice low despite her panic. I know why. This place is empty. It echoes. "Mason. What are you doing? We can't—"

"We're home," I call into the cavernous house, and Charlotte whispers *oh no* under her breath. There's nothing in the once-elegant hallway but a console table shoved up against one wall. I recognize the purple envelope on the top—tickets to the benefit at the botanical garden. No way. They're so desperate to maintain the fiction that they're still wealthy. Still powerful. "Cyrus. Victoria."

Footsteps from a door off to the left, and Cyrus Van Kempt comes into view with his mouse of a wife close on his heels. A glass tumbler shines in his hand. "Charlotte? What is this?"

I brush her hand off my arm and stride over to them. He's smaller than I remember. More pathetic. Still evil. The old bastard doesn't know what to do when I extend my hand. He shakes it with a sneer. "Mason Hill," I tell him, too loud. He flinches. He's drunk. "We've met, but I'm sure you don't remember."

"It's been years." He drops my hand. "You were quite a bit younger then, weren't you?"

"Yes. And I didn't have quite so much money." I reach past him to shake his wife's hand. She's wide-eyed and pale. There's no guidebook for what to do if the person you've screwed over shows up fourteen years later with your daughter.

"Hello, Mason," she says softly. "Were you two out for dinner?"

"We had a wonderful time." I let her see in my face that it was the kind of wonderful time that involves her precious daughter getting fucked in more ways than one.

"Maybe it would be best if we talked later," Cyrus says. He's trying so desperately to regain control of the situation.

"Oh, we'll talk." I step back toward Charlotte and put my hand on her back. Run it all the way around to her hip, where her parents can see that I'm touching her. "I just couldn't wait to introduce myself. Not after your daughter has been such a pleasure."

Cyrus goes red at the mention of pleasure, but he's too much of a coward to turn on me. "Charlotte," he growls. "It's time for your guest to leave."

All the rosy joy is gone from her face. She's so pale it makes her eyes stand out, but she looks me in the face anyway. "I'll call you later, Mason."

I take her chin in my hand, pull her close, and kiss her.

Hard, then harder, until she lets out a gasp into my mouth. Fuck, she tastes good. Fuck, I want her.

Cyrus and Victoria are horrified. He takes one step forward, like he might take a swing at me, but he's too much of a coward to do it. "Get out of my house."

The bastard doesn't wait to see if I go. He steps

back into the room he came from—his office, probably—and slams the door.

Victoria is bone-white, her hand at her throat. "It was…it was nice to see you, Mason."

"Likewise."

I don't want to leave her here, in this decrepit has-been mansion with these assholes. She's sick with embarrassment. Pliant. Everything about the way she stands, the way she looks at me, begs for rescue. If not from the house itself, then from the humiliation I've caused.

Rescue her, a better angel whispers.

I could take her out of here, dress her in diamonds, protect her from the harshness of life. *And you would have her every night.* That sounds more like me. I almost laugh. There's no selflessness left inside. That was crushed the day my parents died. The day my knee shattered. Since then I've had two goals: taking care of my siblings and avenging my parents.

"You'll see me on Friday." I let the meaning settle into the air. A date for her parents to worry about. They'll wonder what I do to her then. No, they'll know. You don't produce a daughter as lush and alluring as Charlotte without knowing what men want from her.

I leave without a backward glance.

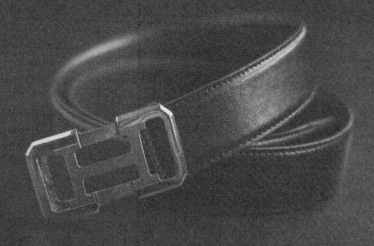

CHAPTER SEVEN

Charlotte

I t turns out a person can survive being kissed by Mason Hill in front of her parents.

A person can survive the still-tipsy climb up uncarpeted stairs to her bedroom and the tumble into bed and the silent weekend at home afterward. She can even survive the memory of the sharp tug of a necklace on her skin. That necklace breaking. Heat in his eyes. A glittering anger. And then that big fist, knocking on the front door.

It was supposed to be separate. He was never supposed to cross the boundary between my real life and the things we did as part of the agreement.

But then…

That kind of separation wasn't in the agreement. He's within his rights to do it. To cross every boundary I have, and then some.

Monday comes, and I go back to the office like Mason didn't pull a necklace right off my neck and say my name like a cruel joke. What I didn't say outside the restaurant is that it's too hard to be Ms. Van Kempt for this. It's too hard to be my father's daughter. I don't want to be a family representative when he has his hand around my neck.

Not choking me. Not really. Just the suggestion of it. Infuriating, humiliating suggestions.

Wednesday.

My father is waiting at his office door when I come downstairs in the morning, his eyes bloodshot. "You making site visits to Cornerstone?"

"One today, Daddy," I tell him. I lean in through the alcohol burn and kiss his cheek.

"Send someone else."

I laugh. "No, it has to be me. I don't want to play a game of telephone with the foreman."

"Don't go near him, Charlotte."

My face heats. "I'm going to supervise the project."

He takes one step forward and crosses his

arms over his chest. "You let him touch you like that in front of the crews—"

"*Daddy.*" I make my voice sharp as the anger rising in me now. If he'd dealt with this himself, I wouldn't be making site visits. "I have to go. Everything will be fine."

The anger simmers on the drive in. I had a couple of orders from my Etsy store last night. It's convenient timing. A quick stop by the post office to send them out before I head in to the Cornerstone site. Phones started ringing at Van Kempt Industries on Monday. It turns out that Mason—and by extension, his company—doesn't waste time. I have to bring some people back from the layoffs or make new hires so Van Kempt can keep up with everything. I can't do that angry, but I'm pissed at my father.

I'm meeting the foreman today at Cornerstone. TThe partnership agreement has a clause that gives Van Kempt or its representative something called "consulting approval," which I'm guessing means Mason will pretend to listen to my ideas about the property and then make the final call.

It'll be good. This is going to work out. A visit to Cornerstone to reassure myself, and I'll be able to walk into the meeting on Friday with my head held high. At the very least, I'll be able to look him in the eye.

He'll make me do it anyway.

I can't think like that now. I turn up the music on my phone and try not to miss the delicate weight of the necklace he let me wear on Friday. Made me wear. He did make me do it. I didn't ask him to bring jewelry. But I didn't refuse. It felt good to have him put it on me. I can admit that to myself with the song drowning out all my conflicted feelings and embarrassment.

It felt good to wear the jewelry. And it felt good to have his hands so close to my skin.

Even if I do hate him.

Which I do.

There's a little parking lot close to the site. It feels good to step out of the car and stretch. I wore ballet flats today. Work-appropriate leggings and a sleeveless top under a structured shirt I made myself.

It takes all of five seconds for regret to set in.

Crash in.

Because he's here.

I see Mason as soon as I turn the corner on what's now a full-fledged construction site. Two weeks ago it was a steel-beam skeleton and empty ground. Now men crawl everywhere over the structure. Trucks come and go along the road, turning into the property. Dropping things off. There's the metal-on-metal rattle of work being done. They've been at it a while.

And at the base of it stands Mason in a pair of dark slacks and a white shirt that's too clean for a place like this. Too perfect. He's with the foreman, a guy named Dave, and the two of them have their heads bowed over an iPad. Mason lifts a hand like he can wipe away all the construction that's already done. The gesture says *forget about this bullshit.*

He's changing things. I know he is. From the way he speaks, even from this distance. The way he stands. His hand cuts another *no* through the air.

Dave notices me before Mason does. Says something to him. Mason turns, and when his eyes land on my outfit, they get brighter. Greener. It's impossible, even in the golden morning sun, but it happens. It makes my heart pound.

I stride up to them and step around Mason, ignoring him in favor of shaking Dave's hand. "It's good to have you back on the job."

He smiles. He's a decent guy. I don't know anything about construction and only a little about the development, but he's walked me through a lot of it step by step. "I'm glad this place is getting done. We've got some adjustments to make, but—"

"What adjustments?" Keep your smile on, Charlotte.

Mason angles himself into the conversation. "I've made a number of adjustments to the construction plan."

"I'm sure you didn't, because this is the plan that's been approved by the council."

"I've had this plan vetted and approved, too. It's gone through my teams at Phoenix. Nothing to be concerned about." He turns back to Dave. "The reduction in units is going to give us the space to—"

All I hear is *reduction in units*. Mason can't do that. I've had to fight to understand all the pieces of this project. It's a thousand times more complicated than making a dress. Designing the pattern itself takes a team of people, and then there are others who have to fit that design into the available money. There is no more available money. If fewer people buy condos in the development, we don't get what we need out of it. If there are fewer units to sell, we'll be screwed. We'll be underwater when the deal is done.

I'll have sold myself for nothing.

"You cannot reduce the number of units in the building," I announce.

Dave clears his throat.

"We've had people working on this for a long time. The design is good. The plan is sound. And we need every one of those units to get a return on our investment."

"Ms. Van Kempt—"

"I don't care what you have to do. Put them back in. Go back to the old plans. We need those units. You're not taking them out."

Construction noise decorates the silence between the three of us. Damn it, I feel so small next to him. So out of my depth.

"The new plans have been approved, and that's what we'll be using going forward." Mason's firm, but there's no bite behind the words.

It doesn't matter. My face burns anyway. "You can't do that."

"I own the majority share, Ms. Van Kempt, so I am well within my rights to bring this project in bounds. It had to be done."

I can't look at his beautiful, terrible face anymore, so I throw a pleading look at Dave. "You saw the original plans. You know they were good."

Dave rubs the back of his neck. "They were a good starting point," he offers diplomatically. "No one expected the project to run so long. Nobody expected—" He cuts a glance at Mason. "Nobody expected for things to turn out the way they did. It wasn't your fault, Charlotte. You did your best. Everybody did their best. But he's right. This is how it gets done."

How it gets done means more than just the development being built. How it gets done means saving Van Kempt Industries. Saving my entire family. That's what this was, and I don't understand how it's going to happen now. I don't see how it works, if Mason is stripping out that ability from Cornerstone in front of my face.

Tears sting the corners of my eyes.

Screw the tears.

I put on my biggest, brightest smile. "Got it. I'm just going to take a look at how things are going. If you need me, I'll be—" I wave vaguely down the street. "Thanks for the explanation."

All my focus goes to blinking back the tears as I move past them. A little rise at the corner of the site gives a relatively safe view of all the construction going on below. My throat squeezes, hot and tight with the humiliation. My own foreman. Dave. *Dave.* How could he? I don't see a damn thing when I reach the top of the hill. I turn my back on Cornerstone and look down the nearest street. All those finished buildings. All those hopes and dreams, made into reality. I'll get there one day. I will.

I don't see Mason following me.

I only feel him, once he's already there. Tall and solid.

"Ms. Van Kempt."

I don't answer.

"Charlotte."

"What—" I wipe away my unshed tears and readjust my shirt. "What do you want?"

Hands on my shoulders turn me around. Not to face him, but Cornerstone.

"We're confined by the construction that's already been started, but the original design only included the bare minimum in safety and stability. You can see a crew on the ground right now. The first thing they're going to do is reinforce the base of the structure." He points, and there they are. Men surrounding a truck. More beams. More concrete.

"It's only forty stories. We didn't need—"

"The original design wouldn't have lasted thirty years. You'd have had sinking in the foundation by year five, and that's not taking possible flooding into consideration. If we'd built on this foundation without making improvements, the whole structure would have been at risk."

"But the plan was approved." All those men, all that movement, all that work. I don't understand it like Mason does.

"It was approved based on construction standards for this year."

"Right, so…"

"So a development like Cornerstone is meant to be a legacy property. It's a new build, which means everything about it has to be forward-thinking to make up for its lack of a past."

"People love new houses."

"In this market, they want it both ways."

"That's impossible."

"It's not impossible. It's a problem of design and position." He sweeps his hand up and up and up until I'm looking into a summer-blue sky. When he's finished, this is where the tower will hang in the clouds. "I adjusted the foundation to anticipate the safety standards that will be in place ten years from now. Storms will be worse by then. Flooding will be worse. Cornerstone will be ahead of its time by then."

"No one will be able to see that, though. It's all hidden."

"No. That's why I've made changes to the

interior as well. Fewer units on some of the floors, but we'll be approximating green space."

"What?"

"Indoor gardens. They have a net positive on the air quality in the building, in addition to top-of-the-line HVAC and filtration design. They're also carveouts for natural light in the event of power failure."

"There are generators."

"The property needs both novelty and luxury to attract the kind of buyer who will make the development self-sustaining. The more sought after the units, the more people will pay to own them permanently. The less they'll fight about building upgrades. People will outbid each other all the way to the moon when one comes up for sale."

"But that won't help me, because we have to sell this to make a profit. We have to sell the whole thing. You—you agreed to sell it as soon as construction is finished."

I turn to face him now, and I find no mocking grin on his face, no sneer. Mason looks back at me. "It's rare to make a profit off obvious desperation. When construction is finished, every unit will already be under contract. There's no imperative to unload the property, in that case."

"We needed all those units."

A nod. "I've added several stories to the design. Adds height, prestige, and overall units. More space between the floors."

"For what?"

"Safety upgrades. Buyers won't find them sexy and desirable at the time of sale, but they'll be grateful."

"What more did you need to add?"

"A better fire suppression system." It sounds like another item he's ticking off a list, but darkness flits through his eyes.

The breeze plays in my hair, cooling the back of my neck. He's too beautiful to look at in this sunlight. Mason doesn't stop me from turning my attention back to the development.

He knows what he's doing.

He didn't gut the units to fuck with me. And I'd bet anything that he's also had his team go through the stripped-down, modern design my father had chosen and made it into something people would clamor over. Something they would outbid each other to the moon for. What we were doing before—it was popular a decade ago. And the things he's changing to make the building more resistant to floods and fire make sense. We didn't go top-of-the-line in the original design because they added so much to the cost, but Mason is right. People will be grateful.

A weird pressure at my collarbone feels a lot like…

Genuine respect.

Does he feel the same thing?

He hasn't made any cutting comments about my clothes, or about getting on my knees, or about how much I hate this, the way he does on Fridays. He hasn't taunted me about kissing me in front of my parents. My father didn't come out of his office all night. My mother won't say a word about it.

"Okay. Show me, then."

"This way."

Mason gestures down the rise and into the construction site, and I find the courage to ask him more questions about the changes he's made. He answers all of them.

"What about the rooftop?" I ask as we navigate a support beam. "Did you change that too?"

He's climbing in front of me. Bags of concrete on the other side. A steep climb around it to another beam. "Yes."

Mason takes a step and something happens to his leg. The fabric of his pants moves in a way I wouldn't expect. It's because of the way he's moving underneath. An unsteadiness. Not right. His next step corrects for it and he's balanced again. He turns back, staying close. I reach for his arm on instinct. Somewhere to hold while we're on unsteady ground.

"What's wrong with your leg?"

"Nothing," he says. His expression hardens, and I'm not imagining any darkness now—it's there in his eyes, like a storm rolling in over the treeline. "No more questions, Ms. Van Kempt."

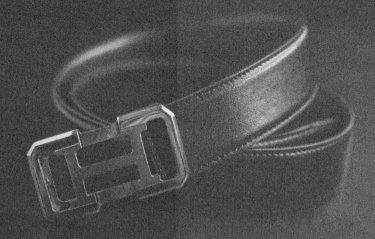

CHAPTER EIGHT

Charlotte

T he package is waiting for me on the polished console table in the foyer. It's one of the few remaining pieces of furniture. My mother refused to part with it. Friday afternoon, and if I stand close enough to the table, I can imagine nothing has changed.

But then there's the package.

Thick, white paper. My name in a neat, black print on the front.

"How was work today, sweetheart?"

My father's voice floats out from his office, and my stomach clenches. "It was good," I call back.

"Come talk to me where I can see you."

We've been avoiding each other since Mason came into the house. He spends most of his time in his office with the door closed. I stay late at work and then stay busy in my room. The three of us stopped eating together months ago, so I'm not missed at dinner.

I put the box down before I get to the open door of his office. "Hi, Daddy."

"I've heard things are picking up at the office. You've done a good job running things there."

Not really, but I'm not going to pick a fight with him about it. "Things are picking up, yeah. We're getting back on track with Cornerstone."

I brought on one new person and two people who had been laid off today. What Mason said at the site has been rolling around in my head since Wednesday. Those people will need something to do when Cornerstone is done whether we sell it or not. I'd bet anything Mason's company is all lined up to manage the property in the event it doesn't sell, so…

"You think you're ready to take the reins full time?"

Um.

"What do you mean, Daddy?" For one thing, I've been full time at Van Kempt for over a year.

He narrows his eyes at me. The glass on his desk

catches the light from the window. No more than one drink at a time. It doesn't matter that he's been refilling it for hours. He used to wait until after lunch to drink. Now he starts as soon as he wakes up. That glass is always there. "We always knew you'd take over the company one day. I think it's time you made it official."

A laugh bursts out of me. My dad scowls, and I cut off the rest of it. "I'm so—I'm so glad you're happy with what I've done, but, Daddy, there's no way I can take over at Van Kempt. I don't know the first thing about starting new projects."

He waves it off. "That's what your executive team is for."

There is no executive team at Van Kempt. There used to be, when my dad still went to the office, but they all bailed quietly, one by one, until there was no one left. It's not worth it for anyone to guide a company that has no money. That's running itself into the ground.

That was running itself into the ground until Mason took over.

"I'm not sure that's what I want to be doing," I admit, trying to soften the blow. When did he get this idea into his head? I've always wanted to go into fashion. I was going to study in Paris after I graduated high school. Two weeks before my flight, I got an email from the apprenticeship program. It was the first FINAL NOTICE letter I'd ever received in my life. Fifty thousand dollars by the end of the week, the full cost of tuition and housing and access to the best designers in the world.

So.

That didn't happen.

"What do you mean?" My dad picks up the glass but doesn't drink from it. "This has been the plan all along. You've proven yourself over the last year. It's time for you to take your place."

"Daddy, this hasn't been the plan."

He scoffs. "Of course it has. That's why you build a family business, Charlotte. To pass it on. Not to let it rot. Which you're going to do, if you don't start putting some real effort into it. You'll go in on Monday and tell them you'll be taking over."

I stare at him across the carpet.

My father's office is the only room in the house that's remained intact. All the books on the shelves. The furniture. The rug. Not a single piece has been sold from here. He's kept his little life around him while I worked my ass off to keep the bills close enough to paid. Every dollar I make goes to keeping my family alive and in the house. With food and electricity.

And on top of that, I've had to keep up with the

minimum social obligations. Tickets to gala events, like the benefit coming up at the botanical gardens. Appearances at dinners in the city. Not because we can afford it—we definitely cannot—but because my mother begs. With tears in her eyes. She thinks it's the only way to save us. To keep showing up.

To say that I've been putting no effort into this—

He rolls his eyes. "Don't stand there with your mouth open, Charlotte. You look like a gasping fish."

His insult hits me square in the gut, taking me backward a step. He's drunk. He's been drinking. That's why he's like this. He doesn't mean a word he says, and listening to him isn't going to help. It won't help anyone.

I back out of the room and keep going. "I have an appointment," I say to no one.

No one answers. The box waits for me outside the door. It comes up to my room with me.

Beneath the white paper is a black box, cool and silky to the touch. The kind of box that used to arrive from boutiques on a regular basis. I pull the top off. It clings to the bottom half a little and pops off with a breath of something that hints at flowers.

White tissue paper. A white note rests on top. I abandon the top of the box and take the note in my hand.

Nothing underneath.

–Mason

P.S. Meet me at the Middlegame.

Oh, Jesus. My face is an inferno at his neat writing. Two words in the privacy of my own bedroom, and the heat slips down over my neck. My breasts. All the way between my legs. *Nothing underneath.* He'll check to make sure I've followed instructions. He'll do it in the bar in the lobby of his building.

Fear follows. He hasn't really touched me. Not yet. Kissed me, yes. Put his hand on my hip, yes. The small of my back, yes.

Nothing else.

One deep breath and I flip back the tissue paper.

One more and I have the dress out of the box, holding it in the air in front of me.

I thought the dress I made was a power move. I was wrong. This piece of clothing is a clear demonstration of Mason's power. He's not even here, and I feel his hands on me.

He'll have full access in this slip of silk blend. Mason will be able to tell instantly if I have anything underneath. It's incredibly short. It's also incredibly backless.

Okay.

I clutch it close to me, partly to hide it from view

and partly because it does feel good in my hands, despite not being very substantial.

I'm terrified.

Because he's going to touch me.

No—that's not true. It's not true, and it causes a fresh wave of embarrassment.

I'm afraid he's not going to touch me.

I'm afraid that I don't want it.

I'm afraid that I do.

There's something else in the box.

I step forward and peer over the edge like I'm looking down into darkness. Like anything could leap out at me. But there's no monster at the bottom of the box.

It's a brand-new pair of Louboutins.

I've never been much of an actress, but I have to be one to walk through the archway at the Middlegame.

I'm pretending to be clothed.

I feel naked.

There's so much flesh exposed to the air that I feel every change in the heat. Every whisper of cool air. Every brush of my thighs. The complete, utter lack of undergarments.

Mason's mean like that. He gives me an order

and then makes me follow it. This dress can't be worn with panties and a bra. They would show.

One man sits at the bar, his jacket slung over one of the padded stools. I keep walking. I have a plan. I will order a Diet Coke. No one will ask me any questions. No one will say anything. He won't look up from his drink and see me wearing this.

No such luck. He glances up from his bottle as soon as my fingertips meet the polished surface of the bar, his eyes glittering. "Make her a whiskey sour," he says to the bartender. "Extra sugar."

"Oh, no—no, thank you. I'm meeting some-one here."

"Sure you are, honey." One hand wraps around the bottle, and he leans over. "How much for the night?"

My mouth drops open.

He thinks I'm a prostitute.

"No." My voice begins to rise. "No."

The man shrugs, a grin on his face like he doesn't believe me. He takes a bill from his wallet and tosses it onto the bar. Grabs his suit jacket. Leaves.

I don't know if I'll ever leave here again. I think I've spontaneously combusted from all the embar-rassment pulsing through my veins.

"He couldn't afford a night of your time."

Mason's voice comes from directly off my elbow.

His scent wraps around me from behind. It's not because he wears too much cologne. It's like my senses are always looking for him. Wanting him.

"My time isn't for sale anyway." It sounds less confident than I wanted because of the shake in my voice.

He laughs, and I feel the air change. I feel how it gets darker. Heavier. "Not tonight. You already sold that to me."

A hand at the small of my back turns me toward him. Right. Yes. *You're not going to look at the ground when you speak to me.* I'm not going to watch an empty barstool, either.

I look into Mason's eyes.

Where I'm required to look.

It takes my breath away.

There are layers to this breathlessness, the same way there are layers to a well-made garment. On the outside is shock at how gorgeous his eyes are. Low mood lighting in the bar makes them seem even more mysterious. Even more complicated. I already know how the sunlight outside throws all the colors into sharp relief.

One layer in is the fear.

The fear extends beyond my inability to breathe. Mason's entire expression is dark. My heart feels like a thrashing tree. Irritation, edging toward anger, is in the set of his jaw. There's no hint of the man who was patient with me at Cornerstone two days ago. No hint of him. He's a towering thundercloud.

But it's not simple, this feeling. No coin with two sides. No dress with an easy lining. There's a third.

Desire. Or arousal. It's a terrible sensation. Forbidden. Wrong to feel any kind of attraction. It's only right that I should hate this, and hate him, and never want him close to me. I never want my body to respond to him. I don't want him to have any effect on me.

He does.

His eyes drop from mine.

I keep looking.

I'm supposed to keep looking, I think, and even if I wasn't supposed to, I'd want to look at him. He's that arresting. That beautiful. The way he considers the dress feels like a physical touch. As if he's dragged his finger beneath the low neckline. Pulled it away from my skin to see underneath. I can feel every place the fabric touches my skin.

I can feel every place it doesn't.

And I can feel the heat of his gaze.

Mason snaps his eyes back up to mine. I startle like he's slammed a door. Scramble for control of myself. "Upstairs, you sweet little thing. I want to get my money's worth."

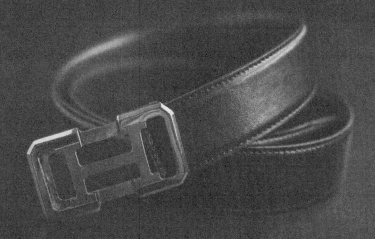

CHAPTER
NINE

Mason

Charlotte's scared now.

She should be.

I'm so tired of waiting. I've been extraordinarily patient. I've dedicated the last fourteen years of my life to my siblings. To my business. Every day. Nights and weekends. Clawing business deals from the jaws of assholes. Clawing what little normalcy I could from the smoking remains of our lives. My knee is killing me.

So casual about it at the Cornerstone site.

What's wrong with your leg?

Of course she'd noticed. She spends all her

time staring at me. But there was no judgment in her voice. No morbid curiosity. She doesn't know the story, then. A true innocent.

And for a heartbeat, I'd considered it. Telling her. She would be kind, because Charlotte Van Kempt is kind, and sweet, and innocent. Amid all those steel beams she was soft and beautiful and I wanted it. The unburdening. The admission. It was the most tempted I've ever been.

I cannot be tempted by her.

Not like that.

This isn't about emotions or giving up the weight of my secrets. This is about retribution. Full stop.

Charlotte shivers next to me in the elevator, but she doesn't cower. She doesn't ask nervous questions. She waits, silent and stoic, all the way to the penthouse.

When the elevator doors open, I stride out into the foyer and through it. A moment of hesitation, and then she's hurrying to catch up with me.

Down the hall. Take a left. She sucks in a little breath as we go into the great room. It looks out over the Manhattan skyline, but I don't care about the floor-to-ceiling windows. I don't care about the orange glow of the sunset sinking into the city. I want her face to burn red. I want tears. I want her to feel as hollowed out and scorched as I do on days like this.

A large, rounded sofa faces the fireplace on the left side of the room. The formal dining table on the right side. But I take her to the center, where four chairs surround a low, white table.

I put the box there earlier. Slim. Black.

She's shaking in her shoes and doing her best to ignore it. I take off my jacket first and drop it into the chair, then reach for the box.

Charlotte's tongue darts out to wet her bottom lip. No questions, though. She stands up tall when I come back with the necklace.

Not the same one as before. That one's in my closet, tossed onto a dresser with its broken clasp. Charlotte watches my eyes as long as she can, but she can't help herself.

She looks.

Her eyes fly open.

Unlike the other necklace, this one has no chain. It's stiff platinum. A collar necklace, glittering with diamonds. Charlotte's chin goes up as I bring it close to her throat, like it might scratch her. It doesn't. There's a breath of space between the metal and her neck. I let it go and the metal falls against her collarbone.

She shivers.

I put my hand around her throat, the diamonds scraping the side of my hand, and look into her huge, blue eyes. My knee seizes and I have to consciously relax for it to let up.

"Kiss me."

Another small breath. This one ignites something at the base of my spine. A thirst for control. A thirst for revenge. It's like fire. Fire everywhere.

She doesn't know what to do, and I give her nothing but impatience.

It doesn't take long for her to find her bravery. Charlotte takes a half-step forward and her hands come up and up and up. Carefully. Slowly. Like I might react to her. Like I might explode. Who knows? Maybe I will. But then her delicate hands are on the back of my neck and she tugs me toward her. Just far enough to reach me on tiptoe.

The kiss is soft. Sweet. I keep my hand around her airway. I try to hold myself back.

Not today. It's not happening today. I turn it on her, turn it into a bite. Too hard for her. She lets out a whimper, and before it's finished, I've taken myself out of her hands.

I take the nearest seat, ignoring the painful throb of my cock, and sigh. She's beet red at my boredom. If only she knew. But Charlotte's never been fucked before. Not in her mouth. Not in her cunt. Not in her ass. She doesn't know what she's doing to me. She won't know until I show her. Once I do, she'll never forget it.

"Put your purse on the table."

She does, then goes back to her spot next to the chair across from me. I've left the lights off. I want her to feel the sun dying around her. I want her to feel time running out.

"Your face is red," I comment. "You're either terrified or extremely aroused."

Charlotte's eyelashes flutter. She whispers something I can't hear.

"Charlotte." Her name—the warning in it, no doubt—brings her eyes back to mine. "I can't hear you."

"I—" She makes a soft noise. "I feel dirty."

"You liked it better in the foyer."

A shake of her head. "I like it when—"

"I don't care."

Her shock is a jerk of her hand.

Straight to the necklace.

It's not what she expects to find there, and she drops it right away. The red splotches on her cheeks spread down to her chest. Her surprise, her sadness—it makes me want to admit that I lied. I do care what she likes. Those are the best things to use against her.

"Undress. Everything but the necklace."

Her lips part like she's going to ask a question. Charlotte thinks better of it. There's no question she can ask that will change what I'm going to do to her. How hard I'm going to push her. I've had enough of teasing. Of taunting. Of the suggestions that make her blush. Tonight she'll get an introduction to reality.

Charlotte slips the halter of the dress over her head and tugs it off over her hips.

"Stop."

She freezes with it down around her calves, her legs tensed to step out of it.

"Try again, you sweet little thing." A flinch at the mocking tone. "Make it sexy. I'm fucking bored."

I'm not bored. I'm the least bored I've ever been. Her naked body in the last light of the day has my mouth dry and my cock throbbing. Charlotte Van Kempt is clean. Soft. Unmarked.

It will hurt so much more that way.

She takes a deep breath, then pulls the fabric back up. Puts the halter back into place. Drops her hands down to her sides again. Starting over, just the way I wanted. Holy fuck. She has no idea.

Her hands shake, but this time, when she lifts the halter over her head, she tips her head back like it feels good to take it off. A quick, searching glance at me. I clench my jaw to keep from praising her. That's not what this is about. Charlotte's trying her best, and it is magnificent, and I want to ruin her for it.

It's a difficult project with a dress like that. It's astonishing how much she makes of it. Showing me one pink nipple, then the next, peeking at me from beneath her lashes. She makes a little sound when she gets it down to her waist. All tentative surprise, like she didn't quite mean to show me her tits, but she doesn't hate it now that it's happening.

A slow slide over her hips.

I hold my breath.

Fuck. I just watched her strip it off not five minutes ago. It doesn't matter. The anticipation makes my skin tight and my cock tighter. It's never been so hard. I've never wanted anything like this.

Charlotte lowers the dress and her pussy comes into view.

Not enough. Not *enough*. She's bare, but it's not enough. I want her legs bound to the corners of my bed. I want all of her on display for me. I want to see every perfect inch of her.

I meet her eyes again in time to see a flare of

hope there. Charlotte circles her hips, tiny motions meant to make the dress fall, and lets go.

It puddles around the heels I bought for her.

One step out of them.

Then another.

She's naked now. Breathing hard. Chin up.

"Come here."

Three trembling steps over to my chair. I take my time looking at her. That's all it takes to make her blush harder. Lingering glances at the tight peaks of her nipples.

She can't take her eyes off me. I'm not a fool. I know what I look like. What I'm doing. I know that the fading light is making me seem more threatening by the moment.

"Ms. Van Kempt."

Charlotte bites her lip, and I know what I've done with those words. I've put her back into my office on the first day we met. *I'm not on my knees. Not yet.* I hold her gaze until I'm sure she's remembering. Until I'm sure the pink in her cheeks is from the realization that the moment has arrived.

"Yes?" she whispers.

"Get on your knees."

She starts to lower herself to the rug. Get it over quickly. I won't have that. It won't be easy for her. I put a hand on her hip and pull her forward at the last minute so she falls between my knees and has to push herself back up. No hiding the quiver in her chin now. No hiding the dimpling skin there. I'll get tears soon.

Except…

There's no except.

I let her wait for as long as I can stand it. "Unbuckle my belt."

"Oh, god." So low. So sweet. So mortified. Charlotte says it almost to herself. She's already reaching for the buckle. I don't do a damn thing to help her. Don't angle my body toward her. Nothing. I just watch her like an asshole. My heartbeat is the timer on a bomb. Nothing seems as essential as knowing when she'll go off. When Charlotte Van Kempt will break.

No fumbling with the buckle. She knows her way around clothes. Charlotte works the buckle open and pulls out the loop. Her eyes meet mine in a silent question. Ah—there's the begging. Wordless. The way I like it.

"Take it out."

Nothing but a hushed breath this time. The tremble in her hands comes back full force. It's intriguing, the way she is with the button and zipper. She's familiar with the pressure and give of fastening and unfastening garments, even when they're on other people.

It's the part where she has to push my pants open, tug them around my hips to get access—that's when she struggles. Her movements become tentative. Each breath comes faster. Tears well in her eyes.

I give her nothing.

Nothing when the pants are out of her way enough to reach my boxer briefs. Nothing when she hesitates for one single, painful heartbeat. Nothing when she slips her hand through my fly and tugs me out.

It's a process, because her hands are small and I'm so hard that I barely manage to hold in a groan. I can feel her preparing to let go, to stop touching me as soon as she can, but I wrap my hand over hers. Take her chin in my other hand. Look through the silvery sheen of her tears.

"Suck me."

"No," she gasps. "Not like this."

Then she's up, so fast it reminds me of a terrified hummingbird. Charlotte slips her hand out from underneath mine. She's light on her feet now, humiliation giving her an adrenaline rush, and it takes her no time to lunge for her purse. Her dress. She flees the darkening great room at top speed.

A single sob trails after her.

I don't.

The elevator doors open, and just before they slide closed again, a metallic thud echoes from the foyer.

My god. She left the necklace.

I take out my phone to text the doormen and tell them to stop her, but I can't bring myself to type the words.

In the empty living room I put myself back together over the screaming protest of my knee and the insistent demands of my frustrated cock. My fist in the shower will make it tolerable until morning.

For a heartbeat, I almost regret this. Regret her fear. Regret pursuing reprisal to this point.

Almost.

And then not at all.

I expected her to break. I went looking for the limit of her humiliation, and I found it.

Now we can have some real fun.

CHAPTER
TEN

Mason

For once, Jameson's early for something. He came home just before I went to sleep at three. Highly unusual, since he's usually not here until we're about to eat. Or until we've been eating for half an hour.

"Where is he?" he asks the server on his way through.

"The den, Mr. Hill," she says.

"Cool," he answers, and then he comes through with wide, what-the-fuck eyes. "What happened? Did you get in a fight last night?"

I don't get up from where I'm sprawled on the

couch with a pillow under my knee. It will do nothing to improve my mood. "I'm surprised you didn't. Are you sure the entire NYPD isn't about to burst in behind you?"

He rolls his eyes and flops into an armchair. Jameson might not have been up to his usual bullshit last night, but the bruise-colored circles under his eyes are evidence that wherever his mind went, it was rough.

My youngest brother pretends not to be looking at the photo on one of the built-in shelves surrounding the TV. An eight by ten of us in a simple white frame. My mother loved those lifestyle photo shoots where we stood by the front door or in the yard somewhere or on the beach where we were vacationing. In this one, we're all gathered by the red door of the house. The three of us are barely contained by my mother's arms, and my dad holds Remy, who's three and beaming at the camera with her baby teeth and scrunched-up nose.

"Uh-oh," Gabriel sings as he enters. "Mason's going to be a nightmare today." I give him the finger over the back of the couch. He grabs for my hand and misses. "Go too hard at the gym?"

"Whose apartment are you coming from? You smell like a flower shop."

"No one's apartment. I was in the flower shop."

"Then where are my flowers?"

He snorts. "Why the hell would I bring you flowers?"

"For having to put up with your obnoxious ass."

Gabe pretends like he's going to hug me, and I scowl at him until he backs off with a laugh. My knee is a mess today. "So sensitive," he taunts.

"At least I care about something other than my nightly fuck."

"That's because you don't have a nightly fuck. And that's a shame. It would improve your mood." My brother drops into another armchair, and I just don't care. My knee hurts. My head aches. I couldn't sleep most of the night, after Charlotte left. Easiest to blame it on my knee. Easiest to lie on the couch and not move. "Where's Remy?"

"Oh my god," our sister says, like he summoned her with the question. "Oh my god, guys are such assholes." She's a blonde, irritated storm cloud this morning as she sits down on the other end of the couch with a huff. It's an extra-long couch, but with me lying the way I am, she doesn't have quite enough room. Even though she's pissed, she's ultra-careful as she slips her arm under my calves and slides her body underneath.

I let her do it. Not because it doesn't hurt. It hurts like someone's driving a fist into the muscle around my knee, making it pull too tight to bear. Fighting her on it would only make the situation worse. Remy studies my face while she slings her arms over my calves and stretches her own legs to the ottoman.

"Guys are the worst," Jameson says. "Did you just learn this information today?"

"I grew up with you, so no," she shoots back, but her mouth quirks with a smile. Jameson is her favorite. She won't admit it out loud, but she doesn't have to. "You're the only ones I don't hate."

"Aww, Remy, out of everyone in the world? You're cute."

She scowls at Gabriel. "That's what the guys in my Classics lecture say. That I'm cute. Never mind that I'm scoring the highest out of all of them. And they won't shut the hell up. Every one of those boys is in love with the sound of his own voice. And then there's the one who wants to take me out."

"Who?" An echo reaches my ears at the same time as my own voice.

Not an echo.

My brothers, asking the same question.

"Who cares?" Remy rolls her eyes. "See? All you care about is what he wants. When are people going to ask the women what they want?"

"I don't give a fuck what he wants." I curl my toes, trying to relieve some of the pressure in my knee. Remy rubs absently at my shin. It doesn't help, but it doesn't hurt, either. "I want his name so I can kill him."

"Get in line," says Jameson. "You can kill him after I kill him."

"This is why I never tell you anything," Remy teases. She segues into a story about a group project with Jameson and Gabe needling her for the name.

I don't hear any of it.

If someone treated my sister the way I treated Charlotte, I'd lose my mind.

I was only half-joking when I said I'd kill that motherfucker for harassing Remy about a date. There's nothing I wouldn't do to protect her. Even if she hadn't been my responsibility since she was seven, with her mess of blonde hair and her lanky limbs and her obsession with digging in the dirt, I'd still be this way about her.

The possibility of an apology, of ending things with Charlotte, floats into my mind and dies a hasty death. I don't want to apologize to her. I don't want to step back.

Revenge is the whole point of this enterprise.

And, like the goals I set at the office, this act

of retribution has been carefully calibrated to get the Van Kempts where they're most vulnerable. It's too perfect that both of their biggest weaknesses are all wrapped up in one another right now. Charlotte and the company. The company and Charlotte. I'll wreck one and profit from the other.

In order for me to do that, she needs to come back.

I pick up my phone from my lap and send a text. An order for flowers to be delivered to one Charlotte Van Kempt, along with a note.

The chef sends her assistant with breakfast trays, and Remy shifts my legs gently off her lap so I can sit up and get a plate together.

"Do you remember when we used to do this in Brooklyn?" No idea why I ask the question while we're all leaning over the coffee table, avoiding collisions with each other's hands to put fruit and omelets on plates.

"No, because we didn't do this," Gabriel says. "We had plastic plates and Eggo waffles."

Jameson adds melon to his plate. "I like Eggo waffles."

"Everyone likes Eggo waffles." Remy leans back on the couch. "I don't know if I remember the first place. Was it the one with the balcony?"

"No. That was the second one. Or the third," Jameson says. "You spent all your time digging in plants we kept on the balcony. The Brooklyn apartment was a real shithole."

"The one with the balcony was just before the house." Gabriel stabs a strawberry with his fork. "It was such a pain in the ass to get that place."

He'd just turned twenty when I got us into the house. It took both of us on the mortgage because none of the brokers wanted to believe I owned a business at twenty-two. It had been a string of sleepless years for a revolving door of reasons. If it wasn't the nightmares, it was the ever-present pain in my knee. If it wasn't the pain, it was the never-ending difficulty of getting Phoenix off the ground. If it wasn't Phoenix, it was trying to make a home for my siblings while the world spun out of control.

Gabriel was the one who recovered the quickest—or the one who seemed to, after our parents died. Jameson regularly lost his shit. But he would pull it together for Remy, whose grief seemed the most unpredictable. Some days she seemed fine. Like our parents had been distant relatives. Like she hadn't wanted to sleep next to our mom every night until she was five.

Other days, she was not fine.

"I remember that prick," Jameson says around a mouthful of omelet. No complaints today. He makes the face he uses to mock the jackass we had to meet with every hour of our lives for the five weeks it took to close on the house. He puts on a ridiculous voice to imitate him. "Son, are you sure you can't convince your father to co-sign? It would speed things up with the underwriters."

Gabriel stabs his fork into a strawberry. "He really thought we were lying."

"I bet that guy's nervous about running into Mason to this day," Jameson says.

"What? Why?" Remy's been focused on her plate, her mind elsewhere. She glances over at me. "Where was I during this?"

"You were there, too. We couldn't leave you with anyone, so you came to all the meetings when we had to bring in documents and sign papers. What the hell was that book called? It was a mystery book, with pictures. Puzzles to solve in the book. All of it took place near the Pyramids."

"The Curse of the Lost Idol." Her nose scrunches with her laugh. "I still have that."

"You loved it so much you missed Mason's first death threat."

Her eyes go wide. "You did not threaten a mortgage broker."

"No. No. It wasn't like that. All he had to do was stand up," Gabriel says. "Jesus, he was so pissed. That guy wouldn't shut up about getting a co-signer, and he would get on the phone with our father if it would help, and on and on and on, until—" He puts his plate on the coffee table and frowns. More than frowns. His imitation of me, pissed as hell and ready to do something about it, is dead-on. I've seen it plenty of times in the mirror. Gabe gets up out of his seat and towers over Remy, who shrinks back.

"Oh my god," she says.

"One more word out of your mouth," Gabriel intones in a low voice that I assume sounds like me, "and I'll walk. My first stop will be at the CEO's office. He'll fucking fire you himself."

"You've seen him," Jameson says to Remy. "You know what he's like."

I sigh. "I'm in the room, motherfucker."

"And my second stop," says Gabriel, still pretending to be me, "will be to your house."

"I hope you didn't leave your wife alone," Jameson and Gabriel say together, and then the whole thing collapses into laughter. Gabe sits down again and pulls his plate back into his lap.

Remy grins. Jameson shakes his head.

Even I can't help the grin that tugs at my lips.

I watch the moment crest and fade with an ache in my chest that seems permanent now. It ebbs and flows but it's never really gone. Remy moves her fork slowly over her plate. "I liked that place, I think."

"You spent all your time digging in the yard." It was why I'd gone to such lengths to get it in the first place. It had a yard, and it had a decent school for Remy, and even at eleven she knew what she wanted to be doing with her life. "We took turns dragging you inside for dinner. You were a treasure hunter. Always convinced you'd find something out there."

"And I did."

"That was garbage." Jameson studies a bite of waffle on the tip of his fork.

"Those were antiques."

They really were antiques. Glass bottles a hundred years old, from when the suburb had been more of an outpost. Everything had grown up around it. The house had changed hands again and again, its property value fluctuating with the years, and by the time we got there, it was verging on ramshackle. All the value was in the land itself. The location.

It was the first time Jameson had looked at a building on a lot and called it. He was about to turn nineteen with a wild, haunted gleam in his eyes. It was hell to keep him in school. To keep him from disappearing into the city and never coming back.

"Dad would have liked that place," Gabriel says. He makes a show of looking around for the remote. It only takes him a second to find it next to the breakfast tray. He picks it up but doesn't turn on the TV.

"Would he have?" Remy's voice is quiet. Aching. It reminds me of the way she would ask questions after they died. *Where are they, where are they?* The middle of the night. My knee twisted up with pain. Holding her in the first shitty apartment in Brooklyn, the only one that would rent to us. My back propped up against the wall so she wouldn't drown in her own tears. Jameson and Gabriel in the streetlight glow. *He's gotta lie down, Remy. They're not here. They're not coming back.*

"Yeah." Jameson's not eating anymore. "He would have made it into one of his pet projects and driven Mom crazy working on it himself when he had the whole company to run during the week."

I finally find the voice to speak.

"Not himself. He wouldn't leave her for that long on the weekend." Part of the reason they're both dead now. "But he would have hired a separate contractor and asked for constant updates." That's how he was when we were growing up. Always consumed with one project or another. Multiple things on his mind at any given time. But he'd drop his phone for my mother. Just let it go. Down onto the tile by the pool or the asphalt on the driveway or the hardwood floor. Cracked so many screens like that.

"I miss," Jameson starts, but then he blinks hard, like he's just waking up. He puts his plate onto the coffee table, runs a hand through his hair, and walks out.

It's the thickest silence. One crowded with heartache and emptiness. Those two things shouldn't take up any space, but they take up all of it. All the air. A pressure around my knee tightens like a vise.

Gabe clears his throat. "I think we should watch the one you like, Remy. The one with all the maids."

"Downton Abbey?"

"That's the one." He picks up the remote. The TV comes to life. "Mom would have liked it, which would have been terrible."

Remy doesn't take her eyes off the screen, but the corner of her mouth lifts. "How come?"

"She would have done the accent all the time," I tell her. "It would have driven us crazy."

CHAPTER ELEVEN

Charlotte

O ur house is always quiet in the mornings. My dad doesn't go to bed until late, and my mom doesn't wake up early. Maybe that's beyond her now.

Past nine, and I can't bring myself to leave my bed.

No matter how I try to calm my fears about Mason and the agreement, to reposition them in the new sun, I can't do it.

I am, as businessmen say, in breach of contract. Null and void. Canceled after non-compliance with terms. I broke the contract by leaving Mason's penthouse last night before he was done with me. Now everything is going to fall apart.

More tears tease at choking me like a hand around my throat. I do deep, steady breathing to keep them from dropping onto the comforter. I broke the contract. I ran away from him. I ran away from him naked, clutching an expensive dress to my chest. That necklace hitting the floor was the loudest sound I've ever heard. He's allowed to break necklaces he owns. What if the one I threw snapped, too? What if I've added even more to my family's debt?

I stare out the window, finding landmarks to look at. A broken branch on a tree. A cloud cleaved in half by a slice of blue sky. These are not the kinds of things I should be focused on. He has the necklace, at least. I didn't take it out with me and risk being accused of stealing. I'm not sure what to do with the dress. It's on a hanger in my closet.

I search out a rose bush in bloom despite the lack of regular gardening. The curl of a new pattern up against the windowsill. How white the clouds are against all that blue.

Maybe I should have stayed.

It would have been an option. Steel myself to what was happening. Get through it. Keep my head up. That's been the game all along. Sell myself, save my family. I knew that was the trade going in.

Maybe I should go back now.

I wrap both hands around my mug of tea. These thoughts aren't completely honest.

It's hot tea, and good. Perfect amount of milk. Perfect amount of sugar. It bolsters me enough to open another bill from the stack on my bed. The power company's not happy. We're rapidly approaching another FINAL NOTICE. I pick up my phone and dial the number. My call is important to them, but all their representatives are busy assisting other customers.

I'll wait.

I'll wait as long as it takes.

The hold music is decent background music for some honesty. For some one-on-one reckoning with myself.

I ran naked into an elevator and fought my way into that dress because I was terrified.

I was terrified of Mason. Of course I was. It seems totally reasonable to have been shivering and near-tears in the face of all that masculine power.

But—and this is the part that's tough to admit, even with my bedroom door locked and the hold music playing in my ear—I was also afraid of myself.

It terrified me, how wet and hot I was. For how mean he was being. For how cold. It was demeaning, being ordered to my knees and commanded to take his cock out and suck it. He talked to me like I was a thing. Like I was his property as much as the rug under my knees. As much as the Cornerstone building.

It's not right to want that. It's not right that I lay awake last night, thinking of how it felt and replaying it over and over in my mind for all the wrong reasons. More than replaying it, actually. I rearrange my legs under the comforter. There's a silver lining. Now that everything's done with, now that the contract is in shambles, I won't have to admit to him that I touched myself thinking of kneeling at his feet with his cock in my hand. Imagining the scent of him, and his voice.

"Good morning! You've reached Eastern Electric. My name is Sarah, and this call may be monitored or recorded for quality assurance purposes. How can I help you today?"

"I—hi. Yes. Hi. I just got a bill for—for electricity." Well, this is not the best introduction I could make for myself. I take a deep breath and think of a room without Mason in it. This room doesn't have him in it. I rattle off the information she needs to verify it's me. "We're having trouble keeping up with the account, and I wanted to know if you would accept—" I'm not ready for this call. I put her on speaker and switch to my banking app.

There's practically nothing in the account. "Fifty dollars toward the balance to keep us in good standing until I can come up with the rest."

A long pause.

I hold my breath.

"We can do that for you today, Ms. Van Kempt. I do have to inform you that we can accept no more than three partial payments in a calendar year. This will be your second."

I was worried about my dignity last night. Keeping as much of it as possible. I'm not sure I have much left at this point. Is that scrap worth my family's life? Should I have given it to Mason Hill without a backward glance?

That wouldn't be the end. I know that now. It wouldn't, because I might like the way he strips me of my dignity. I might like it.

It might make me wet.

I can't think like that now. If that were true, if I gave in to it, how could I live with myself?

I've got my debit card in hand by the time the woman on the phone asks for it. When I hang up, I've bought us another few weeks.

"Charlotte? Are you here?"

My mom's voice spirals up the stairs to my room. Good thing my tea's half-empty. I didn't spill it when I startled. "I am," I call to her through the door, and climb out of bed.

"Could you come down here?"

I'm in leggings and a tank top. Smoothing my hair into place improves things enough to pad downstairs. My mother's waiting in the middle of the foyer near her console table. She frowns in its direction.

I can't see why she's frowning until I'm all the way down on the main floor.

A bouquet dominates the center of the table. The blooms are a riot of summer colors. My mother cocks her head to the side and studies them from one angle, then another. She brushes her fingertips over pale coral petals. "Amaryllis," she murmurs. "Expensive this time of year."

My pulse is in my own fingertips. "Why this time of year?"

"Weddings," she says. "Brides love them for weddings. They symbolize splendor and determination and…" She sighs. "Beauty." My mother drops her hand. Shakes her head. Meets my eyes. "They were delivered a few minutes ago. I didn't look at the card."

The cream-colored envelope blends so well it's like another bloom, only this one has Charlotte on it in neat print.

My mouth goes dry, but I'm not going to hint

at nervousness in front of my mother. It will only set her off. First the fretting, which she'll distract herself from with her roses. It won't work. She'll be in her room with a headache by late afternoon. No hesitating. I pluck the envelope off its plastic stem and open it.

See you Friday.

–Mason

It can't possibly be relief that I feel, this cascade of heat and chill that expands my lungs like a too-deep breath. The contract is still on. No. It's not just relief. Dread, too.

My mother looks over my shoulder before I can do anything but breathe.

"Friday?" she asks.

"We have a standing date," I hear myself answer.

"Is it like the last time he visited?"

I want to disappear back into my room, shut the door tight, and hide. It makes my face flame to remember Mason escorting me into my own house and shouting for my parents like he had every right.

And it's not like the time he visited, which my mother is being incredibly diplomatic about. Mason didn't visit. He barged in and marked me in full view of the people I'm trying to save.

"No. It's not like that." I tuck the card back into the envelope and slip it into my pocket. "He owns the majority stake in Cornerstone now. He's making sure it gets built, so we need to spend time together."

She touches the flowers again, then studies my face. "Is it serious?"

It feels deadly serious. I swallow the instinct to laugh. "What do you mean?"

"The two of you." My mother folds her hands in front of her, her back straight. I've seen her stand just this way at so many parties. So many events. It's the way she would stand in a circle of other women, waiting for her turn in the conversation. I'm the only one to talk to. I'm the only one to wait out. "Is the relationship... committed?"

"We're in business together." I furrow my brow. "That's our commitment."

That, and spending Friday nights with my face red and Mason's voice in my ear and his hands on my body.

Her nod is noncommittal. Not approving. Not disapproving. But her eyes slide back to the flowers.

The only way to talk about the kiss is to side-step it, the way she is. I'm deploying her own skills against her now. Mild confusion, followed by a silence that's meant to be easy. "What, Mama?"

She sighs. "We have a bit of a history with the Hills."

"We do?"

"Natalie and James were part of our circle. Friends of ours. Their deaths were a tragedy." Her hand flutters to her throat. "Shocking. There was a project—a development they were working on. It was finished when it went up in flames." Her eyes flicker to the side, as if she doesn't even want to imagine it straight on. "James and Natalie were in the building when it happened. They both died in the fire. All the children…"

My stomach sinks. I never looked up Mason Hill on the Internet. Couldn't bear it. And if I had, I'd have known this. I wouldn't be red in the face right now. I wouldn't have tears in my eyes. People always say they can't imagine a scenario happening to them, but don't we all do that? Don't we all imagine what it would have been like to find out your parents died?

And then I think of the painfully casual way he said *a better fire suppression system* at the Cornerstone site. Did he see the ruined building? Is the image seared into his mind?

"What did you do?" I press a knuckle to the corners of my eyes. "For Mason. And his siblings." I didn't know he had siblings. I didn't know anything, and now I feel ridiculous.

The corners of her mouth turn down. "I'm ashamed to admit this."

Cold, down in the pit of my gut. "Tell me what happened."

"We could have done more, but your father—" Her eyes plead with me now to understand. That's all she has to say, and it's code for a lifetime of living with Cyrus Van Kempt. *Your father.* "I wanted to help. I wanted to do more. We were in a position to help."

"But you didn't."

"No."

"It's been a long time," my mother says quickly. "Fourteen years. I would hope for your sake that the past hasn't colored your interactions."

Of course it has. Of course it would have. I might have kept myself in the dark about Mason to spare myself the humiliation of knowing how powerful he was. How successful. But Mason knows about me. He sought me out.

He's been so cruel. He's been so awful.

But then…he's also saving us. Saving me.

The bouquet throws its colors onto the bare wall behind it. Our house has been emptier and emptier by the month for more than a year now, but with the flowers, it feels almost right again. It's made the echoing house a home. Absorbed some of the sound from all the hardwood where furniture and rugs used to be.

Mason sent me those flowers.

Another display of his money, and of his power over me. This gorgeous bouquet says that the contract isn't dissolved until he says it is, and not a moment before.

But, like everything else we've done, it contains layers of meaning. He could have sent the note with no flowers. He could have sent a text message. An email. A voicemail, for God's sake. He didn't have to send the flowers.

See you Friday.

Three words on the card, but more are implied. *I want to see you. I'm thinking of you. I miss you.*

"I don't want to assume the worst," I say, because he *is* saving us, despite how mean he can be. I don't know why he's so rough when he has sex. Or why he demanded Fridays in the contract. Is it because of some random attraction to me? Is that just the way he has relationships?

Does it matter? He's our only chance.

"I felt so awful," she says, her voice dropping. "Natalie and I were friends. We spent summers together in Monaco. I wanted to help the children when it happened."

"I understand."

"Your father made the decisions," she says, sounding urgent. "He was the one who decided." Her hand comes up and she presses three fingers to her temple. "I have a headache, sweetheart. I'm going back upstairs."

CHAPTER TWELVE

Mason

I'm not like my brother Gabriel in many ways, but one of the main ones is our approach to events like the gala at the botanical garden. By their nature, these events attract assholes. They're catnip for wealthy people who have everything, and they select for people who crave recognition for how rich they are. The fact that it's a charity benefit is a thin veneer thrown over a pissing contest. Who has the most money to throw at a problem that could be better solved if everyone in our society chipped in? It's all bullshit.

Gabriel's the opposite. He looks at every

invitation as an opportunity. He uses his obnoxiously charming party personality to gather secrets, which he tucks into his pocket to use later. His business has benefited from more than one deal made over a cocktail at a standing table while one prick was honored for having more disposable income than all the other pricks.

Perhaps I'm being unfair. There's money to be made at galas, if your name is Gabriel Hill. He has the advantage of an easy smile. People want to see it. They want him to smile at them.

Whatever.

He sticks his head into my office an hour early, dressed in his finest tux, adjusting one of his cufflinks. "I came to pick you up for the ball, and look at you. You're not dressed."

"Funny. I told security not to let you in."

A half-smile. "If you're going, you have to get up and get dressed."

I don't want to get up and get dressed because getting up is going to hurt. The ache from standing most of the day at the office hasn't faded yet.

However.

I will be attending the benefit.

Charlotte will be there. The purple envelope on that table in her parents' house is proof enough. A family in a situation like the Van

Kempts' won't go to the trouble and expense of buying tickets they won't use. Their attendance at the botanical gardens will be for the purpose of hiding the ruins of their lives.

Also, I want to see her. To surprise her. The flowers were meant to reassure, but this will be a test of whether they worked or not. I can't take revenge on a woman who continually flees the scene.

"I have to read this first."

The email came in a minute ago.

SUBJECT: Shipping delay

The lot with the necklace didn't arrive with the rest of my purchases. I suspect it didn't leave Italy. Poseidon's decided to extend his visit.

–H

Well, fuck. This is one of the pieces I'm more concerned with getting back. A family heirloom, and my mother's favorite. A blue sapphire surrounded by diamonds. Its distinguishing feature is the engraving on the back of the pendant. A tiny slope with an even tinier castle on the top of the hill.

This message means Hades' brother will be on the ground in Italy, tracking down the pieces that mysteriously didn't make it into the ship-ment. Or else he'll be confirming that they never existed. I'm not sure which will be worse for the seller. Knowing Hades, neither will result in a pleasant outcome. Poseidon is rumored to be more bloodthirsty than Hades, though I'm not sure anyone could be more ruthless.

SUBJECT: RE: Shipping delay

You owe me a visit when this is said and done, asshole. It's not polite to keep people waiting.
Mason Hill
CEO, Phoenix Enterprises

I send my reply and get up. It used to be harder to keep everything in check. My expres-sion. The knee itself. Early on, it gave out at incon-venient times. Caused more pain than I expected when I stood. Now, covering it is a matter of habit more than anything else. It might hurt like hell, but it won't show on my face.

Not if I can help it.

Gabriel steps out of my way and ambles into the living room, taking out his phone as he goes. "I'll be waiting for you, big brother," he sings.

I roll my eyes hard enough to send them tum-bling out of my head. Twenty-five minutes later we're in the SUV, both of us peaceably on our phones.

SUBJECT: RE: RE: Shipping delay

Oh, you'll get a visit. Don't fret, motherfucker. I want to see your face when you tell me how much you missed me.

–H

There's traffic—there's always traffic—but none of it seems to bother Gabriel. He's ready as soon as the driver pulls up next to the curb. "Jameson have other plans?" I ask him as we move past the check-in table. No one asks us to show an invitation. They all know Gabriel.

"He always has other plans."

The botanical gardens are filled with lights and conversation, the glow increasing as the sunset dies out. At first I have the impression of butterflies. Jewel-toned gowns next to black tuxedos, all of them fluttering through leaves and blooms. Then the faces resolve. It's a gala like many others we've attended, and it plays host to the same performers. Rich assholes who pretend to be generous, to be kind, but turn out to be frigid underneath.

I recognize two or three of them immediately. Friends of my father's, until they all turned their backs on us. Cyrus Van Kempt was the worst of them all, but they all had a hand in freezing us out.

No idea how Gabriel wears that big, open smile on his face. I feel like a knife's edge in here. I feel like everyone's looking at me for proof. Well, look, assholes. I did it. I rebuilt the family fortune and I have the money and the time to be here with you sons of bitches. My brother puts his hand on my shoulder and heads off toward the sound of his name. I don't look to see who it is.

It's a slow stroll into the gardens, past standing tables and waiters with trays of champagne and a thousand glittering fairy lights strung through the plants. Lanterns on gold wire. They've spent money on every possible thing. Remy's first birthday after our parents died could have used a lantern on sparkling gold wire, but I didn't have the money yet. I never wanted to be the kind of man who bristled at the sight of all these things. They're meant to be beautiful. I get it. A pleasure to look at.

A pleasure that hides a dark underbelly. I'm partially to blame. The only way to get here was to become a fortress, too. A cold motherfucker.

Speaking of sons of bitches, there's Cyrus with Victoria, standing in a clutch of people in the spill of light from one of those lanterns.

It's just like the night at their house. Hate

propels me forward, my own face arranging itself into a threatening smile. *Soften it, just a little, Mason. Don't let them see how badly you want to see them toppled and broken.*

They are broken. They're barely making it. It's up to me to deal the final blow, no matter how well they're hiding it tonight. Cyrus and Victoria Van Kempt are only doing a serviceable job. His tux is starting to wear at the cuffs, and her gown isn't new. Victoria has hidden her too-pale skin beneath layers of makeup. Her smile looks nearly genuine. She's not as much of a mouse, out here where it counts.

Their circle opens for me as I get closer. They're all old, but they know money when they see it. I shake hands all around. A neat little checklist of first names and closed deals and *I heard, I heard, the market's a beast.*

Cyrus keeps himself turned away, his grip too tight on his drink.

"Cyrus," I boom, and shove my hand across the table on him.

He looks at me too slow. The man's drunk, and I don't have to be a genius to know he was drunk well before they arrived here. His gaze slides to the right, and to the left. It's an eternity too late when he reaches out to shake my hand.

It's quick. Glancing. Pathetic. And as soon as he lets go, he turns away. There's nobody there, but he turns away and searches drunkenly for someone to talk to.

"Hello, Mason." Victoria has the same eyes as her daughter, but she doesn't look as hopeful, or fiery. Relief and a certain embarrassment take turns in her expression. Could be about anything. Relief to be here at all, or relief that her husband has turned away? Embarrassment that he snubbed me, or embarrassed that they'll never measure up to me again? "Please excuse Cyrus. He hasn't been sleeping well lately."

"I'm sorry to hear that."

Victoria has mastered the art of the sad smile with the sad sigh, as if I actually meant what I said. The circle of friends she'd been standing with has closed a few steps away. Charlotte's mother drifts back toward the nearest standing table. We're several feet off from Cyrus now. She checks to make sure, then uses her champagne glass to gesture at the arrangement in the center of the table.

"These remind me of Natalie. She used to love orchids." Victoria pats at my elbow with her free hand and steps away.

Cyrus and Victoria's friends float back into place around me and the table like a plume of smoke. More handshakes. More comments on the rising real estate values. The rest of the benefit rolls around us. A sea of fancy people in fancy clothes, and me in the middle of it.

Why did I come?

I have nothing to prove to these pricks. The glances they throw in my direction are proof they think I don't belong. They're right. I don't. No matter what my net worth is, I don't belong here. I'm not one of them. Maybe I would have been, if things had gone another way, but they didn't. My parents died on the same day. Together. And what remained of our family lost everything. The house. The business. Everything gutted and sold. My mother's jewelry, scattered across the planet. All the money gone.

Two of the older men at the table are drunk. More conspicuous about it than Cyrus, but he's a seasoned alcoholic. These two are drinking for the occasion. "Hill," says one of them. We were introduced five minutes ago. "You're James's boy."

Christ. They're all going to drive their knives in, aren't they? The orchid. James's boy. I wish my father were here to laugh at him. *You're my boys.* He'd say that all the time. A teasing joke that we thought we were too old for. We thought we were too old, too grown up. We thought a lot of ridiculous shit that hurts in retrospect.

Regardless. I'm not going to deny it.

"His oldest." I don't bother with a smile.

The second old man purses his lips. He's drunker than the first. His drink sloshes from side to side in its tumbler. "Tell us, Mason, is it considered new money or old money if you lost it and then regained it?"

A nervous laugh goes up around the table. Then the man who asked the question blinks. Grinning like a fool. Proud of his joke. My knee is already sore. Maybe I'll punch this motherfucker in the face and make it worth it.

Or maybe I'll walk out of here. Turn my back on all these people and their laughter and the flowers. Walking out means gathering myself. My chest aches. Tight throat. I swallow against it and will it away. Fuck this asshole for making a joke out of this. Everything's a joke to these people. Everything.

"Oh, darling, there you are."

Her sweet voice. Her delicate hand, slipping around my elbow.

Charlotte.

It's a show for the men at the table. Living this life these past fourteen years has meant learning to play along, and it's easy. It's the easiest thing I've ever done—patting her hand and looking down into her eyes.

And Charlotte.

That sweet little thing.

She smiles up into my face with an honest-to-God grin, blue eyes sparkling in the fairy lights. Her nose scrunches. "Everyone changed places while I was in the ladies' room. It took a while to find you," she says. "Hi, Mr. Kloster. Hi, Mr. Peters."

My god, she's committed. There's no rush to haul me away from the table. No excuse to end the conversation and get the hell out of here. None of the men nearby can take their eyes off her. I want to step in front of her to shield her from view. It's absurd for two reasons. First, because standing in front of her would shield her from these men, but not the rest of the party. Second, because I shouldn't be feeling jealousy. It squeezes at both my lungs.

But this show is going to involve me playing my part, too. When the two drunk men are finished greeting her, I look them in the eye one by one. "How do you know Charlotte?"

"Friends of the family," one says quickly. It's dawning on him. It's dawning that I hate him, and that if it weren't for Charlotte at my side, I would have punched him.

One hit would have taken him out at the standing table. It would have been a kind of relief. To let out some of the pain and emptiness, use it to do something real, like break a man's nose.

"Have you been out to your summer house yet, Mr. Peters?" Charlotte tilts her head at what I can only call a high-society angle to communicate that she's interested in whether this fool has gone to his place in the Hamptons.

"You'll have to find out another time, sweetheart. We're being summoned."

Charlotte waves at the chorus of goodbyes from the table and doesn't resist when I steer her away. Too crowded here—too oppressive. Too many people I don't care about in too small a space. Too many prying eyes for the way I want to look at her, and speak to her, and a thousand other filthy things I won't do in front of people unless she begs me.

I can't explain the sensation I'm having with her on my arm. Charlotte Van Kempt is the daughter of my enemies. She's my enemy. The object of my revenge. The body I'll use and mark to make things right. No—fuck that. To make things even.

And.

And.

Her presence bolsters me. Of the two of us, I'm the only one with the money and power to be standing in this room, but her hand on my arm grounds me. It makes me feel less like a house on fire.

I steer her underneath an archway of white flowers. Another archway. We need to be further out from the light, from these assholes. I need the dark. And I need her.

CHAPTER THIRTEEN

Charlotte

Mason leads me through the glittering, glowing heart of the gala. Humid summer air brushes over the skin exposed by my gown, soft and light in comparison to the strength of the arm underneath my hand and the hard-pounding heart in my chest. With all those people and all those tables and all those lights, I had the impression that the gala went on forever. We pass through one archway bursting with roses in blush and cream, more tiny bulbs alight in the blooms like they might lift off and float away at any moment. Another archway. Another.

His movement is different. Whatever is wrong with Mason's leg is affecting him now. A subtle hitch whenever he lifts his right foot off the ground. I can feel it through the palm of my hand. If I turned my head to look, I bet I'd barely see it. But I would see it. It would have to be bad for a man like Mason to let anything show. His expression tells me nothing.

Is it considered new money or old money if you lost it and then regained it?

A foolish, drunken question from a foolish, drunken man. I heard the words come out of Mr. Peters's mouth, and I saw them reach Mason. He didn't flinch. The change was entirely in his eyes. He hadn't looked happy to be standing in that crowd to begin with. Danger in his smile and the set of his jaw. I saw that danger zero in on Mr. Peters.

And I saw something else, too. The fallout. I've seen how that bristling anger plays out at galas like this one. At best, the insult is smoothed over with more alcohol or a change of topic. At worst…

We avoided all the worst possible outcomes, and for a single moment, I thought I saw a relief in Mason's eyes. Relief, as if I'd rescued him, as if he'd been all alone and out of his depth and not one of the most powerful men in the city.

I might have been wrong about that.

He leads us through a garden glade decorated for the gala with shimmering falls of tulle and lights, then makes a turn. I'm touching him, trying to move with him, so I feel how his balance shifts to one side and rights itself.

The illusion of the forever-gala falls away into shadow.

The illusion of the polite couple bursts like a broken lightbulb.

Mason pushes me up against a pillar, my back to cool concrete, and then his hand is skimming along the side of my neck and up to my jaw so he can tip my face up to his. It's so fast, so fast, and I only have a second to try to catch my breath, a second to register darkness and heat in his green eyes.

"Fuck," he says, and then he kisses me.

My whole body tumbles into the kiss. There's nowhere else to go. A concrete pillar at my back, a man who might as well be made from marble holding me in place. My pulse becomes a racing, dancing thing, completely out of control. I find the lapels of his jacket in my hands, pulling him closer. I didn't make any decision to do that. My hands turn to fists. My nerves turn to sparks, then fire. His tongue is in my mouth, his teeth are on my lip. The chatter and music from the party is no louder than a whisper. It's miles away if it's a hundred feet.

Mason is the only one here, and he's the most dangerous one of all.

Who was I trying to save, going to him like that?

Not me, not me, not me.

I saw the threat of him and then I let him take me away.

He wraps his hand around the back of my neck, testing my lip with his teeth. Again. Again. Like he wants to bite hard but won't let himself. Like he wants to draw blood. I haven't had a sip of champagne at the party but I feel tipsy from the taste of him. A hand on the small of my back hauls me closer in to solid muscle under expensive fabric and the hard ridge of his cock.

His belt buckle.

Ridges of metal and man. Steel digging into softness. It's one thing to see his hands near the buckle. It's another thing to feel it through the insubstantial fabric of my dress.

I've never done this before, I've never submitted to a kiss like this before, never even been offered one, but it's good. It's good. It hurts. It's good.

It's heat on my skin, so much that I part my thighs under my dress so I don't combust. Mason feels me do it and both his hands tighten. Mistake, mistake. The fabric of my thong makes more contact with the air. Cool against hot, wet—

I moan into his mouth. Can't help it. Can't stop it. Don't want to. He licks the remains of the sound off my tongue and laughs. Mason shifts, moves his hands to grip my face, and stares down into my eyes like he's deciding whether or not to kiss me again. Whether or not he's going to do worse. "You sweet little thing. I can't fucking believe it."

"I didn't know you would be here." I can't for the life of me let go of his jacket. He doesn't brush my hands away. "I didn't know."

"Why wouldn't I be here? These events are for people with money."

Money is bitter in his mouth. A dirty word. But it can't be, because he has so much of it that he can buy anything. He bought me. He's gone to my head. My fear of him—of his strength, of his beauty—is like a drug. His hands on me make my blood run fast and my brain run faster. I know better than to bring up what Mr. Peters said about his money. About losing it. About getting it back. But it's the thundercloud hanging over us right now. It won't go away until the lightning cracks.

"My mother—"

"Your mother isn't convincing anyone."

"She told me about your parents."

Mason digs his fingertips into my face. He doesn't mean it. It happens so fast it's over before I can blink. "I don't want to talk about it."

"I'm sorry my dad didn't help you."

A laugh like a knife bursts out of him, followed by another one, the sound so cruel I flinch. "You think our little meetings are about that? No, it's much worse." He backs me up against the pillar again. Nowhere to run. Nowhere to hide. No way to let go of his jacket. I can't do it. "He didn't just decline to help. He stole our money. He used my father's death to make a profit."

His smile is the scariest thing I've ever seen. A painful delight in telling me something I didn't know, telling me something terrible about my father. "That's—how would he have done that?"

"Don't be ridiculous, Ms. Van Kempt." I never thought my own name could sound like such a taunt. Such an insult.

"Charlotte," I whisper.

A shake to my face that makes heat sprint across my cheeks. "You've been running that worthless excuse for a company for long enough to know the basics. How did he take the money?"

"I don't know. I don't know."

"Think."

"It's hard." I can hardly breathe, and when I do manage to inhale, the scent of him is on the breeze and I want more of it. "It's hard when you're—"

He angles my face up, absolute control in his two steady hands, and being forced to stand still sends electricity running through every one of my nerves. "This isn't hard," he snaps. "This is nothing. What's hard is when both your parents die before your eyes. What's hard is when your family fortune is stripped from you overnight. What's hard is having to look into your seven-year-old sister's eyes and explain to her that no, she can't go back to second grade with her friends because your parents are dead and there is no money."

"I'm sorry." Anything to soothe the storm I've brought down, but I'm not calm myself. I'm caught in a million cross breezes and breathing is difficult when I look at him. He's so close. He's so angry. "I'm sorry that happened. It sounds awful. But it didn't happen because of my father."

"Right." There's such a dry bite to the word

that I feel it on my own tongue. "He had nothing to do with it."

"My father's a lot of things. He's—he's not always nice. He drinks. He makes mistakes." I don't want to think badly of my own father. I don't. "He always cared about money and work and he missed every one of my ballet recitals, but he's ultimately a good man. He's honest." *Don't ask it, Charlotte.* "Isn't he?"

Mason laughs again. I close my eyes, then think better of it. When I open them again, he's watching me. Waiting. We're close enough to be kissing. We're so close that if anyone came upon us in the dark, they'd think we were lovers. That we wanted to be this close. And maybe I do, because I'm trying to pull him toward me. Mason stands tall, solid, unmoving. He'll only come closer when he wants to be closer, and right now he wants to laugh at me like I'm the most foolish person he's ever met.

I probably am.

He bends his head. Leans in. I don't know why I inch my legs apart. Hope, maybe. That this will go somewhere hot and unthinking.

But Mason doesn't kiss me.

One of his hands drops and the other locks around the back of my neck to turn my head. This way I can't see his face, only feel the heat of him near the shell of my ear. "I don't give a fuck if you believe me about your daddy. If you want to know how he stole my money, it's quite simple. The next time you're snooping in his office, take a look at the family financials." The low, mean suggestion of a laugh. "And, Charlotte?"

Hard to speak. "Yes?"

"Close your legs." His hand tightens again—half a breath, and then he's detaching my fingers from his lapels. My hold on him was nothing. "Unless you want me to take Thursdays too."

Mason turns and stalks away, his dark suit blending with the shadows. The heat of his hand lingers like a slap, and I put my own hand there in its place. There's no one to hide my embarrassment from. No one to hide my humiliation. I squeeze my thighs tight together. My fingers ache from how I tried to hold him here. Why would I do that? I have no idea what I look like, but a few tentative touches at my hair says it's fine. Mason could have undone the knot at my nape. He could have left me out here a disheveled wreck and made it difficult to walk back into the party.

I'm a bit of a wreck, with swollen lips and a slick, aching pussy and a nervous pressure in my lungs. But I'm okay to go back to the party.

It isn't far. Closer than I thought. Mason's words ring in my ears all the way back to the fairy lights and the tulle and the champagne glasses.

My mother was vague about the details. A fire, she'd said. They didn't help.

She didn't say they lost everything. Not a word about that. And she wouldn't have. I would have asked questions, and there's only so much uncomfortable conversation she can handle. My stomach turns. They knew, then. They both knew what had happened to Mason and his siblings.

It feels like being torn in half. I change my mind with every step I take in my Target heels. *Left*. There's no way my father would have been so callous. *Right*. Mason's correct. *Left*. My father is a decent man, and if he couldn't help them, it was for a good reason. *Right*. There's proof in our own financial records. Mason wouldn't have dared me to find it if it wasn't there.

But then.

The pain in his voice.

Anger, but a wounded anger. He'd expected better from my father. His parents and mine were friends, and Mason must have thought—

I turn a corner and there it is. The gala. The women in gorgeous jewel tones. Summer silhouettes that let the hems play in the breeze. Men in tuxedos, standing tall and proud and laughing. From here, it looks lovely. Perfect even. Good, beautiful people having a nice time. I recognize more than a few of them. There's Jax Hunter and his wife, crossing through. He says something into her ear and she grins. Yes, her nod says. Yes, please. The instant she approves, he straightens up and guides her in another direction.

My pulse races under my fingertips. It's so strong because I've put them up to the hollow of my throat.

Mason's the only one who dresses me in jewelry.

The crowd shifts, and my parents come into view. Around another standing table this time, surrounded by people my father scoffs at when we're at home. He's wearing his tux. Its age is starting to show around the cuffs and buttons, but it's Armani. He wouldn't sell it, even when I started pawning my own clothes. Making sales on eBay and Etsy to cover the bills. He kept the suit. Refused to give it up.

He couldn't have done what Mason said.

He couldn't have.

CHAPTER
FOURTEEN

Mason

I t takes forever to leave the gala.

I'm not sure why I agreed to ride here with Gabriel like a fool who doesn't own several vehicles, but here I am. On the way through the crowd I spot Jax and his wife, Cate, coming in. I motion toward the exit like I'm being called out for an emergency meeting. He shoots me a look of pure, cold skepticism and rolls his eyes. He will give me shit for bailing early at the next card game. Knowing that prick, he'll put a hand to his chest and say *I hope you're all right, Mason. We were so concerned for you after you fled the gala. Now tell me what the fuck that meeting was about.*

Scott finally arrives, and we wend our way through the city. Takes forty minutes to get to the parking garage.

Which is exactly when my phone starts ringing.

Some lucky motherfuckers have the option to ignore calls from unknown numbers. I don't. Not for fourteen years. You never know when some random teacher at your sister's school will call from a field trip or when one of your brothers will call from—

"You are receiving a collect call from the Westchester County Jail. If you want to accept this call, please press one. This call is subject to monitoring and reporting."

I let out a string of *fuck*s and stab my thumb on the screen.

Scott looks at me in the rearview. "Do you need—"

"I'm taking the SUV," I tell him. It's the vehicle I find least painful to drive at times like these, when I have to show up at whatever new and exciting place my brother is being detained. "What did you do now, Jameson?"

"I'm at Westchester, and I need bail," Jameson

AMELIA WILDE

says, and I swear I can hear that bastard grinning over the line.

I bite back the urge to ask him if he is fucking serious, if he knows that Westchester is an hour away in good traffic, if he knows how much I worry that one day this call will be from a local hospital instead of a local jail. "Are you okay?"

"I'd be better if I wasn't in jail."

Then, Jameson, stop doing shit that lands you behind bars.

"I'll be there."

It takes more than an hour to drive to the Westchester County Jail. I would have been better off leaving from the botanical gardens. It hurts to drive. It hurts more when I'm stressed. Even more when I've just said too much to Charlotte Van Kempt in the botanical gardens, kissed her hard enough to feel something, and left her standing there at that ridiculous pillar.

And now I'm the asshole handing my ID to one of the officers on duty in a goddamn tuxedo while my knee pitches a fit.

"I'm here for Jameson Hill," I say.

The second officer snorts. I pause in the middle of sending Remy a text to say I've arrived to give him a look. He presses his lips together to stifle a real laugh. I don't know how anyone could laugh underneath all these atrocious fluorescent lights, surrounded by cinderblock walls and the people they've collected from God knows where. Apparently Jameson's ludicrous behavior was enough to give this guy some entertainment.

At least it wasn't close to home. The good people of Westchester County don't care nearly as much about me or my money as the people in Manhattan. A couple of Jameson's arrests have made the news, but I had enough time and enough money to keep his name out of the press. Partly for him, since he might not want to be known as a petty criminal all his life, but partly for the rest of us. Jameson works for me, which means his actions affect the reputation of Phoenix Enterprises.

The first one hands me back my ID. "He's looking at breaking and entering and grand theft. Cash or credit?"

"Breaking and entering where?" I'll hear all about this from my lawyer, but if this cop over here is laughing about it, then I don't want to wait that long. I also don't want to ask Jameson himself. I hand over my credit card. He takes it.

"A farm half an hour up the road."

Of course. A farm. Christ.

They take their sweet time getting Jameson

from his holding cell. He's in jeans and a black button-down with a bruise on his cheek. Doesn't look too bad. The second officer rifles through a plastic bin full of manila envelopes, finds one, and hands it over to Jameson. "Thanks," he says, like he's been offered a prize instead of his own belongings. "Been a pleasure."

We're both silent on the way back to the SUV. Jameson pauses a few feet off. "You want me to drive?"

"No," I snap at him. "I don't want you to drive. I want you to get in the car and come home and not get arrested again tonight."

"No guarantees." Jameson waits to see if I change my mind. I don't. He shrugs, then goes around to the passenger side and climbs in. I wish I could let him drive, but I don't know what's going on with him. I don't know what he was doing at the farm. If he's truly sober and fine or if he's acting like it for my benefit. I'm as sober as it gets. Irritated. Tired. But I'm good to drive.

I climb in too and get us the hell away from the Westchester County Jail.

Jameson relaxes the instant we're out of the parking lot. He lets out a heavy breath and tips his head back. Closes his eyes. It hurts every time I have to move my foot on the pedal.

252

"A farm?"

"There were pigs." A smile quirks the corner of his mouth.

What the fuck. There are endless questions I could ask Jameson, but they won't do any good. I don't know how to explain to him that I'm not pissed that he keeps doing these things. It's part of how he grieves our parents and always has been. Am I frustrated at having to drive two hours in the middle of the night to get him out of jail because there were pigs? Yes. But mostly I have a gnawing dread in my gut that this ends with the rest of us attending his funeral.

"Are you actually okay, or should I go to the hospital?"

He doesn't open his eyes. "I'm actually okay, big brother. Just visiting some friends of mine."

"You need something to eat?"

"I can wait until we're home."

Is it home to him, though? He's almost never there. Half the time he comes home closer to dawn than sunset. I hate it. That nagging fear that everything I've done has been inadequate beyond words.

It's almost one by the time the elevator lets us into my foyer. Remy rushes in from the living room in leggings and an NYU hoodie and throws her arms around Jameson. "What did you do? Oh my god," she says. "You cannot keep ending up in jail."

"It was a noble cause." Jameson moves them into the living room.

Remy finally stops clinging and pushes him into an armchair. "I want to know what happened," she demands.

I want to sit down, but I don't. I'm too pissed. I'm too worried. Jameson won't stop with this bullshit. He does fine at Phoenix. I settle for leaning against the arm of the couch.

He folds his hands behind his head and grins. "One thing led to another."

Remy falls onto the couch and pulls a throw blanket over her lap. "Okay, but how did it lead to you getting arrested?"

"Because nobody else was willing to go to bat for the pigs."

"Jameson," Remy says.

"It was one of those farms where they test things on the pigs. Worse than a lab, though. Called themselves a rescue." Jameson's lip curls. "I thought the pigs would be better off in another location."

"Were you there by yourself?"

"Yeah." His grin reappears. "Just me and six pigs who were sick of being science experiments."

This won't be the truth, but my brother won't give up the other people who were there with him. Not even to us. I'm shaking my head before I know I'm doing it. "Dad would have kicked your ass for this."

Jameson narrows his eyes, the grin staying in place. "Well, he's not here. Are you volunteering?"

"Would it keep you from being such an immature asshole? Fuck, Jameson. It's not a joke."

He gets out of his seat at the same second I straighten up. I don't know who moves to the center of the living room first but we're there at the same time. I don't know what I'm there for. To block him? To shout at him? To grab his shirt and plead with him to stop being so reckless? Jameson shoves at my chest.

"You're right. It's not a joke." He pushes me again. "You're the joke."

"Don't fight. Please," Remy says. Her blanket slithers to the floor behind me. She hovers off to the side, barely visible when I'm looking at our brother. "Jameson, please."

"Right." Another growl at my tone. "You're getting arrested over pigs, and I'm the joke."

Jameson lunges for my shirt and gets it in

two tight fists. Gets into my face. "Here's the joke, Mason. You've had a stick up your ass for years. You spend all your time trying to act like Dad, but you're not him." He laughs. It's a rough sound. Almost wounded. "And by the way, no one asked you."

"You asked me. You called me for bail." I can't shove his hands away from my shirt without risking my own balance in the process. My knee whines, the pain and pressure increasing, and all I can do is wrap my hands around Jameson's wrists and stay on my feet. "And for the record, you were all minors when they died. Social Services wanted to take the three of you to God knows where, and you're going to stand here and tell me nobody wanted this?"

Remy's crying now. I can tell she's torn over whether to come closer or stay out of it. I understand.

"No. Nobody wanted this." He shoves me, and it's almost too much for my knee. I shove him back.

"You wanted to be split up? Because that's what would have happened if I hadn't stepped up."

"What do you want?" Jameson laughs. "An embossed thank-you card? Should we hold a gala in your honor? Maybe a statue in Times Square would suffice."

His last shove is the hardest and he lets me go, no doubt hoping I'll fall over. I don't. I've had fourteen years of practice with keeping myself on my feet even when it hurts like hell. It hurts that way now. He didn't want to be split up. I saw his face when the social worker came to my hospital room after our parents died to tell us the plan they'd decided on.

"You want to thank me? Do us all a favor and take a day off from being a reckless piece of shit."

"Fine." Jameson's grin widens, but it does absolutely nothing to hide the hurt in his eyes. The grief. It feels like having nerves exposed to a sharp wind. I know.

My phone buzzes in my pocket.

A delivery is here for you in the lobby, Mr. Hill. Should I send it up?

Jameson waits until I read the damn thing to saunter across the living room, brushing past me as he goes.

"What the hell did you send here?"

He turns his head but doesn't stop walking. "There was a baby pig. I said you'd keep it in your bathtub."

CHAPTER FIFTEEN

Charlotte

I make a new dress for Friday night. Black and fitted, with a skirt that moves on the air when I walk.

Maybe it's just an excuse not to go through my father's office and the offices at Van Kempt to look for the proof Mason was talking about. Maybe it's because everything else I own is already steeped in humiliation. It doesn't feel right. Doesn't feel sexy.

I need something fresh, and right, and sexy.

Because this is the first Friday after Mason has told me something about himself. Something real. Something that put a bend in his voice, an edge, like it hurt to say the words.

It's the most raw he's ever been with me.

My heart pounds to think of it. The tiny flares of light caught in his eyes. His mouth on mine. How exacting he was with his hands. In control of every inch of me, even the places he didn't touch.

I stay up all night with my cheeks on fire and my fingers trembling against the fabric I'm using.

Close your legs. Unless you want me to take Thursdays too.

I'll never forget it. Even when this contract ends and Mason Hill is nothing but a memory, I'll have that burned into my brain. Those words in his voice and the way I felt afterward. I could have moaned. I could have begged.

So screwed up. So wrong. Even imagining it is wrong. Feeling this hot and scared and conflicted is wrong. It should be simple between me and Mason Hill. A transaction. Me in exchange for my family's safety and security.

I leave the Van Kempt office early so I can go home and change. I'm so tired from pretending that everything was fine at the gala and from staying up to work on the dress and from thinking about Mason. My head swims. I feel like I have a full-body sunburn, though I haven't had time to spend in the sun. I'm already oversensitive.

It takes loud music and intense focus to drive

into the city, but the nice part about bringing the car is that I can leave on my own terms. It would be worse to have to climb into the back of a car that belonged to Mason with a driver who would tell him everything I did.

It would be more humiliating. I'm not actually sure if it would be worse.

Mason's waiting for me when the elevator doors open.

He's leaning against the table, arms crossed, eyes as dark as they were in the gardens last night. A shiver makes my nipples peak underneath my dress. Shit—they're already so sensitive, and now, looking at those eyes—

They're darker. I see it as I step out into the foyer and the doors close behind me. Take my first breath of the air. It's like the snap of fabric in a stiff wind. A warning. Something worse is coming. Or—something worse already happened.

The pain in his voice comes back to me. That memory attaches itself to another one like the inner lining of a garment to the outer. He was different at the Cornerstone site, the day he told me about the new plans. There's more to him than what appears on the surface. All that's on the surface today are Brioni slacks and a perfect white shirt, the sleeves rolled up to the elbow to show off strong forearms.

He straightens up. Looks me up and down.

Then he lifts something from the table behind him.

It's the collar necklace from last Friday. The one with diamonds. The sight of it in his hand makes goose bumps run from the top of my head all the way down to my shins.

Mason hasn't spoken a word, and the realization dawns that he won't until I do what he's demanding. It doesn't matter that he hasn't said it out loud. It's an explicit order, as plain as the ones on our contract.

I'm supposed to go over to him and let him put it around my neck. He won't come to me.

He won't come to me, which means he won't block my path to go back into the elevator. He won't stop me from leaving. No, I have to choose my own debasement.

My shiver makes the air in his penthouse feel even cooler. It makes my dress feel even thinner. It might only be the illusion of a choice, but dangling it in front of me like this makes me more ashamed than if he'd walked over here and put that necklace on himself. This is a reminder of what I did last week.

It's a challenge. My last chance to walk away from him. I won't get another one.

So it makes no difference that my face feels

feverishly hot or that mortified heat pools low between my legs. I have to do this thing.

My heels click on hardwood all the way across the foyer. I've never wanted to look at the floor so badly in my life. There's always something harder to survive with Mason Hill. Always. I keep my eyes on his anyway. When I'm well within reach but not touching him, I stop.

He studies my eyes. Carefully. Assessing them the way I imagine he'd assess a property to determine if it had value. Like I'm a blank, beautiful gemstone.

I want him to think that I have value. I want it so badly. There's no good reason why. There's no good reason for anything I feel about Mason Hill. There should only be room for hate. Instead, all the emotion has bunched up like a crinoline under a skirt. There are so many layers it's impossible to separate them out.

Oh—but one of them is fear. Fear that he'll tell me that the contract is canceled. That he wanted me close so he could see my face when he told me. My heart feels attached by a single thread. It could throw itself right off my body and that thread would snap.

He makes an indecipherable sound in the back of his throat and lifts the necklace to my neck. I keep my hands at my sides in fists, one around the strap of my purse, so I don't give in to the urge to slap it out of his hands. I'm terrified enough to do it, but I'm even more determined.

I'm going through with this.

The necklace settles onto my collarbone and Mason steps back for a better view. "You'll do this necklace justice tonight, Charlotte."

The words *or else* hang in the air as clearly as if he'd said it out loud. I know what the consequences are for screwing this up. I know there are no more chances.

Mason leads the way back to his living room. To the center sitting area, with its round table and chairs. The same chair he sat in last week.

He takes that seat again. Something changes in his expression when there's no more pressure on his knee, something eases. What happened? I want to ask him again. Those things he said to me in the botanical gardens made me curious.

They made me care, in a strange, forbidden way. And I want to know.

Curiosity will be the death of me.

"Come here." His voice is low and velvet.

"Mason, what you said last night—"

"Don't."

The word feels like a slap. I'm not even sure how I meant to finish that thought. I want more of the intimacy between us. More of his pain in exchange for mine. His dark expression makes it clear I won't be getting that tonight. In fact, it seems like he regrets it.

Like he'll make me pay for what he told me.

"You aren't angry with me, are you?"

His lips carve a humorless smile. "I'm afraid I am."

"But I haven't done anything wrong."

"That's the unfortunate part, you sweet little thing. You don't have to do anything wrong. I can be angry with you for a million reasons. For making me hard. For making me want you." His eyes turn dark. And mean. "For what your parents did."

A shiver runs through me. Protest lodges in my throat. Except what can I say? I don't want to know the truth about my father. I have to take what Mason gives on behalf of my family. I don't need to know.

I go, dropping my purse onto the table on the way. I'm hoping—oh, it's so fucked up—but I'm hoping he'll kiss me again. That felt right. In the gardens, so many things were wrong, but the kiss was right right right.

He takes me by the waist and pulls me into his lap, arranging my legs as he does it so that I'm straddling his hips, hovering over his too-expensive-for-words pants and his Tom Ford belt buckle.

Mason threads his hands through my hair for leverage and pulls me down into a kiss.

Yes.

Yes, yes.

He tastes outrageously good. Outrageously clean. And when he kisses me like this, hard and vicious like I'm property he paid for, it chases all the thought from my mind. There's no anxiety about the future when the thing you were anxious about is happening—and it feels so good. It hurts, too. His teeth hurt, and his grip hurts, and it should be too much but it's not, it's not.

I kiss him back. I'm going to keep up with him. Would it be bad to give in completely? Probably. I won't rock my hips into the front of his pants. I won't. I won't.

My panties make contact at the same moment he takes my mouth with his tongue. All that sensation feels centered over my clit, but he shifts underneath me so I can't touch where I want. I can't get the contact I need. Mason kisses me for a long time like that. So, so long.

And then, with an abrupt laugh, he extricates himself from the kiss and puts me on my feet.

Mason stands up after me and I can see the outline of his cock through his pants. He's hard. This could be it. This could be the moment he takes my virginity, which already belongs to him as per the terms of the agreement.

My thoughts go haywire. He won't be gentle, but I'm not sure I want him to be. That moment between us shouldn't be sweet. He'll make it hurt. I might cry from the sheer relief at having the moment finally arrive. The anticipation is its own kind of pain.

"What's going to happen next?" My voice comes out shaky. "Are we going to—"

"Are we going to fuck? Say it out loud. I want to hear the word."

Heat courses through me. It's both desire and humiliation. They're tangled up together, cross stitched in my body. I can't tell them apart anymore. "Are we going to fuck?"

That laugh again. "You would like that too much. No, we're going to do something more painful." A considering look. "Then again, you might get off on the pain."

Mason's hands go to his belt. He doesn't scold me when I look. It's just how I imagined. His hands, so confident on the buckle and the leather. One quick tug and it's free of his pants. He holds the belt by the buckle and the end, forming a loop.

"Give me your hands," he says.

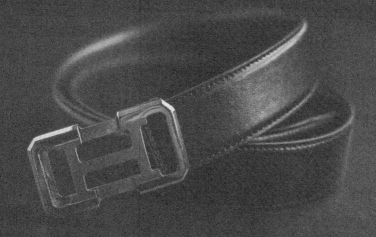

CHAPTER
SIXTEEN

Charlotte

No. *Absolutely not. Never.*
Everything inside me revolts against his words.

I thought I could stand up to Mason Hill. I thought I could bear anything he dished out—for the sake of my father, for the sake of the company. For my family.

Not this.

"What will you do to me?" I sound terrified. And I am, I am. It's one thing to obey his commands. It's another to be tied up so that I can't escape. With my hands bound I would be unable to fight. Unable to push away. Unable to stop what he does to me.

"Whatever I want. I thought the contract made it clear."

The leather looks supple. It's probably warm from his body, but it would have no give whatsoever. These are not fluffy pink handcuffs. This isn't velvet rope. Panic rises in my throat. "I'll do what you say. You don't need to tie my hands."

"I don't need to," he says, his voice dangerously soft. "I want to."

Fighting seems useless.

I hold my hands out to him, palms up. They shake in the faint light.

Mason's smile is a gorgeous slash as he steps closer. With one hand, he pins my wrists together, and with the other he wraps his belt around them. I suck in a breath. I watched him take off the belt. I heard his order. And somehow, my mind never made it this far.

It never quite got to the sensation of warm leather tight around my wrists.

I had no idea what it meant to be trapped before. This is what it means. Having my hands bound by a man who tests the binding with his finger to make sure it's not too tight, then hooks that same finger through the loop and yanks me across the room to the sofa.

"Come along. We have so much to do together. I've been waiting for this. Waiting to have you at my mercy. Waiting to use your sweet little body however I want."

He bends me over the arm of the couch. No explaining. No coaching. He just does it, and I gasp at how much it feels like falling. At how awful it is to be in this position, with my hips held up by the furniture. How exposed I am, even though I'm fully clothed.

My first instinct is to struggle. To pull against that leather as hard as I can. Again and again and again until Mason puts a hand on my head and pushes it down.

Then I can't see him anymore. He's out of my field of vision. My cheek presses against the cushion of the couch. His hand on the inside of my thigh makes me jump, but he just laughs and pulls my legs apart. Wide, then wider. When they're as spread as he wants, he pats the sensitive flesh at the crease of my thigh with enough force to show me he's not afraid to hurt me.

"You're very pale here. Very tender. No one has put you over their knee and spanked you, have they? Daddy never had the nerve. You probably needed a good whipping."

My mouth goes dry. "Wait."

Mason flips up my skirt, bunching it up around my hips, and curls his fingers through the waistband of my panties like he'd curl them through the loop on a garbage bag. He pulls at them slowly until the pressure of my hips makes the thread snap.

One by one, they give out until he's torn them away.

I can't get a full breath. It was better when he made me strip off my dress and start over. There was no belt to fight against then. Now there is. "Wait," I say again. "Please."

"Wait for what?" he asks, very casual, very calm. "Wait for you to be comfortable with this? I don't want you comfortable. I like you afraid. Haven't you figured that out by now?"

He runs a palm over the curve of my ass, patting absently at the small of my back like I'm a wild animal who might break and run. He doesn't have to worry. It would be too hard to get up with him standing over me like this.

Mason's hand delves lower, and my thighs snap shut.

I haven't had time to blink when he shoves

his hand between my thighs and pulls them open again. His hard grip tears another gasp out of me. "I'm sorry. I'm sorry."

"Keep them open." He sounds impatient, and fresh shame makes my whole body flush. "I bought the rights to this, remember? Was there anything excluded from the contract?"

"No." Tears sting my eyes. "You get everything."

"And what does that mean, Ms. Van Kempt?"

"That I won't close my legs," I whisper.

It's hard to keep them open when he slips his fingers back to that place. He drags his fingertips through the wetness I've made, and I turn my face into the cushions to try to hide from him.

He lets me. He must know that this is killing me. I shouldn't be wet for this. I should never, never be wet for this, or him. Ever. But the proof is on his fingers. Mason searches out my opening and pushes a finger inside me, knuckle by knuckle. Then he fucks it in and out. In and out. Curses under his breath. Curses some more.

"Goddamn." A twisted-up comment in a stretched-thin voice. "You're going to be so fucking tight for my cock. You're going to squeeze the cum right out of me."

Panic comes down hard and I pull at the belt.

271

It does nothing. The position makes me helpless and I can't move my arms. I can't get them free. The worst part is that some sick part of me wants to do what he said. That's the part that keeps my legs open wide and my heels planted on the floor while Mason finger-fucks me. No one has ever done this. Ever. Ever. Ever. Except him.

He adds another finger and I whimper into the cushions. It's not painful but it is intense. Mason sets the rhythm and forces me to take it. My thighs quiver with the effort of standing this way. Of being bent for him this way. "Wait," I pant. "No, no, no."

The chant is useless. It's nothing. It doesn't stop him from fucking me with thick fingers. It doesn't stop him from doing it so well, so precisely, that it makes my hips rock against the arm of the chair. I'm fucking a piece of furniture, and he's fucking me, and I thought I knew what rock bottom was. I had no idea. None at all.

He laughs. "You whimper *no,* but you love it. You could walk away from me if you didn't want this. You could walk away and never come back. You've already run once. But you won't do that, will you? And it won't only be because of the contract. It will be because you love the way this feels."

Mason takes his fingers out and finds my clit. Circles it in the rhythm I want—oh, Jesus, I've wanted this for so long. But not from cruel Mason Hill. The conflict becomes a battle in my mind. I want it. I can't. I shouldn't. I want it. I can't. I shouldn't.

He said it would be painful, and the painful part is how much I need this.

I pull harder at the belt around my wrists. Struggle with it. Fight with it. "I don't like this," I say, my teeth clenched. He won't care, but something inside me wants to make it known. Hot tears fall from my lashes. "This doesn't feel good."

"I didn't take you for a liar."

"I'm not lying."

A single long step, and Mason Hill is behind me. I know, because I can feel him there. The heat of his body. The space he takes up in the room.

There's a sound, fabric shifting, and then two hands nudge my thighs apart another inch.

"Then tell me to stop, sweet little thing. Tell me to stop licking your swollen pussy."

His tongue comes next.

It's sexy and skilled and hot. I can't take it. Tears come on so quickly I have to turn my face to the side to keep from drowning in the couch cushion. Mason ignores the crying completely. It doesn't make him pause, doesn't make him stop.

Neither does fighting.

And I do fight, as he licks every inch of every fold, as he finds his way around me with his tongue. Mason holds my hips in a tight grip and keeps me open for him to eat.

Stop. The word is on the tip of my tongue, but I can't make a sound.

No more words. No more real thoughts. Only the battle. My thighs shake and so does the rest of me. The belt doesn't budge. Neither does Mason. He only moves his hands to hold me open for him more thoroughly. The belt pulls back. I yank on it again in a frenzy of panic. But the thing is—the thing is—I don't know what I'm more afraid of. Being bound, or that he's going to make me come like this.

"That's right," he murmurs, his breath hot against the inside of my thigh. "You're so slippery. So hot. You want this, even when it hurts. Even when you're scared, your body knows it belongs to me. *Me.*" Mason spreads me a fraction of an inch wider and does something with his tongue that brings on the apocalypse.

No. That's not what this is. This is an orgasm.

It rolls through my body like a summer

lightning storm. I can't stand up because of the way he has me. Can't close my thighs to him. It's the best orgasm of my life. It goes on and on and on and so does my fight against his damn belt. The second orgasm comes before I can try to stop it.

I sob into the cushions, keeping my thighs wide for him in case he wants to fuck me with his fingers or his cock. I'm braced for it. I'm ready. I agreed. And what does it mean if I keep having orgasms with him? What does it mean if no one else has ever made me feel this way? I didn't know about this wrecked, drugged-out feeling. I'm shocked. Rattled. With Mason Hill. I can't believe it. Couldn't have fathomed it a year ago.

Mason reaches in front of me and helps me stand by the leather of his belt. His eyes shine with satisfaction when he undoes the buckle and slips it off my wrists. He inspects the rubbed flesh there, the pads of his fingers a warning on my skin. "This is the least of what I'll do to you."

The *least*. Why does that excite me as much as it scares me? My wrists feel raw. I tried my hardest to get away.

"Time for you to leave." Mason delivers this casually, then turns and paces across the space to the dining room area on the other side. He sticks his hands in his pockets and bows his head.

He looks forlorn, standing there at his window.

So lonely.

How could a man like Mason Hill be lonely? Having money can be lonely, but Mason has more power than I've ever had. Maybe that makes it worse. I can see a loneliness to that.

The real luxury penthouse doesn't seem to matter. He looks alone.

Alone enough that I go to him.

He glances over at me with a flash of something unnameable in his eyes. "I told you to leave."

I clear my throat. "I didn't go."

"Don't, Charlotte. I'm not in a good mood right now. You do not fucking want this."

A shiver goes down my spine. It's the most open he's been with me, ever.

"You just look like you might need—"

"I need you to leave." The loneliness snaps away, and he's back at his full height again. Dangerous. Prowling. "Do you remember what I said?"

No more chances to run from him.

So I don't run.

I get down on my knees instead.

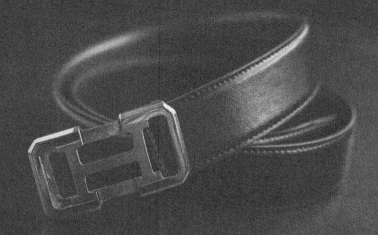

CHAPTER
SEVENTEEN

Mason

S he's just as afraid, just as ashamed, as she
was the night she fled the penthouse in tears.
Only now she's given into it. She's submitting to the fear—and to me. Charlotte trembles on
the floor at my feet, looking up at me with enormous
blue eyes, and *goddamn*.

She's never looked more glorious.

I should send her away right now. I should walk
her to the elevator myself. Taking her throat wasn't
the plan for tonight. I wanted her to fear it. I didn't
want her to offer it to me because she thinks I need
comfort from her.

I don't need comfort from her. From anyone.

But I do want to fuck her mouth. So much it hurts. My abs are tensed with it. My erection has never been so hard. It's already leaking. I'm trembling with how badly I want her heat around me, her tongue against the crown of my cock.

The diamonds wink around her neck. I haven't taken it off her yet. So there's time. And I've been waiting so long. It feels like I've been waiting my whole goddamn life for this.

Decision made.

"Put your hands behind your back."

Her tongue darts out to wet her lip. "Are you going to tie them?"

Part of me wants to say yes. It would probably scare her into backing away, scare her into leaving the penthouse. That's what I want, isn't it? "Only if I have to."

I see her resolve to be obedient in the set of her shoulders. Fuck me. Maybe I should wrap my belt around those wrists to teach her a lesson about asking questions like that.

Another time. I need that mouth.

I free myself of my pants and Charlotte sucks in a breath.

"More than you bargained for, you sweet little thing? It doesn't matter. Breathe deep while you still can. You offered me your throat, and I'm going to take it."

I see the tiny shift in her body toward the door—she wants to run, and her instincts are on a hair-trigger. *Go, go, go. Leave for your own good.*

Charlotte stays on her knees. No words, only the sound of her breath. Too quiet, so I fist a hand in her hair and twist. She cries out, which has the fortunate side effect of parting her lips for me. It turns into a noise of shock. A noise of intoxicating fear. The soft slide of her tongue is so good I could come now.

"This is a kindness," I tell her, breath hitching with the effort of not fucking her as hard as I want to. I want to shove all the way inside. "I'm being… patient. Make it worth my time. Lick."

She does, tentative until I use my grip on her hair to force her in closer. Then Charlotte licks me like she wants to be the society queen of cock-sucking. I won't let her use her hands, so it's hard, it's messy, and Jesus, I love it.

That sweet little thing starts sucking on her own. Ah—fuck. She's frantic to avoid a brutal throat-fucking. And maybe I could go easy on her. Maybe I could—

Charlotte does something with her tongue at my base that yanks a grunt right out of my mouth.

"Be good," I order her, and then I have both hands in her hair, I have her pinned. I shove my cock down her throat like I own it. Which I do. I own her entire body.

She gags on the invasion and I pull out for just long enough to keep her from suffocating. Tears streak down her cheeks. I gave her a chance to run. She didn't take it. And now this is mine, the tight hold of her throat, the slip of her tongue, the panicked crying sounds she makes around me. I hold her hair tightly in my fist, using her the way I need.

A panicked moan.

Another one.

I thrust harder. She can't breathe, she can only cry, and that cry has turned into begging, but it's not begging for me to stop. Charlotte doesn't turn her head. Doesn't pull away. No, she leans in closer.

And then—

Hands. Hands on my thighs, holding on. I'll give her this one. I won't punish her for this because I'm fucking her with all the intensity I've kept bottled up for years. I'm making her cry. Her touch makes my knee seize, makes the muscles react, but I don't care, because Charlotte works harder to make me come.

She's doing her damndest to let me have this.

My cock jumps. I want to do this all night, but

she makes a sound when it happens and that sound curls my toes. My balls draw up.

I pull myself out of her, fuck me, fuck being nice.

"Breathe." My voice is so rough, but Charlotte's already doing it. She's already gasping air into what are probably burning lungs. The image of her this way, with tears silver on her cheeks and my diamonds around her neck and her mouth open to take me, burns into my mind.

I'll never forget it. Fucking never.

Not even when the contract is over. Not even when Cornerstone is built. Not even when I've had my revenge, and this night should mean nothing to me.

Can't wait anymore. Charlotte struggles beneath me, choking, crying, and I hold her head in place and spill myself into her mouth. The orgasm clenches my entire body. There's a roaring sound. It's in my head. No, it's me, filling the penthouse with pleasure. With pain. With a pent-up anguish that comes out in a gush.

"Oh, fuck." The *swallowing* while she tries not to drown in me, audible and hard, tears leaking from her eyes. "Fuck, Charlotte." Again. Again. Again.

Her hands inch up my thighs. She's at her limit

now, but I don't let her go until everything has drained out of me. I make her take every single drop.

Charlotte sits back on her heels, shaking fingertips to her lips. I want to kiss those lips. I want to lay her down on the leather couch and taste her pussy again. And worst of all, I want to drag her into my bed and hold her. Hold her, as if she's a lover. A girlfriend. Not a woman I'm taking revenge on. This is a disaster. I feel too exposed. Too intimate. Rough sex would have been fine, but this was something else. It was a goddamn communion.

I have to get away from her. Have to walk away. Have to put some distance between us, because otherwise I'll screw everything up. It felt wrong to send her away.

But I can't do the things that feel right.

I don't know what's wrong with me, that her innocent curiosity would make me want so many things from her. Not just from her—with her.

It's a problem.

"I'm going to shower." And catch my breath. I'm being a bastard. I know that. Even for a revenge fuck, she deserves better than this. A napkin for her lips. A drink of water. At the very least a *thank you*. But I can't give her any of that. I can't give her anything, because I'm feeling too raw right now. "Stay. Go. I don't care."

My knee puts up a fight all the way down the hall and through my bedroom and has a problem with every move I make to strip off my clothes. Hot water is an improvement, but it doesn't solve my second problem, which is that I'm already hard for her again.

Too hard to ignore.

I wrap my cock up in my fist and brace one hand against the wall so I can get some of the pressure off my knee.

Jesus, her mouth. Fuck, her throat. How am I supposed to live without her on her knees for me after this is over? It was hot, of course, but it was more than that. It was... sweet. It was a dark, sensual comfort that I'm already addicted to.

It takes less than a minute of fucking my fist to come again. Just remembering her lips stretched around my cock is enough to send me over. My abs were already tense before I got into the shower, but now every muscle is shaky. My heart is an earthquake.

Not only because that sweet little thing has a mouth I need wrapped around my cock again, but because my want for her has burst like a diamond into a million cutting shards. Each one of them refracts things I can't want and can't have.

Shampoo. Soap. Both of them follow my cum

down the drain, and I try not to think about what I want from Charlotte Van Kempt. It's impossible. If I'm going to go back out there and look her in the eye, I have to let it happen. Imagine it so I can discard it.

I wanted to lift her off the floor and kiss her hard. Not so hard she bleeds, but softer, so I can tell her how much I loved her lips on me and her struggle and her tears. I want her to be in here with me now so I can work shampoo through her hair and let her lean on me while I rinse it out. I want to dress her in my clothes. Sit on the couch with her in the den, not the living room.

I want to take her to bed.

My bed, so I can take her some more. I want to own every boundary of hers right now, tonight, and I don't want to wait another second. I want to make her cry. Make her sob. And then I want to hold her afterward and tell her what a good girl she was, what a sweet little thing.

I want her to sleep next to me.

But I can't.

I definitely can't let her stay here. Not now. Not ever. It would reveal too much. I don't have women spend the night at the penthouse. Not the women I've dated and left behind, and not Charlotte Van Kempt, whose body I've bought.

It can't happen. She can't ever spend a night in my bed.

None of it can happen, because this isn't about her feelings, or even mine. This is about making things right in a world that's taken so much from my family I can hardly think about it. It's good, though. If I'm going to imagine Charlotte breathing peacefully in the night next to me, then I also need to remember what got us here in the first place. Both of my parents are dead. The way they died fucked all four of us up in various terrible ways. In their absence I've had to fight to take their place and I've done a terrible job. It's possible Gabriel and Jameson and Remy might never recover.

My knee aches, deep in the muscle. I've been standing too long. All day at the office. All this time with Charlotte. In my shower. I'm still shaky. Shaken. I'm rough with the towel so I can get a grip. I can't tell if it works or not.

Another problem—an aching desperation to look at her again. To have her in my sight. I make myself dress at a leisurely pace. Slacks, though I have no interest in pulling them on over my aching knee and would prefer pajamas. A henley. I'm not putting on a dress shirt again. Socks. I shove the sleeves of the shirt up to my elbows and let myself lean on one of the shelves in my walk-in closet. The bed has never been so tempting.

And yet.

There are things I need to do before I go to bed.

It doesn't matter that I can't touch her again. The electric need to fuck her until she's out of tears and out of words would be impossible to deny. It would be like snapping the clasp on that necklace. Once I started to pull, breaking it was inevitable. I had to feel it come apart in my fist. I can't wait to feel Charlotte come apart under the invasion of my cock, but—

Patience.

I've wanted to fuck her since she took that first step into my office. But doing it now will take away her fear of it, and I want her to be fucking terrified.

One step out of the bedroom, and I discover the night's not over yet.

Charlotte didn't leave.

Well, isn't that a surprise.

She's at the end of the hall, peeking in to the half-open door of Remy's bedroom. I meant for her to get into the elevator and *go*. She had to summon some bravery to go snooping through my home while I was in the shower.

From the looks of it, she washed her face in one of my bathrooms, and then she went to make coffee.

One of my sister's mugs is cradled in her hands. It features a cartoon drawing of a pebble with a big smile. A script font reads *My life is in ruins*! An archeology joke Remy grins at every time she sees it.

The delicate flesh of Charlotte's wrists is pink from my belt.

All the muscles around my knee clench like a fist, and my heart does the same thing. Charlotte could be coming home from a night out in that dress. She's kicked off her cheap heels so she can go barefoot through the penthouse. I ruined her hair, bending her over the arm of the sofa and keeping her there, but she's done her best with it.

Home from a night out with me.

Fuck—no.

I take another step into the hall and she jumps a little, controlling it in time to avoid spilling the coffee. For a split second, there's pleasure in her eyes—I've caught her, and she's pleased to see me.

Then she remembers.

It's like a gem tumbling away from the jeweler's light. That pleasure becomes opaque. It's hidden behind her nerves and her shame and her desire. It's separated from me by the loops and falls of her signature on our contract. There's no such thing as Charlotte Van Kempt taking simple joy in me stepping into a room.

"You didn't leave."

"No." Charlotte glances down into her coffee, then back up—always back up, like I told her. "This—" A motion toward the door with the coffee mug. "This is your sister's room?" Her eyebrows lift, and I see why she was looking into the bedroom like she was.

I don't want to talk about Remy. It's too personal. That may be a joke, considering I just had my cock in her throat, but I don't care. "Yes."

"What's her name?"

I'm not going to have a conversation with her from this distance, so I go down the hall to meet her. Every step hurts like a hairline fracture, sharp and thin. Charlotte stays in her place as I brush past and pull Remy's bedroom door closed. For her privacy, yes, but also for mine.

And for the excuse to be near Charlotte.

She backs up a step when I'm finished, and there's plenty of space for us where the hall makes a turn and keeps going. "Remington," I tell her.

Charlotte nods, her eyes wide and curious. "There are textbooks."

"She goes to NYU." I should shut up about my family, but something about the intimacy of the night keeps the words flowing. "She was the oops baby. My parents weren't expecting her. And when my mother found out she was pregnant, she was sure it would be another boy. Even when they found out she was a girl, the name stuck."

A small smile. "It's sweet that she still stays with you."

"My brother Jameson has the room next door." I gesture down the hall. "That one used to be Gabriel's. He moved out as soon as he could."

Of all the things I've said and done to this sweet little thing, naming my siblings and their living situations seems to shock Charlotte the most. "But Jameson lives here?"

"He has a room here, but he barely sleeps in it."

"But he is here ... sometimes."

"Yes."

Charlotte's cheeks turn red. "Are your siblings ever here on Fridays?"

"Oh, look at you. Worried someone might have heard you choking on my cock. No, those sounds are only for me, unless you need an audience."

A quick shake of her head. "I don't need that. I just didn't want to leave yet."

"You wanted to snoop."

She smiles, and I can't believe it—smiling when I just fucked her throat until she was in tears. "Yeah," she admits, looking sheepish and goddamn beautiful. "I wanted to know more about you."

And I want to take you to my bed and make you cry all night. I want to ask you a thousand questions about why a girl like Charlotte Van Kempt is curious about me, of all people. I want to know everything about you.

"You're making a mistake, Ms. Van Kempt."

"Because I made coffee?"

I take the step toward her I've wanted to take all this time and take her chin in my hand. Lift up her face. "There's nothing about me you need to know," I tell her. "You don't worry about that. You worry about surviving this arrangement. Don't worry about me."

She shivers. "Okay," she agrees, because she's like that, because she fights me and gives in. "I won't worry about you."

I don't believe her, but I don't know what to do about it. It occurs to me, as we stand outside Remy's room, that they're almost the same age. I would kill anyone who treated my sister the way I'm treating Charlotte. Unlike Remy, no one's around to protect Charlotte.

It's a goddamn shame.

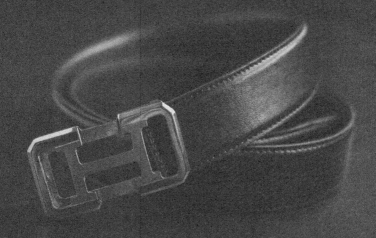

CHAPTER EIGHTEEN

Mason

A week is an eternity to think about what I'll do to Charlotte Van Kempt. I feel cursed, somehow. Every second feels like an hour. The world continues at a breakneck pace while I'm trapped. Waiting. Thinking of her.

I thought the weekly schedule would intensify things for her. I've had to live with a certain sick dread for fourteen years—why shouldn't the daughter of my enemies feel something similar? Why shouldn't she lie awake nights afraid of what's coming?

I was right—it has made things more intense for

Charlotte. The weeklong intervals between Fridays have her breath shallow and her cheeks flushed by the time she steps off my elevator. Her emotions have become more outsized. The crying—

The crying is exquisite.

But my emotions have become more outsized, which, like a fool, I didn't anticipate. I didn't think the urge to bend and punish and lick and taste could get any stronger, and it has.

It has.

Stronger and infinitely more complicated. Sometimes I can't sleep for how much I want her in the bed next to me. My lungs ache from it. My muscles burn. The pillow and sheets on the other half of the bed badger me. *This is how the blanket would fall over her shoulder. This is how it would pull and curl as she turned over on my pillow. This is how her blonde hair would spread out on the pillow case. You can see it now, can't you?*

It's unbelievably fucked up. Because the other side of that want is a need that bristles and burns. It has the shape of anger but it's more than that. Anger is too simple, too blunt, for what I feel. Retribution requires more. It requires patience. It requires commitment. Above all, it requires focus. It took several years for me to be able to set aside my seething rage and grief and see the way forward. Planning for this has been another one of my projects, nested inside the others the way every property I fought for in those early years was nested inside rebuilding Phoenix and keeping my siblings alive and together and regaining the fortune that had been taken from us.

So. My conflicting feelings about Charlotte won't have any impact on the ultimate goal.

I won't let them.

Regardless, I'm hard as steel from thinking about her when Scott pulls up to the Cornerstone development late on Friday afternoon. I've waited as long as possible to make the visit. Set it up as the final task between the interminable week and the moment when the elevator doors will part to reveal a nervous, blushing, wet-between-the-thighs Charlotte Van Kempt. A reward of sorts for surviving the agony of not fucking her for another week.

I step out of the car into a golden summer afternoon. The sky is the color of Charlotte's eyes.

"Mr. Hill," Dave says, approaching from deeper within the site. It looks more like a building now. "Do you have a few minutes? I wanted to show you some of the progress on the ground level."

Cornerstone's a building now, which is nice. There was a certain stark possibility to all those steel beams. There's more in framing and floors. I've hired extra people, extra teams, to accelerate the construction. Pushed it to the very limit of speed. I half regret it now, climbing around inside a space that's nearing completion.

But.

An accelerated timeline on the development means an accelerated timeline with Charlotte. At the beginning of all this, I thought I could strike the perfect balance between terror and loss. Break her. Ruin her for every other man. Turn her into a panting, crying slut for me, and then drop her by the wayside. Long enough to bask in the fullness of my revenge, and no longer.

My knee doesn't hurt nearly as much moving around on the inside. That's the mark of real progress, if a person with a permanently fucked-up knee can get around without trying to surreptitiously search for a bench.

Dave rattles off plans and figures and I pay attention to him. I really do. It's just that I pay more attention to thinking of Charlotte.

Charlotte on her knees in my living room.

Tears racing down her cheeks while she tried her best to take my cock in her throat.

The taste of her—fuck. The taste of her, the swollen heat of her, the way she sobbed when she realized what was happening. When it finally set in that I was going to make her come on my tongue. Sometimes pleasure is a far more effective revenge. It's all in how well you blend it with pain.

My cock throbs as we make our way down to the main level. It's a matter of hours now. I have some decisions to make. Some pain to prioritize. Some pleasure, if she's very good.

Ah, fuck. Especially if she's not.

"—ahead of schedule," Dave is saying. "I'll have the information to you by the end of next week unless something else comes up. Don't foresee that happening."

"You have my number," I tell him. "Remember—"

We step out of the building, and the thing I was going to tell him to remember disappears in a puff of smoke.

Off to one side of the site, Cyrus Van Kempt stands near a pile of bricks. Charlotte's father. The years haven't been kind to him. He looks older. More bloated. More gray, but I see the same hardness in his stance. The prick scowls at the building. His expression is visible even with his hand shading his vision. His hand falls, and he says something—not to anyone, because there's no one around. It looks like a curse.

And then he sees me.

The scowl shifts to bare his teeth.

The part of me that wants to kill him bares its teeth.

"Mr. Hill?"

"Go back to work, Dave."

I don't look back to see if he follows my orders or not. I walk toward Cyrus, every muscle involved in the effort. My knee already throbs from his presence alone.

It takes so much work to look invulnerable. To cover up the signs of pain. To keep my guard up. I have no choice but to meet him this way. Turning your back on a man like Cyrus Van Kempt only invites him to chase after you. I won't allow it. Not only because I'm not a fucking coward, but because running for any real distance hasn't been on the table for years.

I'm two paces away when he comes to an abrupt stop and shoves a finger into my face. "You made a deal with my daughter."

I cock my head to the side and furrow my brow. "Of course I did, Cyrus. You signed off on it. Did you have too much to drink and forget about it?"

A wild grin spreads across his face, his teeth clicking together, and my god. He came here drunk. "I don't have to be sober to know you've been fucking her."

"Have I?"

I wish.

The grin melts into a sneer. "I know my daughter. I know what you've been doing to her. I hope you've had a good time, because that's the only thing of mine you're getting."

The only thing of mine. Like he owns her. Like this man, this drunk piece of shit who's standing on my property, has any claim to Charlotte.

"Do you still think she's yours? That's cute, Cyrus. Why don't you concentrate on making some money for your wife instead of obsessing about your daughter?"

"Don't you say shit about my wife. Or about Charlotte."

"How does she afford the latest season of Dior?" I ask, putting on a mystified expression. "Right. She doesn't. Your wife must not go out in society anymore."

"Not my fault the economy's a mess."

I snort. "How convenient. When you're on top it's because of your hard work. But when you're failing, it's because of the economy."

"You don't know fuck-all about my business."

"Actually, that's not true. I've read every document. That's what the majority stakeholder can do. And you signed that over to me." A pause. "Along with your daughter's body."

"You son of a bitch." Cyrus overemphasizes every word, but he comes down hardest on *bitch*. "In the flesh. Your mother was a bitch. Natalie Hill was always a frigid—"

The punch I throw is so hard it hurts my knee. Of course it fucking hurts my knee. The force of a punch comes from the ground up, and the twist in my body puts too much pressure on the knee. But fuck this guy.

His head snaps around and he stumbles back a step, then loses his balance completely and crumples to the ground. His palm splays out to catch him and he lets out a soft grunt. I hope a piece of building shrapnel went through his hand. I hope it breaks all his fingers.

Gingerly, he lifts his hand from the ground. That's all the time I give him before I put my hands in the front of his shirt and haul him off the ground. Up toward me. So I can get into his face. He's too heavy, and goddamn it, if it weren't for this bastard maybe it wouldn't feel like a knife through the knee to do this.

If he had helped me, if he had done any fucking thing, then I'd have had a chance. I was supposed to spend six weeks in rehab to fix my knee. I was supposed to spend three more months in physical therapy. But there was no money. There was no money, and if I'd gone away to repair the shattered knee they would have taken my siblings. They would have taken them. I couldn't let that happen. I wouldn't let it happen. Fucking ever. They're my family.

Rage feels pure, and hot, and deadly. It feels like sitting in a hospital bed while some unholy shrew from social services looked up from her clipboard and told me that there was nothing to be done while my six-year-old sister sobbed in my arms and the morphine wore off. It feels like tens of thousands of excruciating steps. It feels like fire.

"If you ever say her name again, I'll kill you," I growl into Cryus's face. "You're a piss-poor excuse for a man and the world would be better off without you."

His eyes go out of focus. He's had more to drink than I thought. Did he drive here? Another spike of fury. I don't give a fuck if he wants to drink himself to death, but he's not going to take anyone else with him.

"Why don't you do it then?" Cyrus doesn't slur, but I can tell it's a near thing. He's had years of practice with this. He wraps both of his hands ineffectually around mine but doesn't have the strength to shake me off. The counterweight of his body is too much for the tendons, too much for the muscles. "Or are you as much of a pussy as James? Like father, like son."

The world drops behind a red curtain. Fuck it.

Fuck him. It's over. I'm ending it. The muscles in my shoulder tense. Have to plan for this. Have to stay on my feet. Let go of him and draw back the fist—

Shouting all around us breaks into the act. Somebody's got a hand on my shoulder, and somebody else is unhooking my hand from the front of his shirt and pulling him away. I try to throw off the hand that's on my shoulder but he doesn't let go. Doesn't put any backward pressure on me, either. A hand comes around to my chest. "Stop. Jesus."

"You okay?" It's Dave, with Scott coming up on my other side. Scott takes one look at me and goes to supervise the removal of Cyrus from my sight. "Mr. Hill. Mason. You okay?"

Scott and two other guys hustle Cyrus around the stack of bricks. One of them glances back over his shoulder at me.

"He's drunk," I shout. "Get him a ride."

Get him a ride before I kill him. Everything I am wants to chase after him, to run until I can catch him in a flying tackle and put him down forever, but I can't, because I can't chase him, because I can't risk the damage.

Ha, ha. What a goddamn joke. The damage has already been done.

"Mason," Dave says again, and I feel it then—my face. The expression on my face. Cyrus didn't land a single blow, but my knee hurts like a motherfucker. I know I'm letting it show—all that pain and hatred, and underneath that the shock and confusion of hearing that prick tell me he wasn't going to help. I can feel the shape of *It's for Remy* on my tongue. See the shake of his head, and the self-satisfied smile.

"I'm fine." Dave hasn't let go. "I'm fine. I'm not going to go after him."

"You want me to get people out here?"

Security, he means. Beyond the company we already use. People to make sure he doesn't come back. The technicalities of our agreement are such that while the building is under construction, the property is effectively mine. I can bar him from the site. "Monday. Have them here on Monday. You can let go of me."

Dave hesitates, then pats at my shoulder and releases me.

Like my dad did when he was alive.

Scott reappears, moving directly to my side. "Car's waiting, Mr. Hill," he says. "It's a good time to go home."

CHAPTER NINETEEN

Mason

It's not enough.

Punching that motherfucker across his face wasn't enough. The things he said about my family were like a hand grenade shoved down my throat with the pin already pulled, and a thousand kinds of old pain have splattered across my insides.

Scott drives me back to the penthouse in silence. I try to answer emails. I can't read the words on the screen. I'm not done with the Van Kempts, and I'm not done with Charlotte, but if I lose my shit right now I won't be in control of myself to take my revenge on her. That control is slipping out of reach. I need it back.

I'm the rude piece of shit stalking through the lobby without saying anything to the doormen, but it's better that way. People are so foolish. They think silence is always less polite than speaking. They're wrong. When I'm silent, it's because my words would leave scars. I had to learn to bite them back years ago. I had to learn to become precise with what I said, and what I did, because any step in the wrong direction would lose what little stability we had. It's a heavy weight. I was eighteen then, but it doesn't seem to matter that I'm older. It's still a relentless pressure on my shoulders.

I let myself lean against the railing in the shower. Sore knuckles from punching that prick. A knee on fire. The man in the steamy reflection looks wrecked. He looks like he needs a drink, or five.

I don't. I need a sweet little thing named Charlotte Van Kempt.

The heat of the shower makes no impression. My knee throbs and my gut is an acid mess of rage and tension.

She's going to know.

Last week, when she stepped off the elevator, she knew that it would be different from what came before. I saw the knowledge flicker across her eyes. I saw the nervous swallow. I saw her face flush deeper. I've always hated these bullshit tricks to manage the pain and the anger. All the deep breathing. All the visualization. Fucking hated it. But it's possible to loathe something and use it to your benefit, so I do. I breathe deep.

I visualize punishing Charlotte Van Kempt for the sins of her father.

I visualize how good it will feel to finally have done it. I'll have a sense of calm. A sense of peace. A sense that I've made things balanced in the world again. They're never going back the way they were. I came to terms with that a long time ago. My parents will stay as dead as they ever were, but someone will pay for it. The world won't have destroyed our lives without giving up some of itself, too.

When the shower is finished there's time before Charlotte arrives. I need all my balance and all my strength to keep myself in check. I don't want the gym—don't want the windows, or the equipment, or the sight of myself in the mirror.

The bedroom floor is fine for what I need.

Which is to run through the routine of exercises I've been doing, and loathing, for a decade now. I've hated them from the very first day and I hate them now. I hate having to do this. I hate that they keep some of the pain at bay. I hate that if I stop doing them, it comes back with such intensity that it's difficult to stand at work. There's no such thing as sitting through a meeting for me. I know what the whispers say about me—that I'm a mean, power-obsessed bastard who wields it over everyone at every opportunity. That's true. It's just not the whole truth.

Anyway, in order to remain in control at times when I need to be on my feet, I need the goddamn exercises. They steady my breathing. Disconnect me from the pissed-off knot in my gut enough to think. Enough to wait through the rest of the minutes until Charlotte arrives.

She's always a few minutes early. My phone buzzes with the text from the doormen exactly when I expect it to.

Derek: Ms. Van Kempt is in the lobby. She's entering the elevator now.

Mason: Thanks.

I push my sleeves up to my elbows and go out to meet her. I'm stepping into the dim light of the foyer when the doors slide open to reveal her.

Her dress is a purple, floating thing that reminds me of flower petals. But her eyes are what demand my attention. They're blue like topaz, shifting in the light until they've taken on the impression of sapphire, and they are innocent.

She doesn't know what's happened yet.

Charlotte's chest rises in the shallow rhythm of her sweet nervousness, but she takes the necessary step into the foyer. The doors slide closed behind her, and it's that sound that undoes all the care I've taken with the breathing and the visualizing and all those goddamn exercises.

I want her. And I want to break her. I want her to come, and I want her to cry.

I want her to understand.

I leave space between us so she can feel the distance. "I saw your father today."

Shock makes those blue eyes fly open. Genuine—her daddy didn't call her to tattle on me. Her hand comes up to the hollow of her throat and she doesn't stop herself. "What do you—where?"

"At Cornerstone." Out there in all that sunlight. I saw every twitch of that fucker's mouth, every glimmer of satisfaction in that bastard's eyes. "He came to see me."

"No. There's no reason for that. I told him I would handle everything."

She doesn't believe me. The struggle is written in her features. Charlotte Van Kempt is still trying to make her father into a good man. She's still trying to believe the best of him.

"What else did you tell him? That I licked your cunt until you came on my tongue?"

A gasp. "No. I didn't—no."

I advance on her, eating up the distance in two strides, and make a collar of my hand on her throat. Force her head up and back so she has to look into my eyes. So she can see what she's walked into.

See that there's no escape.

"He had a lot to say about you." Her neck tenses under my hand. I'm squeezing too hard. *Let up a little, Mason. Don't make her run.* "He thought we'd been fucking. A lot to say about my parents, too, which is about when I punched him."

Her mouth drops open. Charlotte doesn't know what to say.

"He's wrong about that. But not for long." I take a deep breath. "Now that you're here, I think it's time you made yourself useful. All this aggression has to go somewhere." I run my thumb up and down the side of her neck. "It's not healthy to keep it bottled up."

She's trembling now. "I can't believe you punched him."

I laugh at her and she blinks like it hurts, like this humiliation causes her physical pain. "The black eye I gave him could have been a lot worse. I wanted to pummel him into the ground. But I knew I'd have you later, wouldn't I?"

"Yes." Her lips form the word, but it doesn't

make any sound. It doesn't have to. She's been mine to use in just this way since she first let my office door close behind her. Charlotte would try to insist that it was when she signed the contract, but she would be wrong about that. I owned her as soon as she took the meeting with me.

"It will be significantly more entertaining to beat your pretty little ass until you're red."

Charlotte jerks backward, trying to free herself from my hand. Cute. I use her own movement to back her against the doors of the elevator. Her chest heaves. "Because of him? You're doing this because of him?"

"Not only because of him, you sweet little thing. I've been a patient man. I'm done waiting."

Her eyes fill with tears. "You don't have to do this."

"I don't have to do anything. I'm not sure how many times I have to explain it to you. This is what I want."

"To hurt me?"

I lean down and press a kiss to the side of her neck. "Yes. You'll be sitting at the dinner table with Mommy and Daddy tomorrow, and they won't have any idea that you're bruised beneath your dress."

Charlotte makes a sound that's closer to a moan

than a protest, and I pull back so I can look into her eyes. "But how will you—how will you—"

"Punish you? Go ahead and say it."

"How will you punish me?"

"However I fucking want."

She's trembling. "Oh, no—no. Please. I didn't do anything wrong."

"Is that what you think?"

"I didn't," she whispers.

"You're fighting me right now."

"I think—" A swallow that I feel in my palm. "I think you like that."

I've never been harder for anything in my life. I love the way she can't help herself. Charlotte likes what I'm doing to her—loves it even. But she hasn't been broken.

I'll continue with that tonight.

"Oh, you sweet thing."

I want to hurt her so badly. I need to hurt her. And Charlotte needs me to hurt her. She needs that because that's the way to save her father's company and her family's lives. Submitting to me in any way I want is her only guarantee for pulling Van Kempt out of a bankruptcy tailspin.

But she also needs it for another reason.

It makes her hot. It makes her wet. And she can't stop thinking about it. I can't stop watching the reality of me and the fantasy of what she wants collide in her eyes, over and over and over until I'm forced to lean down and kiss her. Lick her. Taste her tongue, and drink in the little whimpers she makes when I bite her bottom lip.

She sags forward when I let her go, almost as if she's going to go to her knees in the foyer. Charlotte catches herself at the last moment and holds tight to her purse. Determination flares in her eyes. The subtle lift of her chin tells me she's already working on a story to tell herself about tonight—that it was necessary in order to save her family. That she had no choice but to put herself in my hands every Friday like clockwork. Even after I made her cry. Even after she ran from me.

There's no more running now.

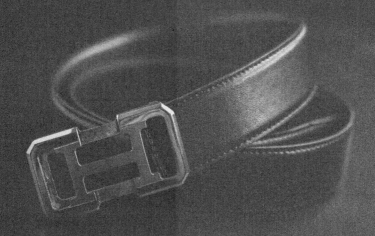

CHAPTER TWENTY

Charlotte

The first time I met Mason, I had a strange dread that he'd do something impossible—that he'd make the windows of his office turn to nothing and let in the thunderstorm that roiled in the clouds around his building.

I was mistaken. The rain and the lightning outside were no threat.

The storm was already in the room with me.

It was still contained that day behind all his self-control. He deployed his cruelty with precision. I expect him to be precise now, but his fury is out in the air. It feels like gathering electricity. The kind of friction that builds and builds until it tears apart, and all at once, you see how weak the seam was.

His words are like sharp gusts of wind, here in this silent space, and they make it hard to breathe. Hard to think. My father was at Cornerstone. Mason gave him a black eye. No one told me. I stayed late at Van Kempt today. I didn't want to risk another conversation with my mother or another status report in my father's office. I brought all my clothes and my things to the office and used the small employee gym to get ready. They didn't call. No one called.

My heart beats out of time. A part of me thinks I should go home to make sure my father's okay, but that would mean walking out on Mason.

I won't do that.

I can't.

And maybe the scariest part of all is that I don't want to. My curiosity is too strong to let go. It's like the feeling I get when I see a garment I need to make or a pattern I need to put together—I *need* to do it, almost like a compulsion. Fresh air in my lungs and a tug at my core. It doesn't matter if I have to save my pennies and hoard coupons for the fabric store and stay up late to do it.

I wanted some of his pain in exchange for mine. I wanted that.

I'm going to get it.

Mason watches me, impassive. He takes in my trembling, my shaking. I'm within reach of the elevator. I could reach behind me and push the button and try to escape. But there is no escape—I see that now. He'll live in my mind. The question of what we might have done will never leave me.

"Everything off," he says.

"Here?"

A vicious smile. "I've been too lenient with you, Ms. Van Kempt. No purse. No clothes. Not another step until those things are on the floor."

Heat floods my face at *Ms. Van Kempt*. It's worse, somehow, to have to undress in the foyer. But there's no getting around it. The promise behind his words is that he'll take my dress for me. It's purple and summery and soft. I don't know why I keep making things for him. Every Friday seems to demand something new for him to see. A fresh layer of armor.

I reach for the hem and pull it over my head in one motion.

Mason laughs, and I could cry. It's the meanest sound. Beyond that, he's right to laugh, because of what I've done. "Nothing on underneath, Charlotte? Did you think I would be impressed?"

"You tore them last time." I drop my purse onto the dress and step out of the shoes. It's a relief to let it drop. I couldn't stop shaking if I wanted to. I step out of my shoes next. "I thought it would make things easier."

His smile is beautiful and dark. "Nothing will be easy for you tonight."

Mason puts his hand into his pocket and takes something out. A necklace—one I haven't seen before. A medallion made of diamonds in light colors, radiating out from a center diamond in white. Even the chain is a delicate twist of diamonds.

He puts his hands around my neck and I stop breathing. His fingers work at the clasp and it seems so final, this necklace going on. My last chance to escape sails away. The medallion makes contact with my skin. It's heavier than the other pieces. It must have cost a fortune. Worth more than I am. The cold of the metal sends goose bumps racing down my ribs. It makes my nipples pull tight.

Mason makes a sound—a noncommittal, observational one—and takes the medallion in his fist. "Keep up," he says, "if you deserve to wear this."

As if I have another choice. I know how much necklaces like this cost. If it snaps, it won't be because of me.

Shame is cool metal on hot skin. I get ready to go left out of the foyer, toward his enormous great

room with its living area and sitting room and dining table, but he goes right.

Toward the bedrooms.

This is where he found me snooping last Friday.
This is where he sleeps. He's never taken me to his
bedroom before. Mason pulled his sister's door
shut tight in front of my face. He doesn't hesitate
for even a second. An abrupt left turn and then, on
the right, a set of double doors recessed into the wall.
He throws one open and drags me inside.

More hallways. It should be simple to keep up
with him, but I'm off-balance with this pressure
around my neck, in these unfamiliar rooms. My
lungs are on fire with a wild, ridiculous curiosity.
A desire? I don't know. I want to be familiar with
these rooms. I'm desperate to know more about
him. Maybe then I wouldn't be so afraid. But I don't
know, and I am afraid.

Another turn into a huge walk-in closet that's
bigger than mine at home. Through a wide archway is a gleaming bathroom, but he doesn't take me
there. He stops at a drawer and opens it. Takes something out.

It's one of his ties.

More fear. I begged him not to tie my hands last
time, and I want to do it now, but I know he'll do it
anyway. I press my lips closed to keep from doing it.

Mason's eyes on my skin are intense and un-readable. "You'll do one thing before I bind your hands, Ms. Van Kempt."

Anything, I almost say. "What?"

"Reach down and put two fingers inside yourself."

This is what it must be like to burn alive. "I—but—"

He narrows his eyes. "If you insist on wasting my time with bullshit protests and cute questions, I'll insist on a gag, Charlotte. I'm running out of patience."

And so I have to do this horrible thing, I have to inch my thighs apart in Mason Hill's walk-in closet so I can push two fingers into a tight space that's dripping wet and so sensitive a sound escapes me at the contact.

A moan.

I can't look at him.

Mason leaves me behind the dark of my eyelids for long enough to feel my fingers there, for long enough to feel myself contracting around them, for long enough to want to die.

"Take them out," he says. "And hold out your hands."

I only open my eyes again because I know he'll make me, and when I do I find him stepping closer.

His eyes burn with a dangerous satisfaction. My hands shake in the air between us. Mason takes my right hand in his and holds it between us. In front of my face.

"When you're crying and begging me to stop, Ms. Van Kempt, remember that you wanted this. Here's the proof." And then he takes my fingers into his mouth. Wraps his tongue around them. Licks the evidence of my humiliation off. This is how I die. This is how Charlotte Van Kempt leaves the earth. Here in Mason Hill's closet.

Somehow, I'm alive when he pulls my fingers out of his mouth with an audible pop and binds my wrists together with his tie. I'm too mortified to fight it, but then my brain catches up with the situation. It finally puts all the pieces together. The tie, instead of his belt.

He has other plans for the belt. He told me about them, and I imagined his hand, I imagined—I don't know what I imagined. My mind was all over-heated by him, my body overheated and need—

I make a motion toward the door, but Mason has his hands on the tie and he jerks me back toward him. Turns me around. "You had the right idea, you sweet little thing. I need more room for what I'm going to do to you."

Back out into his bedroom. A single lamp glows

on his bedside table. I resist him with every step, pulling back as hard as I can, but it's not just him I'm resisting. It's myself. Because part of me wants to go forward. Part of me wants to go with him, to see what he'll do. To know him like this. Whatever happened with my father wounded him somehow and I want to know why. It's so sick. It's so wrong.

Mason doesn't seem to notice the fight. He drags me out to a sitting area in front of a fireplace. There are glass doors opposite, but I only catch a glimpse of the skyline. One final pull on my wrists and I'm over the arm of the chair. The diamond pendant lands first. I can feel it there, underneath me.

This won't be like last time.

This won't be like when he bent me over the arm of his sofa and licked me. Mason shoves my hands into the side of the cushion, the end of his tie spilling out like a loose thread. "I'd suggest holding on tight. Too much thrashing, and I'll have to tie you down."

"Don't do that," I plead. "You don't have to do that." I'm already gripping the cushion with all my strength and oh, Jesus, I shouldn't feel this torn. This terrified and hot. This ashamed and aroused.

"We'll see."

It's new upholstery, the cushion firm, so it pins my hands better than I would have expected. And here I am, helping, my fingertips wrapped around as far as I can get them. Mason traces a path down to my spine. Everything seems supersaturated and intense, even the pad of his finger on my skin, and I shake under it like he's already keeping his word.

Like he's already leaving marks.

He pats at the curve of my ass.

Too late. I'm too late in realizing what that pat was for. It was a small kindness—to tell me where the first blow was going to fall.

Mason's hand cracks against my ass so hard I cry out. It stings. Oh god, it stings. It burns. And he doesn't stop, doesn't hesitate. He does it again, on the other cheek. A pressure on the small of my back intensifies as he spanks me—his free hand, holding me in place. I'm trapped by the chair but the rest of my body doesn't know that. I lose count almost immediately. It's such a shock, this pain—it's so different from anything I've ever felt. His hand feels so enormous but his power seems even larger. It fills the whole room. The whole world. "Why?" I gasp. "Why?"

He lands ten more—*ow, ow, ow*—before he answers. "For you, sweet thing."

My heart is wild in my chest. Mason rubs his palm over the places where he spanked me. He laughs when I gasp. Every touch is heightened. I'm shaking like a leaf torn free in a storm. He slips his fingers between my thighs. Nudges them apart. Strokes through the center of me with one finger. "I'm not," I whisper. "I'm not."

"Yes, you are. You're soaked. Which is it, Charlotte? Do you like being the sacrifice, or is it the pain?" I open my mouth to answer, but then his other hand covers my lips. "Tell me when I'm finished."

He takes his hands away and steps into view. I can't crane my neck far enough to look up into his face. I'm too embarrassed to do it anyway. But adrenaline beats down the door to my veins at the sight of his hands on his belt.

On the heavy belt buckle.

It's out of his belt loops in a second. The supple leather never catches, never hesitates, and then I can't see what he's doing. When I can bear to look I can only see the side of him. Only see the perfect line of his waist meeting his hip. The expensive slacks.

He returns a hand to the small of my back, and new panic comes. "Please. Please."

Mason reaches underneath me, takes the pendant, and slides it between my teeth.

I bite down on it through a blaze of shame, tears already falling.

"Stay where you are. And don't let that necklace drop."

Then he's not touching me, and that's scarier than everything else, because I don't know what will happen next, I don't know, I don't know, I don't—

The belt lands.

It drives a shocked howl out of me around the metal in my mouth. Jesus, it hurts, and it hurts in such an entirely new way. It's a wide, deep pain. It goes through my entire body. And my entire body reacts.

The belt comes down again and I burst into tears. I'm not in control of myself. Not at all. He's in control of everything. Why do I like it? Why do I like this even a little bit, feeling him towering over me? I'm so terrified. I've never been so terrified. And it's hard to cry when I have all these diamonds between my teeth.

Again.

My legs kick up and it's the fight of my life. It's the most I've ever fought, because I'm fighting to do two things at once.

To get away.

And to hold on.

Again.

It just keeps coming, that long snap of pain across where he already spanked me. Over and over.

Tears stream over my face and I can't wipe them away. They drip down onto the cushion beneath me and keep coming. "Please," I say once, the sound distorted by the necklace. I say it a hundred times. "Please."

"That's better," Mason says, as cool and casual as he would be if he were standing in his office. "That's begging. But I'm not going to stop until you learn."

Learn what? I want to say. I can't. I can't let the necklace go.

Again.

He doesn't tell me, and it's the most difficult problem to solve in my entire life. Harder than how to run a company. Harder than how to pay the bills. I'm naked and bound and trapped and fighting—

Fighting.

Kicking. Pulling. Trying to get my body away from the chair. Away from him. The belt strikes and—oh, god, oh shit—I see what I have to do. I see.

Again.

Again.

Nothing is harder than putting my feet on the rug. Nothing is harder than pressing my cheek to the cushion and promising silently to keep it there. Nothing is harder than taking a breath to steady the quaking in every muscle.

"Good girl," Mason says, and then I feel him

draw the belt back. I feel the movement of him in the air.

I feel it land.

My lungs crush another sob out of me, but I don't fight it this time. I just keep my ass still, where he wanted it, and wait for what comes next.

Which turns out to be the soft impact of leather on rug. The muted clink of his buckle. "Fuck. I can turn your ass red, but look what you do to me." I blink more tears away. Turn my head until it hurts. Bent over like this, I can just see his pants. The rigid outline of him beneath. "How am I supposed to give this up? We're running out of Fridays, you sweet little thing."

Pure heat between my legs, intensified by the heat of my ass, the bruised flesh that he's left. I don't mean to moan. It just happens.

In answer, Mason makes a sound like he's in pain. I'm the one bent over and belted, but his groan is all ache. "I have to have you." I lift up on tiptoe, mind hazy from pain and want. He curses under his breath and reaches between my legs. "So fucking wet," he comments. "Jesus." Then he pulls me upright by the tie around my wrists. Takes the pendant out of my mouth. My jaw was so tense, my god. I haven't been lifted in someone's arms for a long,

long time, but he does it now, and he carries me to his bed.

My back meets the comforter and I let out a hiss—he's just punished me, and it still hurts. The pendant swings around behind me, the chain tugging at my neck. He makes another sound like he can't stand to wait. Like it's hurting him to wait even more than it's hurting me. Mason pushes my arms up above my head in a silent command. Clothes hit the floor, and then he's over me, shouldering my legs apart, spreading them wide. Lowering his head.

His tongue feels so good it brings on another sob. I don't know what he's done, only that it's too much, too good. He pauses. "How much does it hurt, Ms. Van Kempt?"

"A lot," I gasp. "But when you—when you—"

"Say it."

"When you lick me it feels better. It feels so much better."

He glides his tongue along the crease of my leg. So close and so torturously far. "When I lick you where?"

I can't say it. I can't.

"My pussy. My cunt. Please."

The sound he makes is half growl, half groan.

He gives me more of this, and it's beginning to feel not like a punishment, not like anything but pleasure. I should fight this too. I shouldn't let him make me come after what he did. But I want to. I have to let him. I'll die if he doesn't. So when he drills into my clit with his tongue and wrests a shaking orgasm from me, I submit to it. This time, I feel the sound he's making through my pussy. Through all that shameful wetness he's created.

Mason's limit arrives. He crawls over me and if I thought he was like a god before, I was wrong—this is it. This is it. He blocks out everything in the room. A lick to the side of my neck. I let my eyes close. My pulse is quick as a sewing machine, quicker than the fastest setting, and I am afraid, I am, but I'm more than that, too. I spread my thighs wider for him, to give his hips more room.

He reaches between us and takes his cock in his fist, and then the wide head of it is pressing against me. It's as intimidating as the belt. I try to breathe through it. It's a lot. Taking the first inch feels like victory. When he's taken a little more of me, Mason comes back. His hands go to my face, my hair, and I'm shaking so hard now. Tears run down my cheeks but they're more from frustration than anything else—I want to be fucked by a man with this much power. I want to be fucked by a man who can hurt me like this.

That man, that god, gives an experimental thrust, and I gasp.

"Fuck, that's hot," he says into my ear. He kisses my earlobe. Strokes my hair back from my face. "Fuck, you're tight. Would it be better if I forced you to come on my cock?"

All I can do is moan.

His hand glides between us again, and it's mortifying how fast it happens—barely any contact with his knuckles on my clit, and I'm there, pulsing around the invasion of him, my muscles out of control.

"Good," he says. "Your cunt feels so good, and I haven't taken all of you yet." A shiver moves through him, and somehow he's even bigger inside me. "Tell me, sweet thing, do you regret signing this pussy over to me? Are you sad that no other man will be able to hurt you first?"

I look into his eyes, my voice taken from me. It won't cooperate. "No," I say. He reads the shape of the word on my mouth. "I'm not sad."

He kisses me with another anguished groan. I can taste myself all mixed up with clean mint. Mason pulls away, breathing deep. Emerald eyes search my face. Whatever he sees there makes him circle my throat with his hand, push my head up, and lean down to speak directly into my ear. "Then break for me. Bleed for me. Show me how much your sweet little virgin cunt loves my thick cock."

Oh, I *want* to.

I spread my legs wider, trying to let him in, but a bolt of fear shoots through my spine and escapes as a whimper. His body settles heavier against mine. "That's it," he murmurs. "It's happening, Charlotte. Nothing you can do to stop it. Ready? Here it comes."

An unforgiving thrust, and my virginity is gone in a sharp pain that makes tears spill. I'm babbling, but I don't know what I'm asking until he answers. "Good girl. Give it a minute. Keep those legs spread…"

What was I saying? *It hurts. Make it feel better.*

Mason fucks the pain away. It dissolves into an ache that turns into a pleasurable stretch and then real, liquid desire. *Blood,* I think. *And juices.* I'm bleeding for him. All over him. It's the wettest I've ever been.

"Your perfect pussy is so greedy for my cock she's crying for me, just like you," Mason says, an edge to his voice. He runs his thumb through my tears while he fucks me. Hard, then harder. "Yes. Fuck. I can feel you getting tighter. Come again for me, sweet thing. I want it."

It hurts to come, but it feels so good this way.

Looking up at the most beautiful man I've ever seen. Feeling him stretch me. Hurt me. Pressure on my throat. The weight of his body over mine. I come one more time from the sight of him. He fucks me with total abandon, like I've always belonged to him, all the way up to some hidden peak.

And then Mason's green eyes close. He whispers *fuck fuck fuck* and then he pushes in so deep it makes me sob again. I've been taken so thoroughly. With such force. Heat spills into me in waves and violent thrusts of Mason's hips until he slows.

"Your cunt was made for me to break." His voice is a million miles away and the closest thing. "It made the sweetest sounds on my cock while you bled for me." He bends his head and kisses me. Tastes me. "It's mine now, Charlotte. You can never take it back."

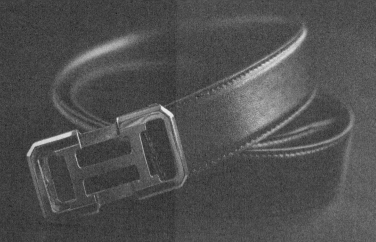

CHAPTER TWENTY-ONE

Charlotte

I've been fucked by Mason Hill.

How do I keep living in the world as if I haven't been? I guess that's not really an option. It happened. He punished me. He fucked me.

He's inside me now.

Mason's careful—or at least not rough—when he pulls himself out. I open my eyes as he moves to the side of the bed and stands.

Oh, Jesus. He's even hotter like this, even more perfect. I can just see how I'd fit a jacket to the angle of his hips. How the hem would land near the thick, proud cock he just used to fuck me. How I'd sew a shirt to hint at the ridges of his abs and hug his strong shoulders. How I'd cut a pair of slacks for his Greek-god thighs. I'm delirious, tracing the long lines of those thighs down to the scars.

One knee. His right knee. A lattice of surgical scars, some obviously newer than others.

My breath comes quicker. This is the secret he hides beneath his clothes. This might be more vulnerable than having him inside me, if it were possible for a man like Mason to be vulnerable.

What's wrong with your leg?

Nothing.

It's hard to feel any fear of this moment when every muscle is under a weighted quilt of pleasure.

I meet his eyes again. The green-gold is shadowed in the low light, and there's an expression on his face that could be pain. Or maybe I'm seeing things.

"What happened?" Speaking is a struggle.

Mason steps closer to the bed. Bends down. Turns my face to the side. "I belted your ass red, and then I couldn't help but fuck you." A kiss so light it's probably my imagination.

He releases me and pads out of the room. I lose track of time. Must not be long, but I'm floating. He's dressed when I look for him again. A soft t-shirt and slacks. Without a word, he unties my wrists. Helps me off the bed. Guides me to his bathroom.

Water runs, and a washcloth appears in front of my face. It's warm under my fingertips, but I don't take it. Can't, really. Mason says something I don't understand and puts an arm around my back. We end up at the ledge of a deep, deep tub surrounded in shining tiles, where he sits and positions me in front of him.

All I feel is warm now.

Until he runs it between my legs. I want to be playing it cooler than this, but a hiss escapes me before I can stop it. "It's all right," he murmurs, steadying me by the hip. Maybe he says something else. It's hard to understand. I'll probably want to remember it later.

My mind is in another place. A gauzy, lifting pleasure. "Ms. Van Kempt," says Mason. I look into his face, his mean, beautiful face. The corner of his mouth curves up. "I wish," I think he says. But what does he wish? I don't know.

For a minute he's gone, and when he comes back he has my purple dress in his hands. It's all I brought with me, aside from my purse and shoes. I stand in front of him on unsteady legs while he shakes it out and slips it over my head. The fabric falls lightly around my skin. "Turn around," he says.

His hands are gentle on the fabric. It's a slim keyhole back, held together by a single button. Mason pauses in the middle of drawing the pieces together. "What's this?" He turns me slightly, angling the dress toward the light to read the tag. "Charlotte Van Kempt? You made this yourself?"

We have very recently finished fucking, but I blush anyway. "I love fashion," I admit. "It's mostly just a hobby, really. Dresses. Skirts. Blouses. I sell a little on Etsy."

"When do you have time to do this?"

"After I come home from the office. Late at night. Whenever I have a spare minute."

His fingers work on the button. "So why don't you do this full time? It's clear you care a hell of a lot more about this than you do about real estate. " I don't have a chance to answer, because he lets out a soft laugh. "Ah. Because you're busy saving your father's business."

"Yeah." I can't keep the longing out of my voice. If I could make clothes full time, I would.

"Poor little martyr," Mason murmurs, his fingers still warm on the button, still testing the flesh beneath. "Giving up your dreams. Sacrificing yourself for your family."

He takes the pendant from around my neck and puts it somewhere I don't see. Mason used it to gag me, but it feels like a loss.

I'm still floating.

Is it possible I sit on his sofa in his living room, drinking water from a slim bottle and eating a shortbread cookie? I come back to myself in the middle of it and blink at him. "You're nicer than I thought."

He laughs, a low, dark sound. "I doubt you'll feel the same way in the morning."

Mason takes me to the elevator, wraps his hands around the back of my neck, and kisses me. He kisses me the way he licked me before. Long and thorough and deep. Almost like he's sure I won't remember. He pushes me backward into the elevator with his mouth on mine, and when the doors shut between us, it's like he disappears into thin air.

He's gone.

I'm gone.

I don't know how long I sit behind the wheel of the town car in the parking garage, waking up. I'm sure I didn't fall asleep, but that's what it feels like.

It's all dark roads on the way home. Less traffic now, but a drive nonetheless. I think about him the entire time. What happened to him? What surgeries left those scars?

My eyes are burning by the time I pull onto the cobblestone drive. It's a small torture, having to slow down to four miles an hour while the car bounces over potholes. My ass hurts from Mason's belt. And his hand. It makes my face hot to think about it. I can't stop. I'm reminded by every. Single. Bounce.

And—nice. All the lights in the house are on. I don't know how many times I have to tell my parents that we can't leave them on like this anymore. Our electric bill is racking up with each second that passes. I'm going to have to go through the entire house and make sure they're all switched off before I can sleep.

The garage door screeches on its way up. Well—soon enough, I'll have the money to fix it. Or I'll have the money to stage the house and put it on the market. I'll have the money, because I didn't run away from Mason. I didn't want to. Even the indistinct memories bring on a shiver. I need to sleep before I can figure out how wrong it is to want more of that. Shit, it hurt so much.

Still does.

But I feel so good.

I step gingerly out of the town car. Close the

garage door. All my muscles ache as I head for the kitchen door and open it.

To the sound of shouting.

I'm instantly, fully awake. My parents don't shout at each other. I know it happens—I've heard them talking about their friends over the years in murmured conversations over small dinner parties. Whose husband got out of control. Whose wife would lock herself in the bathroom. But it never happened in our house.

It's happening now.

There's almost nothing left to deaden the sound, so the roar of my father's voice fills the space. The words themselves don't separate. Only the sharp consonants and the wide, sarcastic vowels. I'm frozen at the kitchen door waiting for it to stop.

It does, and with that moment of quiet comes the guilt. There's no one but my mother for him to yell at like that. Heavy footsteps thud across the upper floor and it occurs to me I've never seen Mason move like that, never seen him try to make himself more intimidating by losing control.

This is bad. This is really bad.

The footsteps come down the stairs and I tuck myself in to where the cupboards jut out from the pantry door. I know it won't matter. My parents will have heard the garage door opening and closing. They might have even seen my head-lights on the driveway. If he wants to find me, he will.

His footsteps pause at the bottom of the stairs.

I hold my breath.

An indecipherable mumble, and the foot-steps stomp down to his office. The door slams a moment later, and I kick off my Target heels and run. Light on my feet. Minimal noise. The pain from Mason's punishment seems far away right now. I take the stairs two at a time and rush down the hall to the master bedroom. This is where my mother has been sleeping all my life—where my father sleeps when he's not in the guest room. I al-ways thought it was because of his snoring or her headaches and maybe I was wrong.

Maybe I was very, very wrong.

I catch the door frame with one hand and swing myself into the room. It's all lit up. My mother hates overhead lights, but that one's on, too. The fan circles lazily above a frantic scene.

My mother's too-thin frame buzzes back and forth from her walk-in closet to the foot of the bed. A suitcase is thrown open there. It's at a lopsided angle, like it took most of her strength to get it down from the high shelf where she keeps it.

"Mama." She tips the clothes in her arms into the suitcase and opens her arms wide. I go into them and hug her tight. "What's happening? What are you doing?"

"I'm leaving, Charlotte. I'm sorry. I'm leaving." Her blonde hair is twisted into a bun on the top of her head. That's not like her. "I have to go." A tight squeeze, and she lets go. I haven't seen her move this quickly, and with this much purpose, for months now. She seems most normal when we go to events like the gala at the botanical gardens, and even then it takes a lot out of her.

"Are you okay?" She's back out of the closet before I can follow her in. Another bag is already packed next to the suitcase—a big shoulder tote that she used to use on summer beach days. Two photo albums stick out the top and the side bulges. "Mama? Are you okay?"

"I'll be okay," she says. "I'll be fine. You should come with me. We can—" Her hands press down on the clothes in the suitcase. There aren't very many. She must be nearly done packing, because I know her wardrobe has been stripped down just like mine. "I have a car coming in a few minutes to pick me up."

No—I can't. I'm not ready, and I don't know what it will mean if we both go on the run. Debt collectors don't care about that. They just want to be paid. "What happened?" I put a hand on her arm to stop her. "Please. Tell me what happened."

A glance at the door. "Your father came home in a strange car with a black eye. I didn't even know he left, Charlotte." Her hand goes to her mouth. "I don't know who brought him back here. It wasn't an hour ago, and he—" She closes her eyes, then opens them to look into mine. "I can't do this again. I can't stand to the side and watch while he destroys himself. Destroys me along with him." Her phone lights up on the bed. "That's my ride."

Dread creeps in. "What's he going to do?"

"It's already done." My mother flips the top of the suitcase closed and jerks the zipper around until it's closed. I help her haul it off the bed and we both stand in the quiet, listening. "Okay," she says softly. "I'm going to go out through the kitchen."

Out through the kitchen and around the side of the house, so she doesn't have to go past his office. "I'll help you carry your things."

My lungs scream with the effort of carrying the suitcase down the stairs one painstaking step at a time. It's heavy with all the important things from her life and at least one secret she can't or won't tell me. We sneak to the back door. My mother opens it with a quick pull and steps outside, taking a huge breath of the night air.

I follow her. The suitcase rolls neatly on the path behind me. The Uber she hired is just pulling into the mouth of the circle drive when we get there, and my mother speeds up. She doesn't want him to park in front of the house. Any moment now, my father could come out the front door and cause a scene. Drag her back inside. The driver pops the trunk as we approach and I shove the suitcase in. My mother checks the license plate and yanks open the back door. Whoever's driving greets her, but she turns back to me. "Are you coming?"

Yes, says every instinct I have.

"Not yet. But I'll be careful. I'll be safe." I don't know what I'm saying. My father is inside the house. Who knows what's waiting for me in there, now that Mason has punched him? "I'll leave if I have to. There are things I need. I'll text you."

Another tight tight tight hug and she sits down, lips pressed into a thin line. "I love you, Charlie Bear."

My oldest nickname. "I love you, Mama."

I watch the taillights of the car until they disappear at the end of the drive. My ass smarts. Mason was right—my parents aren't going to know what happened. He thought I'd be sitting through dinner like this.

Nope.

In bare feet, I'm practically silent going back into the house.

The office door is closed.

I march up and open it before I lose my nerve. "Daddy? What's going on?"

The apocalypse. That's what. He's leaning back in his desk chair, the neck of a bottle in his hand. The purple bruise around his eye is much worse than I thought. His glass sits empty on the desk. "Hi, honey. How was your date tonight? Are you still playing whore for Mason Hill?"

I flinch in spite of myself, but anger steels my spine. He's crossed a line. My father's obviously drunk. Obviously. That doesn't happen. My pulse pounds with the uncertainty. "I know you went to Cornerstone today."

He tips the bottle up to his lips and drinks. There's not much. "I'm allowed to visit my own goddamn property."

"I told you I would handle it, Daddy. There was no need for you to go there."

Somehow, even his laugh is slurred. "I wanted to talk to the man who's fucking my daughter. Didn't I teach you anything about bastards like Hill? Open your legs for garbage and you are garbage."

My stomach turns. I've seen my father be less than kind at meetings. I saw him snub Mason at the gala. He's never turned it on me like this before. "Mason Hill is our business partner. He's the reason Cornerstone is going to be completed. Please don't go back there again."

"Why would I go back? I've done what I needed to do." He gestures at me with the bottle. "First step to getting anything done is to appraise the asset. Just like he appraised you."

"You're not making any sense."

"I'm done with that place." My father drains the bottle. "And so is Hill. I'd pay to see his face when he realizes. It'll probably be the same as his father's. Didn't get to see that either. I felt sorry for his father, but not him. Not the son of a bitch."

I don't know if I can stand to be more horrified than I already am. It's like I've swallowed a bucket of churning ice water. I could be sick on the floor. "Why are you acting like this?"

"Money, sweetheart. You should know by now. This house and everything inside it. How do you think I paid for it? Nothing like a good insurance payout to wash the debts away. Such a clean slate. What works once will work again."

"Daddy…"

"*Daddy*," he mocks. "I'm tired of looking at you. You've been a waste, Charlotte. A good-for-nothing slut who spread her legs for a man who should have died with his father."

I'm shaking with fear. With rage. "What insurance payout are you talking about?"

"Get *out*."

He throws his glass. It's too sudden. Too shocking. The fact that he's done it doesn't register in my mind until it hits the wall to the left of me and shatters. A thin, bright pain cuts into my cheek. It sounds like all my work, and all our plans, splintering into shards. I press a hand to that pain and run.

I'm already gone, already going for the stairs, when he shouts after me.

Not my name. A curse.

I burst into my bedroom and grab for my computer. There's no time to gather all my clothes, and all my fabric pieces, all my tools. One Etsy order, already in its padded envelope. I shove the envelope and the computer under my arm. One more turn back at the door for a photo. Me and my mom on the beach at the Hamptons when I was about six, with missing teeth and wild hair. Both of her arms are slung around me and we look thrilled to be alive.

Back downstairs. Through the house. My purse and shoes lay abandoned at the garage door. I scoop those up, too, and fling myself out of the house as my father calls after me.

"Whore," he slurs. "Just like your mother."

CHAPTER TWENTY-TWO

Mason

I'm awake when the doorman texts me.

Derek: Your sister's on her way up.

Mason: Thanks.

Remy usually comes home early on Saturday mornings and sleeps a few hours. If I'm awake, I go to meet her on her way in.

It takes longer than I would like to stretch out my knee and be in a position to walk without showing the damage, so Remy's on her way into the kitchen when I get there. She pauses in the hall, blinking at me. "You're still up?"

"You're home early."

My sister scrunches up her nose. "You'll laugh at me if I tell you why."

"I will not."

"Want some tea?" Remy goes into the kitchen before I answer, so I follow her. The summer after I bought this place she picked out this antique wall organizer that was a pain in the ass to install. She hangs her purse on one of the hooks and pats it like it's going to bed for the night. "Or coffee, I guess?"

I lean against the island and fold my arms over my chest. "I'm fine."

"Okay. Anyway, I just didn't feel like staying. They wanted to party. I wanted to study. Plus, I wanted to talk to you about Greece."

"Remy, you can't go without your team. It's not something I'm willing to entertain."

"But Gabriel's all over the city without people to protect him. Jameson does all sorts of crazy shit. And *don't* say I'm not like them, because that's bullshit, Mason."

"You're not like them. You're my baby sister. I'm not going to stop caring. And I'm not sending you to a foreign country by yourself."

She laughs. "It's a study abroad program. I'd never be alone." She yawns so hard I don't know how she's going to get through her tea.

"No. You won't."

My phone buzzes in my pocket. Another message from Derek. Jameson, probably, or Gabriel if he's in a particularly obnoxious mood. I swipe the text open.

And freeze.

DEREK: Ms. Van Kempt just came through the lobby. She's on her way up now.

Why? I want to type back, but Derek's not going to know anything about that. Now that he knows who she is, he'll wave her through with mild pleasantries until I tell him to stop letting her in.

Why, indeed. I sent her home a long time ago. It makes my pulse kick up to think she might want to talk about what happened. Cry about it? Beg for more? I don't know.

Remy dips the tea bag into the mug and yawns again. "I'm taking this to my room, I think." Then she cocks her head to the side. "Are you still trying to do that brunch thing?"

"Yes, and you're going to be there." If it were anyone else, I'd be snappish. What the hell is Charlotte doing here? She didn't leave any of her things. I know. I looked for them after she left. Some foolish part of me had hoped there was something left behind. Lord knows why. I don't need her to forget anything in order for her to come back next Friday.

Remy takes her mug by the handle and comes across the kitchen to hug me. "Sleep well."

"Goodnight," she says. "I love you."

"I love you, too."

I should have told her while she was in the kitchen that our mother used to do the same thing—stop there whenever she came back to the house. Kitchen first. Even though we had chefs and cooks and all kinds of people to manage the household work. She liked to go to the kitchen and sit down at the big table there and look out at the backyard. My kitchen looks out over Manhattan, but it's still the same.

The elevator arrives a few moments later, and I go out to meet it, my heart beating harder than I'm willing to give it credit for. I don't fantasize about Charlotte Van Kempt coming back to my penthouse after I've finished with her to beg on her knees for more. Definitely not.

However, I wouldn't hate it.

The doors slide open and she steps out. Charlotte looks down at the floor like she's not sure of the terrain and my pulse stutters. With her head bowed like that, the elegant line of her neck—

She's changed out of her clothes. Into leggings and an oversized t-shirt that looks soft and expensive.

Charlotte lifts her head and meets my eyes.

Cold. That's all I feel at first—cold, rushing through my veins, sloshing through every part of me, head to toe. It's worry, that cold. The certainty that something's gone wrong. It's in her red eyes and splotchy cheeks and the subtle shake of her hands around her purse.

It's in the cut on her cheek.

The cut.

On her cheek.

Blood beads at the line. My own blood rushes to my head.

I'm moving before I can think about compensating for my knee. The first step lands wrong and it gives, a shock going through it like a blade. Charlotte blinks up at me but her face doesn't reveal anything else. A quiver in her chin. Like she's about to cry.

"I didn't know what else to do," she says.

I take her face in my hands and turn it so I can see, my heart trying to slice its way out of my body. Her blood is the color of my rage. It's all I can do not to shout. "Who did this to you?"

Her hand comes up to touch it but she flinches away at the first brush of her fingertips. "It was an accident."

She won't look me in the eye. This wasn't an accident. "What kind of accident, Charlotte?"

All I can see is bright blood and blue eyes. Tears swim over them. "My father was angry," she says. "He threw a glass. It hit the wall next to me."

Oh my fucking god.

I'm torn in two. I want to kill him. And I need to take care of her.

Charlotte is closer.

I have to get her out of the foyer. Remy could walk in any second, and that can't happen. Not with Charlotte bleeding and on the verge of tears and looking like she just wandered off some college campus. I put my arm around her. "It's okay." I don't sound like it's fine. I sound pissed as hell. *Try again.* "You're going to be okay."

She lets me usher her down the hall to my bedroom, and if she has any complicated feelings about what we did here before she left, it doesn't show on her face. Charlotte barely looks. Three steps inside, and she turns to face me while I'm shutting the doors.

One tear slides down her cheek, then another.

For Christ's sake. This is not like when she cried earlier. That was the hottest thing I've ever seen anyone do, the way she sobbed from all that punishment and pleasure. This is different, and I hate it. Her soft cries wrench my heart.

I fold her in my arms without thinking of

349

anything but getting her calm. I don't consider what it means to hold her in the context of our agreement. I don't consider anything. I want my arms around her, and so they are.

Charlotte buries her face in my shirt, her shoulders shaking. Her body trembling. I run a hand over her shoulders, her back. Inside all my cold dread is a hot ember of anger. I made sure she was all right before she left.

Shamefully well-fucked, but fine.

That motherfucker threw a glass at her.

I want to take her to bed and hold her for as long as she needs, but when I lift her face from my shirt, the cut is still bleeding. "We need to take care of that," I tell her. "Come with me."

In my bathroom I find the first aid kit in the linen closet and sit her down on the ledge of the tub. She swipes at her eyes. Tries to stop crying while I get a washcloth and take a spot next to her.

Charlotte blinks at me when I take her chin in my hand. "I'm going to clean the blood off your face and put some liquid bandage on the cut. Okay?"

A nod. Her frown is shaky, but she's trying to be brave. Jesus Christ. More tears come at the first touch of the washcloth. "Shh," I tell her, though she's not making much sound. An old habit from the bad

days, when our parents had just died and there was
no one but me to help my siblings. "I know it stings."

"I can't believe he threw it at me," she whispers.

"You were talking to him?"

A shuddering breath. "I went home. Obviously."
A strained, shocked laugh. "I went home, and he was
yelling at my mom. Which doesn't sound like—I
know that doesn't sound like anything, but it's not
like him." She makes a cutting motion in the inches
between us. "It's really not. Afterward he went down
to the office and when I went upstairs she was packing a bag."

"To leave him?"

There's always more blood from a wound on the
face than you imagine there will be. It makes me furious to see it on her delicate skin. But no one else
is touching her now.

This belongs to me, too.

"To leave the house. To leave him. That's what
she said." Good. Cyrus is a bastard who's never de-
served anything, much less a wife. "That's not like
my mom, either. But then she said that she couldn't
do it again. I never got an answer about what. She
couldn't stand by and watch my father do something
terrible."

"Did you talk to him?"

"He was drunk," she whispers, and her face goes

351

pale. "I mean—he was *really* drunk. He's not—" A hand over her mouth, and then it drops away. "You probably already know all this. You made it a point to learn everything about us."

"Enlighten me anyway."

"My father has always been so careful." Her voice is rising with fear, and I'm honestly going to kill that motherfucker. For scaring her. Whatever he did to scare her, he deserves to pay for it. "He drinks from the glass. Do you know what I mean? He only ever has his glass on the desk, with not much in it. This time he had the whole bottle and it was mostly gone."

I get a dry washcloth and press it to clean skin, then reach for the liquid bandage. "This is going to sting, too, but I don't want to put anything with adhesive on your face."

"Okay," she says softly. "So then—then he started talking to me." Color rushes back into her cheeks. "He was being awful." From the way she's choosing her words, I know it's so she can avoid telling me exactly what he said to her. "But the scariest part was that he kept saying things about Cornerstone. And about you."

"Like what?"

What hasn't Cyrus Van Kempt said about me over the years?

I put the liquid bandage over the cut. One fast swipe. Charlotte sucks in a breath, and on instinct I lean in and kiss her. She relaxes into the kiss like it's taking away her pain. The liquid bandage is almost dry when I pull back. Pull her to her feet. Take her out to the bedroom.

Where I fold my arms around her again, because she looks like she needs that.

Charlotte gathers herself for the rest of our conversation. "He said he visited Cornerstone today to survey it for some—some plan he had with it."

"He's not in charge of any of that anymore." He'll be dead soon, if I have my way about it.

"He said he did what he needed to do. Something about appraising the asset." Charlotte puts both hands on my chest like she needs me to steady her, which is not possible in this life or any other. For the kind of stability she'll want in her life, she'd need someone else.

The drunken ramblings of a man who used to work in real estate and couldn't hack it—but worry taps somewhere deep in my mind regardless. I spent the time after my parents died in a haze of painkillers, with lawyers and assessors who talked about assets in relation to their will. About beneficiaries, most of whom turned out not to be us. Even if I hadn't been high on opioids, I still wouldn't have understood a thing. Both my parents were dead and I was in the process of getting custody of my siblings.

"Are you sure he wasn't remembering his former life?"

I ask this without malice. Cyrus's former life is also part of mine, but there's no way it has anything to do with why she's so upset now. That was separate.

Charlotte frowns, her lips trembling. "Both, I think? He was talking about your father."

My jaw clenches tight. This isn't her fault. "Well, my dad's been dead a long time. If he's still obsessed—"

Her eyes shine in the low lights, a new red flush on her cheeks. "That's the thing. That's the thing that I didn't—he was talking about you. He said…" Charlotte closes her eyes. Swallows. "He said he would pay to see your face when you realized." Her voice shakes. "I don't know what that means."

"Of course not." It takes all my strength to remember that Charlotte Van Kempt is an innocent. She's never been in a building that's burning down. Never suffocated in black smoke. I'm not breathing it now. My lungs are clear.

"I'm sorry," she whispers. More concern fills her expression. Concern for me, I think, which is ridiculous. She's the one with a cut on her face from her bastard father. Until I feel the tension pulling my muscles apart. Until I feel the pain like a thick metal band around my knee. "He—he mentioned an insurance payout. He said, *what works once will work again.* I don't know what he meant."

There's a moment when I feel the knowledge coming. It's a moment before impact, when you're aware your body is going to slam into an unforgiving surface with far too much force and terror has never felt so pointless because there's nothing you can do to fight gravity.

What works once will work again.

The building my parents died in was all but complete. Only a few inspections remained. Normally that would have been a cause for celebration. It would mean a big payday. But the real estate market had taken a downturn. The neighborhood that had been poised for a renaissance was now dead in the water. None of the luxury stores and restaurants wanted class A space. A hundred million dollars spent on construction and high end finishes—down the drain.

My father was prepared to take the loss. It would have been substantial, even for the Hill family fortunes, but we would have survived. Every development carries risk.

Then the fire happened.

An insurance policy recouped most of the debt.

It would have been a windfall, a relief from the real estate downturn… if my father had survived. Instead a quirk of the company's operating agreement meant the payout went to the other members of the corporation. It didn't go into probate with the rest of my father's estate. Which meant we absorbed the loss completely.

"He talked about insurance," I say slowly, processing this.

Cyrus Van Kempt was the recipient of the insurance money. I went to him for help, needing something to keep my siblings alive. He turned us down. I knew then that he was a bastard, but I thought he was a lucky bastard. I thought it was pure chance that he had been bailed out by that insurance policy. I thought it was random that the operating agreement had been written that way. But no—it had been carefully orchestrated.

What works once will work again.

He set that fire.

"Yes," says Charlotte. "He talked about witnessing results. He talked about seeing your face when you realized. And how it would look the same as your father's. But I don't know, Mason. I don't know what he meant."

"I do."

My phone buzzes three times in my pocket.

Messages, coming in fast. And then a call. I know who the call will be from. I know what it'll be about.

Time to go.

I take Charlotte by the arm and pull her along with me. If I have to see this, so does Cyrus Van Kempt's daughter.

CHAPTER TWENTY-THREE

Charlotte

Mason knows what's going to happen, and I don't.

It's the story of our entire relationship so far. Our entire arrangement. He knows what's coming, and I have to find out. It's always embarrassing. It's always shameful. It's always hot.

Except this.

This isn't hot.

The shameful part is that he looks sexy behind the wheel of a car, or in this case, his SUV. Sexy with his big hands curved around it and his eyes on the road. I shouldn't even notice those things about him because what we're driving toward is going to be terrible. I know that from the dark look in his eyes. The tic in his jaw every time he moves his foot on the pedal. The anger radiating from him. Filling the air. The night.

What am I trying to do here? Distract myself by looking at him?

Yes.

Something shuttered over his face in his bedroom and it hasn't lifted yet, and maybe that's the worst part of all. I'm grasping for anything. Show me where the thread goes. Show me how the pieces fit together. Show me how the world makes sense.

I came to Mason because my father finally lost it. He finally drank enough to be dangerous, to hurt me, and I couldn't think of a single other place to go.

The information was important—I knew it was. Mason's face when I told him was too carefully neutral, and then it wasn't, and I should know what's happening here. I should know what the terrible secret is. Beyond the insurance money. Beyond the theft.

The cut on my face throbs under the bandage he put on. With careful hands, like he'd done it before. He has, I think. He's taken care of people. It felt good for him to take care of me.

It's all so much.

He makes the final turn onto the block where Cornerstone is.

All this time, I've been trying to hold it together for the inevitable reveal. Trying to seem fine, fine, fine while I'm scared out of my mind and very little is making sense. But I can't stop myself from gasping when I see the wild orange flames against a stark black sky.

It's on fire.

Cornerstone is on fire.

I feel like a seam ripping away from fabric. The whole damn thing is coming apart in my hands. It's on fire.

It's on fire.

Flames shoot out the top of the building. It's already spread. It's in almost every window I can see and orange streaks cut into the light pollution above the city. The air coats my tongue with heat and ash, even inside Mason's car. It comes in through the vents. It saturates the air.

Fire trucks are at angles from the building like needles in a pincushion.

Water jets from hoses, but there's just no way.

There's no way they can stop it, with those tiny streams of water and that huge, roaring fire. And not all of them are trying. More trucks rush by with sirens screaming, and a crew jumps out at the next building over. There should be enough of a buffer. Shouldn't there? There should be enough space, unless the wind picks up, unless the wind carries embers from building to building. Unless the whole city burns down.

I can't think like that. People are coming to help. People are doing the right thing, even though my life is really over now. Even though it's literally going up in a cloud of black smoke.

Mason pulls the SUV to a stop behind a fire truck and gets out.

Something's wrong. The way he's moving is wrong.

A hitch in his step.

It has to be his knee. I don't know what's wrong with his knee. He's never told me. But it's obvious now, as he strides across the empty street. He must have been injured at some point. A severe injury that never fully healed, despite his surgeries and scars.

A pair of abandoned work boots lay haphazardly on the concrete next to the fire truck. Someone was in a rush to get here and had to change—someone ran toward this fire, to try to save what can't be saved.

My hands are numb on the handle but I get out into the heat. It's eating through the humidity of the summer air, drying it out. We're not close enough to be in danger but it feels like it—it feels too close. My heart is in my throat. My heart is on the ground. It doesn't know where it wants to be. I see my father's glass flying through the air and even now I can't get out of the way in time.

Where else can I go, but to his side? Mason's opaque to me. He's been inside me, fucked me, punished me, but I still don't know what's happening in his mind. That's impossible to know unless a person tells you, and he hasn't told me. He has kept himself away from me. Bound by the terms of our agreement.

Flames tower from the top of the building, adding the kind of height that would have made Cornerstone a New York City destination. They lick at the air. Devour it. How can the firefighters stop this from the ground? They can't take ladders up there. People shouldn't die over this. At least no one was inside. No one lives here yet. It's just my life that's ruined.

Oh, god, what are we going to do?

"How did this happen?" I think my question might be swallowed by the flame and the sirens and the spray of the water, but Mason rounds on me. "What happened?"

His mouth is a slash, his eyes cruel on my face, on the cut. "It's your fucking family. Your father did this. He did it now so it would be impossible to make money off the Cornerstone development."

"No," I say, because my mind can't comprehend that. "No."

A mean laugh. "Don't be foolish, Ms. Van Kempt. He told you himself. *What works once will work again.*" Why does it hurt so much for him to throw my father's words at me? They're not mine. I'm not him. "His drunk ass told you about insurance payouts. He wanted to see my father's face. Cornerstone? Fuck Cornerstone. If he set this fire now—which he did—that means he set the one that killed my parents fourteen years ago."

"You're talking crazy because you're angry. It's not true."

I don't know I'm shaking my head until his hands come to my face, his grip as harsh as his belt. Even in his furious struggle, he's careful not to press on the cut. "Don't shake your head at me, you sweet little thing." I gasp at the insult in his tone. "Don't you tell me *no*. He did this."

"Sir, you need to get back. *Sir.*" A cop yells over the roar of the fire, the rush of water from hoses. He gestures hard for us to move away.

"I own this building," Mason says, his voice stark.

The cop stops then. He looks back at the flames.

"Damn," he mutters. Then he gives me a sideways glance. "You still need to back up. It's dangerous here."

Mason curses, so fierce it makes me flinch. "Stay here," he says. The fire is in his eyes now, orange vivid on the green. "You. Watch her."

He strides away, leaving me with a cop who says something into his walkie talkie. Probably something about a crazy man trying to walk into a god-damn fire.

Of course I run after him. Heat from the flames licks over my skin. This close I can feel that itch that can only come from a fire. My senses are over-whelmed. "What are you doing?"

"Stay back." He doesn't even slow down.

"There's no way my father could have done this." I'm not sure who I'm trying to convince, Mason or me. The pieces fit together too well. My father knew this was happening. He made it happen.

"What the fuck did you think he was talking about?" He doesn't stop walking, striding through a barricade and passing a firefighter in full gear. Pain edges his voice, and my stomach drops to where my heart lies on the pavement beneath us.

"Please stop walking. I know it's hurting you," I say, because I can't argue with him, not really. I can't. My father was gleeful when he told me about what he'd done, even if he didn't list all the specifics. He wouldn't have. He likes to leave himself the benefit of the doubt, and that's what I've always given him. He was kind to me growing up, and I knew that kindness didn't extend to everyone, but I can't make myself believe that he's done this. I can't force the two people together in my mind. "I know something's wrong with your knee."

"Like what?" He whirls to face me. The question is deadly soft. Deadly calm. The fire roars and crackles. "Any guesses? You've seen me naked. What do you think happened?"

His eyes are so bright with pain I can hardly breathe. I force myself to do it anyway. "I've seen the way you walk sometimes. And I've seen your scars. Your clothes—" I can't explain the clothes. Not in a way anyone else would understand. "You hurt your knee somehow."

"Right. I hurt it." A vicious laugh. None of the kindness from earlier. None of the softness. "Some high school sports bullshit. A car accident. That's what you're imagining. No, you sweet little thing. My knee broke my fall."

Dry air. Dry heat. Tinder in Mason's eyes. "What kind of fall?"

He passes the building as if it means nothing. Millions of dollars in real estate and construction.

Of course it means nothing. It's on fire. Instead he goes to the next building, where people are rushing to exit. It's an apartment building. I've been to Cornerstone enough times, seen people coming and going, seen children playing on the steps. People rush out wearing pajamas, their eyes full of fear, hands full of babies and pets. They're almost trampling each other in their rush. It's chaos.

"This way," Mason says, his voice cutting through the panic. He takes a small child from a mother struggling with an elderly woman. And passes her to me.

I have no experience with children, but here I am, holding one. Responsible for it in the middle of a disaster. "Shhh," I say, smoothing down curls. "Everything will be okay."

Because of first responders. Because of people like Mason who take charge in an emergency. He organizes the people exiting the building, asking if anyone is injured, finding out if there's a family member left inside. I help him for the two hours it takes the fire department to get Cornerstone under control, passing out water and helping corral terrified pets.

When we're finished, I stagger to the side of the building. My clothes are wet with sweat and lingering water from the hoses. And possibly throw up from a small child.

I push my hair away from my face. Mason looks just as much a mess as me—and impossibly handsome. The hitch in his gait grew stronger as time went on, as he went up and down the steps. He must have hidden his pain all this time.

He comes to me. Without a word, he holds out a bottle of water. I handed out so many, but I never took one for myself. Thirst is a burning sensation. I've never been hungry. Or thirsty. I've lived a privileged life—because my father took care of us. I didn't know he did it at the expense of others. I didn't know he would do something this vicious. The water bottle crinkles in my hard grip. I can't make myself take a drink. Not until I know.

"What kind of fall?" I ask, my voice hoarse.

He's quiet a moment, and I think he doesn't understand the question. It's from hours ago, this conversation. "From the fourth story of a building that was on fire."

"No," I whisper, imagining a scene like this one, ending in tragedy.

"The fire that destroyed my knee. It was the same fire that killed my parents."

"You were there."

"I always knew that your father was the bastard who turned his back on my family. I knew he was a thief." His jaw works. "Until tonight I didn't know he was a murderer."

My throat tightens. How can I defend the indefensible? It's terrible what my father did tonight. What he might have done in the past. But he's still my father. "Mason."

A grim smile. "Do you know why I sent that offer? Do you know why I blocked every other deal? It wasn't because I was interested in the fucking Cornerstone development. Or your goddamn company. It was so I could get revenge on your father."

It shouldn't feel like a physical blow, but it does. "You don't mean that."

"Then you showed up, so perfect and pure. I thought, what better way to ruin her father than to defile his daughter? And it worked. It worked beautifully."

"No. *Please.*"

"There's no point in begging, Ms. Van Kempt. He murdered my parents. No matter how pretty you do it, no matter how nice you say *please*, I'm going to kill him."

Thank you for reading NET WORTH. This revenge romance is scorching hot! Find out how far Charlotte will go to protect her family. And how determined Mason Hill is to take vengeance.

Read HOSTILE TAKEOVER on Amazon, Apple Books, Nook, Kobo, and Google Play!

The stakes are higher than money. They're deeper than secrets. They're life or death when Mason Hill sets his sights on the Van Kempt family. Charlotte's hopes and dreams crash down around her. She questions everything, especially her own father. But she's always understood the value of loyalty. She'll defend her parents' lives—even if it means risking her own.

ABOUT THE AUTHOR

Amelia Wilde is a *USA TODAY* bestselling author of steamy contemporary romance and loves it a little *too* much. She lives in Michigan with her husband and daughters. She spends most of her time typing furiously on an iPad and appreciating the natural splendor of her home state from where she likes it best: inside.

For more books by Amelia Wilde, visit her online at

WWW.AWILDEROMANCE.COM

Made in the USA
Coppell, TX
12 March 2025

46995984R00218